Caitlin Murphy, you are a fool, she told herself.

Quisto Romero was not for her. He was a *cop,* after all.

But he wasn't just a cop. He was also the man who had come in minutes when she called him, the man who had taken her where she would be safe.

And he was the first man ever to make her heart take off on a crazy rampage every time she looked at him. The first man ever to make her dream scandalous, erotic dreams, until she woke up moaning, her pillow crushed in her grip, sadly lacking the heat and solidness of the man she was craving.

Craving. Yes, that was the word for it. And it was a word she'd never used in conjunction with a man before. It frightened her, even as it excited her.

But she would get over it, she told herself firmly. And the sooner the better.

Dear Reader,

Once again, we've got an irresistible month of reading coming your way. One look at our lead title will be all you need to know what I'm talking about. Of course I'm referring to *The Heart of Devin MacKade*, by award-winning, *New York Times* bestselling author Nora Roberts. This is the third installment of her family-oriented miniseries, "The MacKade Brothers," which moves back and forth between Silhouette Intimate Moments and Silhouette Special Edition. Enjoy every word of it!

Next up, begin a new miniseries from another award winner, Justine Davis. "Trinity Street West" leads off with the story of Quisto Romero in *Lover Under Cover*. You'll remember Quisto from *One Last Chance,* and you'll be glad to know that not only does he find a love of his own this time around, he introduces you to a whole cast of characters to follow through the rest of this terrific series. Two more miniseries are represented this month, as well: *The Quiet One* is the latest in Alicia Scott's "The Guiness Gang," while Cathryn Clare's "Assignment: Romance" begins with *The Wedding Assignment*. And don't forget Lee Magner's *Dangerous* and Sally Tyler Hayes' *Homecoming*, which round out the month with more of the compellingly emotional stories you've come to expect from us.

Enjoy them all—and come back next month for more excitingly romantic reading, here at Silhouette Intimate Moments.

Yours,

Leslie Wainger
Senior Editor and Editorial Coordinator

Please address questions and book requests to:
Silhouette Reader Service
U.S.: 3010 Walden Ave., P.O. Box 1325, Buffalo, NY 14269
Canadian: P.O. Box 609, Fort Erie, Ont. L2A 5X3

JUSTINE DAVIS

LOVER UNDER COVER

Silhouette®

INTIMATE™MOMENTS®

Published by Silhouette Books

America's Publisher of Contemporary Romance

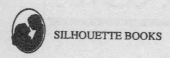

SILHOUETTE BOOKS

RECYCLED PAPER

ISBN 0-373-07698-3

LOVER UNDER COVER

Printed in U.S.A.

Books by Justine Davis

Silhouette Intimate Moments

Hunter's Way #371
Loose Ends #391
Stevie's Chase #402
Suspicion's Gate #423
Cool Under Fire #444
Race Against Time #474
To Hold an Eagle #497
Target of Opportunity #506
One Last Chance #517
Wicked Secrets #555
Left at the Altar #596
Out of the Dark #638
The Morning Side of Dawn #674
*Lover Under Cover #698

*Trinity Street West

Silhouette Desire

Angel for Hire #680
Upon the Storm #712
Found Father #772
Private Reasons #833
Errant Angel #924

Silhouette Books

Silhouette Summer Sizzlers 1994
"The Raider"

JUSTINE DAVIS

lives in San Clemente, California. Her interests outside of writing are sailing, doing needlework, horseback riding and driving her restored 1967 Corvette roadster—top down, of course.

A policewoman, Justine says that years ago a young man she worked with encouraged her to try for a promotion to a position that was, at that time, occupied only by men. "I succeeded, became wrapped up in my new job, and that man moved away, never, I thought, to be heard from again. Ten years later he appeared out of the woods of Washington State, saying he'd never forgotten me and would I please marry him? With that history, how could I write anything but romance?"

For Bob Henry, NBPD,
Who went down in the line of duty March 12, 1995
And to all the rest of that thin blue line
This series is respectfully dedicated.

Chapter 1

The first thing he noticed before she slapped him was the strawberry-blond color of her hair.

The first thing afterward was that she had one hell of a right arm.

His left cheek stung, and he tasted a trace of blood in the corner of his mouth. Quite a price, Quisto Romero thought, for the quick once-over he'd given the shapely redhead as she walked up the steps toward him. First the sergeant's test—which he knew he'd messed up—and now this. It was not shaping up as a great day.

He sensed a movement to one side of him and muttered, "Hold on a minute, partner."

"No thanks, Quisto, ol' buddy," Chance Buckner said, stifling a grin as he began to sidle away. "I'm an old married man now. I never get in the middle of your...domestic problems."

"Normally I'd agree," Quisto said, staring at the petite woman with the wavy mane of hair who still stood on the steps of the Marina del Mar police headquarters, "but I've never seen this woman before in my life." He tried his most practiced, charming smile; it hurt his sore mouth. "And believe me, I would remember."

He'd gotten varying reactions to that smile, both positive and negative, but never had it fallen quite so flat. She simply stared at him, this redhead with the peaches-and-cream complexion—and a pair of blue eyes that redefined the word *ice*. She wasn't angry; she was far beyond that. Fury was rolling off her in waves that were palpable.

"If you're really his partner," she said to Chance, never releasing Quisto from the ferocity of her gaze, "then you have my sympathy. You must have to do his dirty work, too."

"Ouch," Chance said. "You stabbed him right in the machismo."

His partner's gibe, half joking, half wary, had the effect it was supposed to; Quisto's ire, which was sometimes too easily aroused, cooled. And his curiosity—even more easily aroused—began to make itself known.

"A large target, I'm sure," the redhead said.

"Are you just pushing to see how far you can go, or do you have a plan of some sort?" Quisto asked, merely curious. "Perhaps to prod me into arresting you for simply being obnoxious, and then filing a brutality suit, Ms—?"

"Oh, no," she said, ignoring his implied question, her tone turning bitter. "I'm sure you would never do anything that could be construed as brutal in front of witnesses."

"Unlike yourself, of course," Quisto said mildly, rubbing anew at a cheek that he was certain still bore the imprint of her palm.

"So arrest me for assaulting an officer. It was worth it. You're the one who should be dead."

Quisto straightened sharply; Chance went very still. A slap in the face from an outraged female was one thing—and one Quisto had suffered through before, on occasion—but a death threat was something else again.

He saw Chance move with that swiftness that was so striking in such a big man, coming up close behind her, so quickly that, startled, she jumped forward and turned her head to look at him. In that instant, Quisto moved again, catching her wrists in his hands and holding them.

She whipped around, the thick mass of her hair swirling with the movement. Her chin shot up, and her eyes narrowed as she glared at him. Whatever her problem was, it wasn't lack of nerve, Quisto thought.

"Let go." She grated the words out through clenched teeth. She pulled with considerable strength, but Quisto held her fast.

"In a minute," Quisto said. He glanced at Chance. *"Amigo?"*

Chance groaned. Then, with a sigh, he began to do a pat-down search of the slender woman. "Why me?" he muttered rhetorically as he ran his hands up the outside of her leg.

"Hey!" the woman exclaimed, looking back at Chance. "What do you think you're doing?"

"Being late for my vacation." He continued the search methodically, thoroughly. "My wife is at home waiting for me now, the baby's with my parents, and we're going to be alone together tonight for the first time in a year."

"Oh."

The mention of Chance's family seemed to throw her; it always amazed Quisto how people never seemed to realize cops had families, too. Except, he thought sourly, when they saw them at said cops' funerals.

"I'm sorry," she said unexpectedly to Chance. "But what are you doing?"

"It's called a pat-down search for weapons," Quisto said coldly.

"Weapons?" she yelped, jerking around to face him again.

"It's routine for people who are stupid enough to threaten police officers on the front steps of the department."

"Threaten? I didn't threaten you! I just said you were the one who should be dead!"

"Excuse me, but in my line of work, when people start wishing me dead, I have a tendency to take them seriously."

"I don't doubt you have to," she snapped, as Chance finished his search and shook his head. "I'm sure you have a lot of enemies, Detective Romero." She rolled the title off her tongue as if it tasted bad.

Quisto lifted a brow in an expression that some women had described as whimsical, some as sardonic, depending on whether he was still seeing them at the time. He didn't release her wrists.

"I see," he said. "So this is a specific attack, and not a campaign against cops in general."

"I have nothing against cops in general. I respect them. There are only specific examples of the species I loathe. Let go."

"In a moment—"

"Not even enough courage to face an unarmed woman?"

Quisto sighed. "You know, you keep punching, and pretty soon that machismo of mine is going to be bruised. And I get very cranky when that happens."

She ignored the warning. "I shouldn't be surprised. Not from the kind of man who sends a child to do his dirty work for him."

Quisto stiffened. And his voice took on a low, quiet note that had Chance watching very warily, because he knew it so well.

"I'll have your name now, please."

Her hands still held tight, she gave a short shake of her head, tossing the red-gold mass of her hair back out of her eyes. "It's Murphy, for all the good it will do you."

"That was a very specific accusation...Ms. Murphy. Would you care to explain what the hell you're talking about?"

The very evenness of his tone made the curse somehow more potent. For the first time, a touch of caution came into her eyes. He had to give her credit for that, too; she seemed to have sensed she'd gone too far. Even when Chance searched for weapons, she hadn't been wary. Which meant she trusted them—well, Chance, at least, probably due to those blue-eyed-and-blond farm-boy good looks—to behave as most people expected cops to behave, with more restraint than would ever be asked of an average person.

The only problem was, Quisto thought as he looked at her thoroughly once more, she had run through his quota of restraint for the day in one big hurry.

"You know very well what I'm talking about." It came out through gritted teeth, as if she were having to hold back an even stronger anger than she'd let out. "And you have no right to hold me like this, now that you know I'm not *armed*."

The last word was bitten off sarcastically. Quisto held on, trying to maintain his grip while not hurting what seemed to be inordinately delicate wrists. "I do if you're going to slap me again the minute I let you go."

"I won't." She sighed, and he felt some of the tension go out of her, and her constant pulling, her testing of his grip, eased. "I didn't want to slap you in the first place."

Quisto's mouth quirked, and then he winced slightly, as the movement pulled on the sore part of his lip. But she seemed calmer now, so he released her. "Then you sure did a good imitation of somebody who wanted to slap me, lady."

Her chin came up again. "I wanted to slug you."

Quisto blinked. He heard an odd sound, and glanced to one side in time to see Chance stifling a chuckle.

"Sorry, pal," his partner said, raising his hands, palms out, to disclaim responsibility, "but this has all the earmarks of a scene I've watched before. Often. And Shea's waiting for me."

Quisto knew Chance had reached the same conclusion he had: Ms. Murphy was not likely to try hitting him again.

"Give my love to my favorite songstress," he said, signaling Chance that it was all right for him to go. Chance hesitated, but Quisto nodded toward the parking lot, where

Chance's Jeep was parked. "Go on. I get the feeling the lady's business is with me."

His partner would have stayed, had he asked, but he knew that Chance wanted nothing more than to get out of here before something happened to delay his long-awaited vacation. He was absolutely crazy about his wife, and watching them over the two years of their marriage had had an odd effect on Quisto; he envied them, even as he acknowledged that the thought of being as close to anyone as Chance was to Shea made him very, very nervous.

"So, *Ms.* Murphy," he said after Chance had left, accenting the title slightly, "would you like to explain what brought you here in such righteous indignation?"

He knew the second the words left his mouth that they were a mistake. That chin came up again, and the blue eyes—they were, he noticed, very blue—regained their former icy gleam.

"I suppose I should have expected that kind of belittlement from you," she said, her voice tight. "Putting the little woman in her place would be your style."

"Hijo la," Quisto muttered the expression of disgust under his breath. He glared at her, all attempts at charm now far from his mind. "You are carrying around a bagful of assumptions about me, and I don't appreciate you airing them in public."

"I'll bet. People like you work better under rocks."

"That's it," Quisto snapped, his patience at an end. "Come on."

He reached for her arm. She backed away. "Am I under arrest?"

"Oh, I'm sure I could find something to arrest you for. Some obscure municipal code to do with loitering on the steps of a public building with no visible purpose, or obstructing pedestrians on the sidewalk . . . not to mention assaulting an officer. And I assure you, I could make it a miserable experience for you."

She studied him for a moment. "But you're not going to."

"A decision for which I shall surely pay," he said gloomily. "Now, will you please come inside, where we can talk in—"

"We can talk here."

He let out an exasperated sigh. "Then at least let's get out of the way." He started toward a small bench that sat to one side of the front door of the station, positioned to give its occupant a glimpse of the Pacific Ocean—gray today, in the typical early-spring fog—in the distance. She hesitated, and he said warningly, "Don't make me change my mind about that arrest."

"I don't respond well to threats, Detective," she said, following him, but refusing to sit down.

His mouth quirked again as he resignedly remained standing, and again he winced. "You don't respond well to civility, charm or restraint, either. Or am I assuming too much on such short acquaintance?"

Faint spots of color tinged her cheeks; she had the grace to acknowledge the accuracy of his jab. "I know enough about you," she said shortly. "But I apologize for hitting you. Violence isn't the answer. I'm ashamed that I resorted to it."

"But it was your first instinct."

Her color deepened. "Yes. I wanted to ... hurt you."

"Rest assured," he said wryly, "you did."

For the first time, she lowered her gaze. "Then why don't you arrest me?"

"I'd rather know why." Her gaze shot back to his face. He shrugged. "Insatiable curiosity. Occupational hazard."

For a long moment, she simply looked at him. Her eyes really were incredibly blue, he thought. And he'd be willing to bet that in the summer a trail of freckles marched across that pert little nose. And maybe elsewhere ...

And she'd slap you again if she knew what you were thinking, he warned himself. With an effort that was unusual for him—both because he made it at all, and because of the exertion it took—he masked his appreciation of her long-legged, nicely curved figure and kept his expression even.

Finally she shook her head slowly. "Did that child mean so little to you? Just a tool to be used and then thrown away?"

Her voice was full of pain, and something knotted in Quisto's stomach. His reaction disturbed him, because he couldn't explain it. But something in this woman's eyes as she stared at him was making him very uneasy, like a man who knows something's wrong in the instant before the bomb goes off.

"That's twice now you've mentioned a child. Who," he said carefully, "are you talking about?"

"God!" she exclaimed, her eyes suddenly glistening with moisture. "Do you use so many you can't remember? Eddie, damn you! Eduardo Salazar."

Quisto drew back a little, his brows furrowing. "Eddie? He's what this is all about?"

"You probably thought no one would care, didn't you? No father, no family... And what's one kid more or less? Especially when he was already in trouble—"

"Ms. Murphy," he said, cutting her off, "I haven't talked to Eddie in well over two weeks. So if he's in trouble—"

"My God."

Her eyes were wide with shock as she stared at him. He felt like that man again, only this time he'd heard the final tick of the time bomb.

"You really don't know, do you." The whispered words weren't a question.

A chill raced up his spine; he tensed his shoulders against it. He opened his mouth to speak, to ask her what it was he didn't know, but no words came. He closed it again and simply waited, what she'd said before echoing in his head.

You're the one who should be dead.

She bit her lip, her eyes now wide and troubled, rather than angry. And then she spoke, saying the words Quisto dreaded, but expected.

"Eddie is dead."

He stared at her for a long, silent moment. He searched her face for any sign that she was lying. He found none. Nausea gripped him. Slowly he sank down onto the bench, inanely wondering if his stomach or his knees felt more wobbly. She remained standing, and he could almost feel the heat of her gaze on him.

"He was fourteen years old, Detective Romero. Fourteen, but you sent him into that hell to do what you wouldn't do yourself." Her voice was cold, harsh, and it beat on his ears like pellets of hail in the afternoon sun. "You killed him, as certainly as if you'd put a gun to his head."

Damn. Damn, damn, damn...

Quisto felt a stinging in his palms. He glanced down and saw his hands curled into fists atop his knees. With a conscious effort, he straightened his fingers, easing the digging of his nails into his palms.

"What happened?" He said it, his voice hoarse, still staring at his hands.

"He was murdered, Detective," she said. "Yesterday."

His gaze shot to her face. "Murdered?"

"You sound surprised. What did you expect, when you sent him back in to spy for you again?"

Slowly Quisto rose to his feet. He wanted facts, details, but first he wanted one thing very clear with this woman.

"I did not send Eddie anywhere, not the first time, and certainly not again."

"That's not what Eddie told me." Her voice rose slightly, and Quisto could hear the pain in it, genuine, honest pain. "I tried so hard to keep him out of that life, to keep him away from the street gangs. And he had stayed away from them, too. He was at the Neutral Zone almost every day, after school."

"The Neutral Zone?"

"My club. For the kids. Eddie was doing so well, helping me out there this summer. Until you came along."

"Eddie came to me..." Quisto began.

"And you used him," she said. "He was just a boy, and you used him." Her voice wavered, then steadied as she added coldly, "And I hold you personally responsible for his death."

"And I'm telling you, Ms. Murphy, that I never recruited Eddie. He came to me, with information we needed. We used that information. I won't deny that. But I told him to stay out of it. I told him he was in way over his head, and to stay away, for his own safety."

"And you expected him to listen? He was fourteen and practically drunk on the excitement of being a 'secret informant.' Like on television, he used to say."

"He wasn't an informant. We don't use kids—"

"But you used what he told you."

"Of course we did. He'd already given us the information. We'd be crazy—and negligent in our duty—if we didn't."

"Duty?" The red-gold waves of her hair swirled again as she shook her head. "Was it worth it? Was keeping the Pack out of Marina del Mar worth a boy's life?"

Quisto's head came up sharply. "What do you know about the Pack?"

She gave him a disgusted look. "Please, Detective. Don't insult my intelligence. I live and work in Marina Heights. You can't do either of those and not know about the Pack."

He knew she was right. Even in Marina del Mar, they'd known about the Pack long before they had to deal with them. Bound together not by ethnicity or territory, but by a common predilection toward crime, they were a band of thugs, of many races and mixes, whose ferocity held even the most vicious of the other youth gangs at bay while they conducted their own criminal forays.

"So was it worth it?" she asked again. "Or do the upscale residents here in Marina del Mar think a life is a small price to pay to maintain their pristine little world?"

Quisto had heard that more than once, had even thought something not too far removed on occasion. He and Chance had more than once acknowledged the irony that a large number of the residents in the town they served paid more in taxes than the two of them put together were paid to protect them. Even his small apartment down at the marina took a portion of his income he still winced at when he wrote the monthly check.

But he wasn't about to admit that to a woman who was already, however unjustifiably, furious with him.

"Envious?" he asked.

To his surprise, she laughed. "Hardly. I was born here in Marina del Mar. I grew up here. With the proverbial silver spoon in my mouth."

"Well, well—isn't that a coincidence."

Her arched brows, a bare shade darker than the sunset color of her hair, furrowed. "Isn't what a coincidence?"

"I was born and grew up in a place very much like Marina Heights. Just as rough, and with the proverbial mean streets."

"And now you're going for the silver spoon?"

He laughed. "On a cop's salary? Hardly."

"Protecting them, then."

It was so close to what he'd been thinking moments ago that it startled him, but he'd had a great deal of practice in hiding his reactions in four years of undercover and narcotics work.

Which reminded him of something.

"Just how did you know who I was, Ms. Murphy?"

"Eddie described you to me. Your partner, too."

"And on the basis of that, you slapped me? What if you'd been wrong?"

"I wasn't." She gave him a look that made him feel suddenly empathetic with snakes in zoos. "Eddie described you perfectly."

"Oh? And what exactly did he say?"

"Besides what you looked like? That you were two people. Rough, tough, and straight. Very macho. And also smooth, charming, and very pretty."

Quisto's mouth quirked. "I'd thank you, if I wasn't reasonably certain you meant that as an insult, not a compliment."

"Thank Eddie. But you can't, can you?"

It hit him again, the realization of why she'd come here. He'd postponed dealing with it, afraid the nausea that had taken up residence in his gut would get the upper hand if he tried to think about it now. But he wasn't sure it was going to get any better.

"What happened?" he asked again.

"I told you. He was murdered."

"How? When? Where? Any suspects?"

"Suspects? Do you really have to ask? You know perfectly well who did it." She glared at him. "I notice you didn't ask why. Because you already know, don't you? The Pack obviously found out he'd informed on them."

Quisto gave her an assessing look. "For the moment, let's set aside the myriad of other things that could have happened and say that's true. How did they find out?"

She blinked. "How should I know?"

"I don't know, Ms. Murphy. But then, as far as I knew, the only people who knew that Eddie had talked to us were me, my partner, and Eddie himself." He kept his gaze on her face. "But apparently I was wrong."

It took her a moment, but only a moment. She looked stunned, then, quickly, angry. "I don't think I like what you're implying, Detective Romero."

"Then give me another explanation. And," he added as she looked at him, "if you're thinking of suggesting my partner or me, forget it."

"Actually," she said, a dispirited expression skewing her delicate features, "I was going to suggest Eddie."

Quisto didn't react immediately. He was noticing how sad she looked and trying not to notice how much it bothered him to see her like that. He'd only just met her, and just because she'd come upon him like an avenging angel, that was no reason to go all soft because she now looked like that angel cast out.

"Eddie?" he finally said, thinking he must be truly desperate to avoid the reality of the news she'd brought, if he was resorting to that kind of distraction.

"He was always bragging. You know, exaggerating things, to make himself sound like a big man."

"I know." His brows lowered. "It's possible. He was a mouthy kid. He could have bragged to the wrong person. Or to someone who sold the information to the Pack to make his fix money for the day."

She nodded. He should, he supposed, give her credit for not trying to blame him for this, as well. Eddie had been a loudmouth, but Quisto had recognized the symptoms of a kid trying desperately to find his place in a world that seemed to have already condemned him to what it thought his place should be. He'd fought that battle himself, although it had been easier for him, with the big, loving family he had to back him up. And a mother with an indomitable spirit and a will of iron, who refused to allow any of her children to be sucked into the maelstrom of the streets.

Eddie had been small, wiry, bursting with teenage energy, enough energy that he hadn't yet succumbed to the fatalistic resignation so common to his peers, the view that life sucked and then you died. That there was no way out, that in Marina Heights, if you were born poor you stayed poor, while right next door in Marina del Mar lay the personification of the American dream.

Damn it, Eddie, why couldn't you just stay out of it, like I told you to?

His jaw tightened. Even after eight years as a cop, eight years of seeing the wide variety of awful things people could do to each other, Quisto still found himself, every once in a while, astounded by the ugliness. Eddie could have made it; he'd had the drive, the determination. He'd even talked to Quisto once about maybe becoming a cop someday. And he would have been a good one, Quisto thought. He could talk that talk and get people to open up to him, and he'd had those big, brown, innocent eyes . . .

"Damn," he whispered. And he sat down again on the bench, shaking his head, closing his eyes against the image of a kid clinging to some small bit of hope and innocence in a world that did its best to destroy both.

He opened his eyes when he sensed the woman sitting down beside him. She was looking at him with a curious expression that was tinged with doubt, as if she weren't quite as certain about him as she had been.

He should be gratified that he'd shaken her conviction about his culpability in Eddie's death. But he wasn't feeling that way at all.

He was feeling guilty. And responsible.

And very much as if the dauntless Ms. Murphy had been absolutely right.

Chapter 2

Detective Quisto Romero hadn't been at all what she expected, Caitlin Murphy thought.

She stirred the paint in the half-full can, staring at the swirl of cheerful yellow color thoughtfully.

He hadn't been the arrogant tough guy with a flip attitude and a smart mouth that she had thought would be just the type to appeal to Eddie Salazar. Or the kind of man she had pictured at Eddie's admiring description of "Rough, tough, and straight . . . *muy macho*."

And he hadn't been the cool, uninvolved manipulator she had imagined he would be, either.

No, Quisto Romero was none of those. He had an obvious edge, but she supposed that was inherent in the job. He might indeed be arrogant, but it might just as easily be a surfeit of the confidence that she also guessed was necessary for the job. And whatever his attitude, she had no doubt that he had been shaken by the news of Eddie's death.

She lifted the paint can by its wire handle, tilted it and emptied the contents into the roller tray. She'd been putting off painting the back wall of the Zone for weeks now, trying to catch up on everything else her recent battle with the city council over her use permit had put her behind on. But this morning she needed to do something that didn't require her to concentrate on numbers, and forms that went on forever.

But Quisto Romero certainly fit the rest of Eddie's description, she thought, as she picked up the roller and began to immerse it in the paint. *Smooth, charming, and very pretty.* Eddie had said it jokingly, along with some tales about his idol's effect on the ladies that she had thought were exaggeration. But now that she'd met him, Caitlin thought the words perhaps a bit of an understatement. Because Quisto Romero was indeed very smooth, very charming... and, yes, she admitted, he could even be considered very pretty, if you went in for dark, smoldering good looks, perfect golden-brown skin, and eyes that made you think of a choirboy gone bad.

He was especially striking next to his blue-eyed, blond partner, she thought, wondering for a moment what kind of woman had the fortitude to marry a cop, even a good-looking one like Detective Romero's partner. Or Romero himself. If he was married. The teasing comments the big blond man had made seemed to indicate otherwise, but she was too far past the innocent stage of life to believe a wedding ring kept a man from fooling around if he wanted to.

And Detective Quisto Romero's marital status had nothing to do with her, she told herself firmly. Nor did his attitude, or his charm.

But he was an interesting man. Except for those moments when he'd restrained her—easily, it had seemed, despite the fact that she was a relatively strong woman, and he looked more wiry than bulkily muscled—he'd been very gentlemanly. Even after she slapped him, even after she accused him of being responsible for Eddie's death, even when he was angry, he'd been almost courtly in his response.

It was, in part, the slightly formal syntax of his speech that had given her that impression, she knew, but not completely. It went deeper than that, as if this were a man who had grown up with manners. An odd thing to think about a cop, perhaps, but once she calmed down, she had quickly realized that Detective Romero wasn't the kind of cop she'd anticipated.

She lifted the roller to the dark wall behind the soda bar. It was a huge expanse, broken only by the counter that held the soda dispensers, the door to the bathroom on one end and the door to her small office on the other. It had been covered with graffiti when she took over the place, and the brown paint that had been donated had been the easiest way to cover it and get the club open. But now she wanted a brighter mood and had talked one of the local hardware stores into a ridiculously low price on the much more cheerful color. She spread a wide band of yellow paint, looked at it and sighed. Two coats. Definitely two coats. She began to work in earnest. But that didn't stop her thoughts.

Detective Romero hadn't taken the news of Eddie's murder lightly, she admitted. At one point, he'd looked almost ill. And that had caught her completely off guard; she had never expected such a strong reaction from the man she held responsible for that murder.

And she still did hold him responsible, she insisted silently. Charm and manners and looks aside, Detective Quisto Romero was the one who, intentionally or not, had started Eddie down the road that cost him his life. She still held him responsible for that, and that was why he was so near the surface of her mind, not because she'd found him quite different from what she'd expected him to be.

Besides, looks meant little, manners could be assumed, and all that charm could just as easily be a facade. After five years in Marina Heights, she knew all about facades. And she knew that some of them were no more than a thin disguise for viciousness.

Or a coat of paint over ugliness.

He hadn't been to Trinity West in a long time, Quisto thought. In fact, the last time he'd been anywhere near the police station, so called because of its location on Trinity

Street West, the street that had also given the surrounding neighborhood its name, was for the funeral of Chief Lipton, a year and a half ago.

He glanced around once more before turning into the parking lot. Trinity West—the station and the neighborhood—hadn't changed much on the surface. Although it was on the western edge of Marina Heights, just a stone's throw away from Marina del Mar, it was a world apart from the wealthy town in attitude and perspective. There were prosperous sections in Marina Heights, and Trinity West was one of them, but there were still more areas that bore the unmistakable signs of neglect and decay. Areas set apart not so much by ethnicity—there were as many Caucasians as Hispanics or any other group in most places—as by degrees of poverty. Areas marked heavily with graffiti, that red flag of anger and arrogance and territoriality.

But Quisto knew there had been a lot of changes that weren't so visible. He'd seen the statistics, seen the amazing drop in the felony crime rate over the past year. Trinity West had been a department under siege when their chief was murdered. But Miguel de los Reyes, the captain who had replaced him—a man who had also been wounded in that drive-by shooting—had taken hold immediately upon his recovery and appointment as interim chief, running things with almost a siege mentality, adopting techniques that were sometimes called by detractors—most of whom didn't have to live in Marina Heights—nothing less than guerrilla warfare, and would no doubt have been frowned upon if they hadn't produced such spectacular results. The law-abiding residents of the town were ready to nominate Chief de los Reyes for sainthood.

The few Trinity West cops Quisto had run into in the past year were a little rough around the edges, a little cold in the eyes, and he didn't doubt that their reputation for now being the toughest, most effective small police force in the county was well deserved.

He parked in a visitor's space near the front doors, not wanting to deal with the hassle of gaining admittance to the gated, secure lot in the back for the short time he was sure he'd be here.

Unlike the Marina del Mar station, which was a pleasant modern structure on a hill with a view of the Pacific, Trinity West was a square, uninteresting-looking two-story building, with tall rectangular windows all around that mostly overlooked other buildings and a weed-filled empty lot. The regular glass that had been installed when the station was originally built had belatedly been replaced with bullet-proof material when a sniper had explicitly demonstrated what marvelous targets the windows were at night when lit from inside.

Quisto checked in at the desk, displayed his badge and identified himself, and asked for the detective in charge of the murder of Eduardo Salazar. The young cadet, dressed in a uniform that appeared to have been cleaned and pressed just moments before, looked at him blankly.

"A 187? When?"

"Yesterday."

The cadet shook his head. "Haven't heard a thing about it. And I read the log this morning."

"It was a juvenile. A fourteen-year-old."

The young man's brows rose. "Now, I would have heard about that." He smiled proudly. "I know pretty much everything that happens around here."

Quisto stifled a sigh; gung ho was so wearying. He told himself there must have been a time when he had been just as full of energy and enthusiasm; he just couldn't remember it at the moment.

"I'll just wander down to Detectives, then," he said, "and see if I can find out what I need."

The cadet shrugged, as if to say that if he didn't know about it, it hadn't happened. But he pointed Quisto down the hall and buzzed him through the security door into the detective-division reception area.

The older woman with steel-gray hair seated behind the reception desk gave him the same blank look the cadet had.

"No, we had no murders reported yesterday. I'm certain of that, because that set a new record for us. Twenty-two days without one."

Marina del Mar was more likely to go twenty-two years without one, Quisto thought. He'd been there eight years now, and he'd seen only one. And that had been the first one in a decade. Trinity West was definitely a different place.

"This was a juvenile. Age fourteen."

She looked thoughtful for a moment. "We did have a juvie DB yesterday...."

She turned to look at a large book that lay open behind her, apparently listing the cases and the detective assigned to them. Marina del Mar had used a similar system prior to everything's being computerized a couple of years ago. Apparently Trinity West's budget didn't run to sophisticated computer case-tracking equipment. The woman turned back to him, apparently having found the dead-body case she'd referred to.

"Detective Butler is handling that. He's here, if you'd like to speak to him."

"Yes, please."

"I'll buzz him for you."

Moments later, a tall, rangy man with a shock of thick, pale blond hair that fell forward over his left brow stepped out into the reception area.

"Detective Romero?"

Quisto nodded, feeling suddenly old at thirty; this man barely looked old enough to have graduated from any police academy. Tan and fit, he also looked as if he should be lolling on the beach ten miles due west, at Marina del Mar.

"I'm Gage Butler." He held out a hand, and Quisto took it. The man's grasp was firm but not crushing; no challenge or testing here. "Come on back, and we'll see if what I've got is what you want. Want some coffee?"

Quisto declined politely as he followed the man back into a large room filled with desks in various stages of disarray, set up in pairs, back-to-back, in clusters of varying sizes.

Some were occupied, most were not; he'd evidently been lucky to find Detective Butler here. Phones rang regularly, adding to the backdrop of blended voices from those investigators who were here. It was a familiar mixture of sounds to Quisto.

A long, low bookcase on the far wall held books that were also familiar to any detective division, penal codes, volumes of the *Physician's Desk Reference,* and the ubiquitous tools of any investigator, telephone books from all over the country. Above the bookcase was a bulletin board with the requisite Wanted posters, crime warnings and advisories from other departments on missing persons and property and unidentified bodies. It was an atmosphere Quisto, as any cop would, felt immediately comfortable in, although this office lacked some of the modern equipment he was used to, and showed a lot more wear and tear than his home office did. Butler gestured him into a chair beside one of the neater desks behind a low divider labeled with a sign declaring it Juvenile and Sex Crimes. Quisto sat down and relaxed, resting his right ankle atop his left knee.

"Pam said you wanted to know about the juvie DB we turned up yesterday?" Butler asked, setting aside three file folders on his desk and picking up the one beneath them.

Quisto nodded. "I may know him."

The Trinity West detective flipped open the front of the pale tan folder. "We got an ID from someone who said she knew the kid, but nothing from the family yet."

"That wouldn't have been a redhead with a temper, would it?" Quisto asked, rubbing reflexively at his cheek.

Butler grinned suddenly, and he looked even younger than before. "You've met Caitlin, then?"

"Caitlin?"

"Caitlin Murphy. Strawberry blonde, big blue eyes?"

Quisto lifted a brow. "That guess didn't take long. You know her?"

"Not as well as I'd like, but apparently I'm not her type," Butler said, his mouth twisting wryly. "She's...an amazing woman. More guts than sense, but an amazing woman."

Quisto wasn't about to quibble with that assessment. Besides, something the man had said was bothering him. "She identified him?"

Butler nodded. "He had her phone number in his pocket. They didn't have anything else to go on, so they called it. She went over and gave us the positive ID."

Quisto drew back a little. "Unpleasant," he murmured.

"Yes. She was pretty shaken up. I think she and the kid were kind of close. He hung out a lot at the Neutral Zone."

Quisto frowned. "She mentioned that. Some sort of club, or something?"

Butler nodded again, tapping a finger against the folder. Quisto looked down, and saw a note clipped to the folder, with Caitlin Murphy's name and what he assumed was her address and phone number. Below it was another address, in Marina del Mar, that appeared to be for her parents, Mr. and Mrs. Patrick Murphy. Instinctively he read them, filing the information away.

"That's what I meant about more guts than sense. She opened the place in an old storefront on Trinity Street East. In the middle of one of the worst parts of town. We tried to get her to move it up here to Trinity West, but she insisted the need was greater downtown. We told her she was nuts, nobody down there would abide by her rules, but she wouldn't listen."

"Her rules?"

"No booze, no weapons, no drugs."

Quisto let out a low whistle, and his raised foot came down to the floor. "She have an army of enforcers?"

"No." Butler shook his head, his expression tinged with more than a little awe. "Just her. What's amazing is that, so far, she's done it. And most of the time, without much help from us. Oh, we were out there a few times the first month or two, but once they knew she meant what she said about the rules, they seemed to ease up. Rumor has it she faced down some of the toughest guys in the neighborhood, one-on-one."

There was more than just awe in the detective's voice, Quisto decided. Butler hadn't been lying when he said he didn't know Caitlin Murphy as well as he'd like to. For some reason, that didn't dispose Quisto to like the young officer any better, even though he knew his reaction was somewhat childish.

"So she's a miracle worker," Quisto muttered. "A regular saint."

Butler laughed. "Caitlin's much too real and far too stubborn to be a saint. She was just determined to give the younger kids on the street down there an alternative to starting with the street gangs and ending up with the Pack. If they survived long enough."

"What is she, some kind of social worker?"

Butler shook his head. "She's a teacher. English. Marina Heights Middle school. She opens the Neutral Zone on weekends during the school year, and every day except Sunday during the summer."

"The Neutral Zone," Quisto repeated absently.

"Yeah. Sort of her version of a DMZ. A place where there are no affiliations, no colors, no secret hand signals."

"And no gunfire?"

"That, too. Oh, it still goes on outside—even Caitlin can't stop that. But inside...well, she hasn't had a shot fired yet, and she's been open nearly a year."

"From what I've heard," Quisto said wryly, "it's amazing she's still alive, let alone open."

Butler suddenly looked very serious, his green eyes solemn. "Yes, it is. And I'll tell you, as big a pain as she's sometimes been, and despite the fact that we've tried to get her out of there, there are a lot of people around here who would be very upset if anything happened to her."

He turned his attention back to the file, digging something out that was fastened on the inside with the same paper clip that held the note with the addresses. He freed it, and handed it to Quisto.

"That's the first Polaroid from the scene. That your boy?"

Quisto looked at the photograph, which was eerily bright from a too-powerful or too-close flash. Every part of the grim scene was illuminated all too plainly. Including the wide-eyed, gap-mouthed death's-head stare of the boy whose image had been haunting him ever since Caitlin Murphy brought him the news. There was no immediately visible cause of death, but the photograph was no less grim because of that.

She'd had to look at this in person? A dead kid, shirtless, his skinny torso showing every rib, propped against a trash bin like some sort of ghastly comment on a disposable society? No wonder she'd been so wound up she slapped him.

He stared at the photo. Fourteen. So damned young. Still a child, really. Or he would have been, if he lived anywhere else. Here, he'd been older than his years, matured far too early by a life that stole childhood the way the Pack stole cars. Quisto swallowed.

"Yes," he said after a moment. "That's him."

Butler nodded. "Were you working him for something? This maybe clear some cases for you?"

"No." Quisto let out a sigh, handing the photograph back. "He . . . helped my partner and me on something, a couple of months ago."

"Really?" Butler took the photo and clipped it back inside the file. "A snitch?"

Quisto nodded.

"Kind of young, wasn't he?"

Quisto winced at the use of the past tense. He couldn't get past the last time he'd seen Eddie, when he warned him yet again to stay away from the Pack. All the boy could talk about was helping them, becoming a cop himself when he was old enough. And asking whether, if he did good for them, it would make the force overlook the fact that he had a misdemeanor record as a juvenile.

"We didn't recruit him," Quisto said, for the second time today. "He came to us, with some info on the Pack. And his information was good. So we used it."

"The Pack?" The detective looked suddenly wary.

"Yes. They were getting ready to make a move into Marina del Mar. We knew it, but we didn't know where or how. Eddie did."

Butler's eyes widened. "Wait a minute. Romero. Romero and Buckner, right?"

Quisto nodded.

"Hot damn!" Butler exclaimed. "I heard about that! Last year, right? When Rico sent his boys down to pick up that boatload of China White, and you guys were sitting there waiting? I heard that was the smoothest operation the DEA boys had ever seen."

"No thanks to their presence," Quisto remarked.

Butler laughed. "Feds," he said, with the disdain most local cops felt for federal officers who intruded on turf and cases they considered their own.

"Yes," Quisto agreed.

"I heard something else, about a crack house the Pack tried to set up in Marina del Mar, several years back. Wasn't it Buckner who took that down, too?"

Quisto nodded. "Seven years ago."

"I heard that cost him heavy."

"Yes," Quisto said quietly. "His wife and unborn child. A car bomb meant for him."

Butler paled beneath his tan. "God."

"Yes. And that was shortly after his old partner blew his brains out."

For a moment, Gage Butler turned away. He was still holding the relatively thin file, but his knuckles were as white as if he were trying to compress the paper back into wood. Quisto watched him as he swallowed, heavily; something else was at work here, something that greatly darkened the man's otherwise genial and open demeanor.

"That's . . . ugly," Butler finally said, not looking up.

"Very. He wasn't my partner then, but he was still carrying it pretty close when I started working with him, four years ago." Quisto shrugged. "But he's married now. With a new baby. And so damned happy it makes you want to get away, in case it's catching.''

Butler looked up then. And managed a smile that was as wide as, but lacked the genuineness of, his earlier ones; something about Chance's story had struck a deep chord within this man. ''That's good to hear.'' He smiled again, better this time. ''So what's it like, working with the legendary Chance Buckner?''

''It has its moments,'' Quisto said wryly. ''Especially since he's as all-American-looking as you are.'' Then his mouth twisted wryly. ''But it may not go on for much longer. We took the sergeant's test this morning, and, knowing him, he aced it.''

''May lose him to a promotion, huh?''

''They'd be crazy not to,'' Quisto admitted frankly. ''He's the best there is.''

''So I've heard.'' Butler's smile seemed back to normal this time. ''Guess every department has its legend.''

''You mean like Yeager?''

Butler looked surprised. ''You've heard of him?''

''Every cop in this county's heard of Clay Yeager.''

''Yeah. Too bad he didn't come out of his hell as well as Buckner did.'' Butler dropped the folder on his desk and changed the subject rather abruptly. ''Sorry about the kid.''

''Me too. What's the status?''

Butler shrugged. ''We're waiting for some decisions. His mother went to pieces and wasn't much help in making arrangements.''

That wasn't what he'd meant, but an image of Rosa Salazar formed in Quisto's mind, from the one time he'd seen her, two years ago. She'd reminded him of his own mother, in her fierce love for her wayward young son, and he wasn't surprised to hear that his death had left her devastated.

''I'll go speak to her. Perhaps I can help.''

''I'd appreciate that. The coroner needs to know where to send the body.''

''What about the investigation?''

Butler shrugged. "The usual, toxicology and all that, will be back in a few days. Then we'll wrap it up. That's the only good thing about these. They're short and easy."

"These?" Quisto asked.

Butler gave him a curious look. "Yeah. I'm not sure yet what he was using. Nothing I recognized right off. But they're mixing some strange stuff together these days. Once I get the report from the coroner's office, then it's just fill in the blanks on the death report. You know how it goes."

Quisto took a breath. "I'm not sure I do. What exactly was the cause of death?"

Butler blinked. "Sorry. I thought you knew already. Kid shot up a load of something really nasty. Found him with the needle still in his arm."

Chapter 3

"Caitlin," Quisto said patiently, "they found a hype kit, used. Syringe, needle, rubber tubing, the whole gamut of paraphernalia."

"I don't care," she said. "He wasn't doing drugs. I know he wasn't."

Stubborn, Gage Butler had said. That, Quisto thought, was a tremendous understatement. He'd laid it all out for her, and she still wouldn't budge, still insisted that Eddie had been, if not clean as the driven snow, at least free of the ravages of intravenous drug addiction.

"Caitlin—"

"I told Gage it wasn't an overdose."

Gage? He couldn't get her past "Detective Romero," despite having used her first name since he'd arrived here. Perhaps they were closer than Butler realized. They'd make a dramatic couple, the tall, tan, good-looking blond man and the beautiful peaches-and-cream redhead. The thought didn't please him. And the fact that it didn't pleased him even less.

"I told him Eddie wasn't using. Obviously he didn't believe me."

"How can he? Caitlin, Eddie still had the needle in his arm. His own mother said he'd been gone for two days, hadn't even come home at night."

"I don't care," she repeated, her expression mutinous, her delicate jaw set.

She turned on her heel and walked away from him. Quisto sighed inwardly. *Stubborn* was definitely too mild a word for it. He followed her, slowly, looking around the high-ceilinged main room. The bright yellow of the far wall did a great deal to brighten what could have been a dingy, depressing place.

It also, Quisto guessed, explained the two specks of yellow paint that marked Caitlin Murphy's sassy, upturned nose, the splatters on her jeans, a drop on a pair of what seemed to be very small white high-top tennis shoes, and the blue T-shirt she wore. He wondered if she'd done all the painting herself; she didn't seem to have any help around.

And she could use it, he thought. Lots of it.

He'd found the Neutral Zone easily enough, but that hadn't alleviated his shock when he actually saw the place, and where it was. Butler, if anything, had been kind about the location. Quisto would be wary himself walking down this street, even armed; he shuddered to think what could happen to a woman who, from what the detective had told him, presumably came here alone, and stayed here alone. Especially a woman who looked like Caitlin. Not only was she beautiful, but her pale skin and bright hair would make her stand out even more in this grimy place.

The neighborhood was beyond run-down, all the way into borderline derelict, far worse than even the poorest part of Trinity West. Only the Neutral Zone stood out as having had any kind of attention at all in the past decade, if not two. It stood out midblock, lights on amid the darkened buildings on either side and across the street, most of them festooned with crisscrossed boards over broken windows. Some lacked even that much care, gaping holes yawning where windows had once been. A liquor store with heavily barred windows at one corner, and a small old Mom-and-Pop-style grocery store at the other, were the only signs of life.

The Neutral Zone itself hadn't been open yet when he arrived, but he'd found the back door propped open—he'd have to talk to her about that—and Caitlin had answered when he called out.

"This is an . . . interesting place you have here," he said, hoping she'd accept the change of subject.

"It's a place for the kids. The young ones, who haven't gotten sucked up into the street gangs yet. It's a place to get away. To not have to be looking over their shoulders, for at least a while. To let them learn what it feels like to just . . . be kids."

"And just how do you manage that?"

"There are rules here, and the kids all know they're enforced."

"Enforced? By who?"

She drew herself up. "By me. You think I can't? I've only had to call the police three times since I opened, over a year ago."

Quisto held up a hand, as if to stave off her anger, feeling the heat of her gaze, as fiery as her hair. "I never said you couldn't do it. Although I do admit to a certain amount of curiosity as to how."

Suddenly, unexpectedly, she smiled. Quisto felt an odd sensation in the pit of his stomach, as if something there had contracted fiercely.

"I don't really know," she admitted, her smile turning sheepish. "It just seemed to happen. The first day I opened, a bunch of kids came in. I knew they were here to test the waters, so to speak. To try and scare off this "rich bitch," as they called me, who didn't have a clue what life was really like down here."

Quisto could just imagine it. And it wasn't a pretty image; Caitlin, facing down a group of angry young thugs who would no doubt feel no qualms about teaching her a painful, if not fatal, lesson.

"What did you do?"

"I showed them some pictures."

"Pictures?"

"Of two of my Irish cousins. Handsome boys, barely ighteen. One the son of my father's sister, the other the son f my mother's brother. And then I showed them pictures f what little was left of their bodies, after they were both illed in an IRA bombing. They were on opposite sides, but hey were both dead. Padraic probably even set the bomb imself, if the truth be known."

"And?"

"I told them there wasn't a damned thing they could teach ne about blood and territory that I didn't already know, hat they were amateurs at street and guerrilla warfare. My eople have been at it for centuries."

Slowly, Quisto nodded. That was the kind of thing these ids would understand, and they would see her standing up them like that as a sign of courage or craziness, things eserving of almost equal esteem on the streets. He began see why they respected Caitlin Murphy.

"They backed off?"

"After I hung the pictures up to remind them," she said. he gestured toward the wall opposite the yellow one. "That as the start of the wall."

She said it in a tone that was almost reverent. He turned is head. When he came in, he'd noticed the mass of pho- s on that wall, a conglomeration of faces and names, eemingly with only one thing in common: their youth. He urned and looked at her again.

"Who are the others? Your clientele?"

"Some. Most were gone before I got here."

"Gone?"

She gave him a level look. "Dead, Detective Romero. 'hat's what all those kids over there have in common. Every st one of them is dead. Some from drugs, more that were hot, stabbed, run down in the street. And a few suicides, oo. They're all there, on the wall. Friends, brothers, sis- rs, cousins . . . My kids bring in the pictures and put them up there. So they aren't forgotten, like the world wants to forget them.''

Quisto looked at the wall again, fighting a rising tide of queasiness. You'd think that after eight years as a cop he'd be used to this kind of thing, but the sight of all those young faces hit him hard. There, but for the grace of a determined family and a bit of luck, could be any one of his brothers and sisters, nieces and nephews.

''I think it's that wall that really keeps things in control around here, more than me. The kids have come to think of this place as a shrine as much as a club. And even though they may not have much respect for anything else, they do have respect for the dead.''

He turned to face her again. ''And for you.''

''I hope so.'' He saw her lips tighten. ''And now I have to put Eddie's picture up there.''

''I'm sorry.''

''He wasn't on drugs,'' Caitlin said again, vehemently, spinning away from him. ''I saw him almost every day. He helped me around here, more than anyone else. I would have *known*.''

Quisto didn't dispute it; he knew it would be pointless right now. He settled down on one of the stools that sat in front of the long bar, a rather makeshift affair of some dark, stained wood that was nevertheless polished to a high sheen. Caitlin walked around behind it, then stopped across from him. Quisto watched her face. He could see her wrestling with some kind of internal dilemma. Then she took a deep breath and turned to face him.

''I'm sorry. I haven't been very polite. Would you like something to drink?''

Quisto smiled. Widely. ''You're the bartender, too?''

Her answering smile was halfhearted, but it was a try. ''Since I only serve soda, coffee and tea, it's pretty hard to mess up.''

''Do you have any root beer?'' he asked. She looked startled for a moment, and Quisto let out a dramatic sigh.

It's true. I am ashamed to admit to it, but I have a great eakness for root beer."

Her smile this time was wider, and much more genuine. I confess, so do I." She reached for a glass beneath the bar, en stopped. Her eyes were twinkling with humor when she oked at him then. "I've got some vanilla ice cream, if ou're interested. Root beer floats are a specialty of the ouse."

"*Querida,*" Quisto said, pressing a hand to his chest with air, "for a root beer float I would slay dragons."

She ignored the teasing endearment. "I'll remember that e next time I come across one," she said dryly.

He watched her turn to the old refrigerator that sat gainst the wall, humming rather noisily.

"I would imagine you come across them quite often, round here," he said.

She looked back over her shoulder at him. "Don't like the eighborhood, Detective?"

"Please. We are becoming intimate friends. You are fix-g me a root beer float." He grinned crookedly at her. Can we drop the 'Detective'?"

She looked at him for a moment, then turned her back on im without comment, apparently unaffected by the pat-ted Romero grin. But Quisto didn't care at the moment; e'd bent to take the ice cream out of the bottom freezer, eating him to a lovely view of her trim backside and long gs, clad in worn and nicely snug jeans. When she straight-ed, the wavy mass of her hair swayed, falling halfway own her back. He'd never gone in for redheads before, but is one could definitely change his mind, he thought.

This one would also probably take his head off if he even ied. It wasn't just that she was angry at him about Eddie; e seemed immune to his much-practiced charm, which left m at a bit of a loss.

She turned back with a round half-gallon carton of ice eam in her hands. She set it on the bar, pried off the lid, en reached below the bar again and came up with a spoon. ut before reaching in to scoop out the ice cream, she leaned

forward, resting her hands on the bar, one still holding th
spoon, as she looked at him.

"You didn't answer my question."

"Nor you mine," Quisto pointed out. "And mine w;
much simpler."

She lowered her gaze to the carton of ice cream, as if th
answer were frozen there. Her lashes were thick and lon;
and as softly reddish-blond as her hair; they reminded hii
of the finest of artist's brushes. And they would brush ove
his skin the same way.

He drew back sharply, wondering where that thought ha
come from. She was most definitely not his usual typ
however attractive she might be, a stubborn redhead with
temper, and a bleeding-heart surrogate social worker t
boot, was so far removed from the kind of woman wh
usually attracted him that he caught himself nearly laugh
ing. He schooled his face to impassivity as she looked up ;
him once more.

"All right. What should I call you? Mr. Romero?"

"Call me Quisto," he said. Then, grimacing slightly, "(
Rafael, if you must."

"Oh? Then Quisto is... what, a nickname?"

He didn't quite feel like explaining to her exactly whe;
that name had come from. At least not yet. So he dissen
bled, picking a relatively harmless explanation that al:
happened to be the truth. Just not all of the truth.

"It's a family thing. My oldest nephew started it, when I
was little. Now everyone uses it."

She looked thoughtful for a moment, and Quisto wo:
dered if she was truly one of those who thought of cops ;
robots that came completely assembled, without emotio:
or feelings, much less an actual family.

"And you don't like Rafael. Why?"

"A bit... dramatic, don't you think?"

She looked him up and down from behind the bar, h
mouth quirking upward at one corner. "So are you."

Quisto blinked. He glanced down at himself, wonderi:
what had made her say that. He was dressed conservative

enough, in a pair of brown twill slacks and a tan cotton sweater. A bit neater, perhaps, than what she was used to around here, but nothing conspicuously flashy.

"Your clothes," Caitlin said, her tone wry, "have nothing to do with it."

He wasn't quite sure how to take that. He wasn't quite sure how to take *her*. It was a feeling he wasn't used to, especially around women, and it bothered him. Not seriously; it was just a niggling little sensation of wariness that would, he assured himself, go away as soon as he had Caitlin Murphy figured out.

"I like Rafael," she said as she scooped ice cream into the two glasses.

"Then, by all means, use it."

"I don't think so."

She didn't elaborate or explain, just went about filling the glasses with root beer. Quisto watched her smooth, practiced motions, wondering what it was about this woman that had him so nonplussed. He was never at a loss for a quick comeback, yet his brain seemed to have shut down this morning.

Caitlin gave both glasses a quick stir, stuck a straw in each, then set one on the bar in front of Quisto. He took a long sip, then sighed in satisfaction.

"Dragons," he said again.

"Which brings me back to my question, Detec—Quisto."

"Ah. About your lovely neighborhood." He stirred the root beer concoction with his straw before asking, "Are you saying you do like it?"

"Answering a question with a question is a technique used by lawyers, cops, kids in trouble, and adults dodging something they don't want to answer."

"And I'm two for four, is that it?"

She took a sip of her own float, then set it down. "Are you?"

Slowly, a reluctant smile curved his mouth. She was truly something, Caitlin Murphy was. "I am a cop," he conceded, "and I'm dodging giving you an answer that will no doubt make you angrier at me than you already are."

"Are you sure of that?"

"What do you mean?"

"Give me an answer and see."

Quisto looked at her for a moment. "All right. No, I don't like your neighborhood. It reminds me too much of what I escaped, what I spent my teenage years running away from, the fact that this is the kind of place too many of my people lived in. And died in."

"But you did escape."

"Yes. I did. My mother saw to that. She knew education was the key, and she made sure we knew it, too. My oldest brother is a doctor. My oldest sister is a lawyer. A defense lawyer, I might add."

"Must make for some very interesting dinner-table conversation."

"Yes," he said, looking at her speculatively. "You really are not angry with my answer. Why?"

"Because you just proved my point. My whole reason for being here."

"I did?"

She nodded. "Escape is possible. Just because you're born in a place like this, that doesn't mean you have to stay here. You can get out. Rise above it. Or survive to change it. It can be done." Her expression became very solemn. "Eddie was determined to do it."

Quisto had no answer for that. He knew the boy had been determined. His determination just hadn't been strong enough to overcome the lure of his own bad habits.

He bent his head over his glass and took another long, cooling drink. When he looked up, Caitlin was watching him, stirring her float with her straw, as if to hasten the melting of the ice cream in the bottom of the glass. She seemed to be waiting for something, and he wasn't at all sure what it was. He wasn't sure of anything with this woman. Except that, good-hearted though she might be, she was kidding herself.

"Did Eddie ever tell you how we first met?" he asked finally, his tone intentionally casual.

Caitlin's eyes narrowed. "He told me you arrested him once, if that's what you mean."

"Yes. He was twelve then. And he was holding a kilo of marijuana."

She drew back slightly, her motions with the straw stilled. "A—a kilo?"

She wasn't surprised by the charge, Quisto realized, just by the amount. "Yes. A nice big brick." Then, guessing but still fairly certain, "I suppose he told you it was just a couple of joints?"

He saw by the faint pinkness in her cheeks that he was right. And that she had believed the boy. He could understand that; Eddie was—had been—a charmer.

"I could have popped him for sales," Quisto said. "But he insisted he was just holding for somebody else, and I believed him. He was too scared not to tell me the truth. He talked a big game about how tough he was, but when he sat in that cell, looking at those bars, he reverted to a scared twelve-year-old kid very quickly."

He saw her close her eyes for a moment, and he could guess all too well the images that were playing through her mind, images of a boy who had wanted out so badly, but hadn't made it. When she opened her eyes again, they were troubled, but the anger he'd seen yesterday on the department steps was there, as well. And it was in her voice when she spoke.

"He told me that was the first time he became an informant for you. That he told you who gave him the stuff."

Quisto smiled wryly. "I'd hardly call it becoming an informant. In exchange for lowering the charge to misdemeanor possession, and a promise that we'd keep him safe from retaliation, he gave us the name of the dealer he was holding for."

"And you arrested him?"

Quisto shook his head. "Never got the chance. He dropped out of sight, then surfaced six weeks later. Literally. In the water off Pelican Point."

"Oh."

It took him a moment to understand the disappointment in her tone. "Caitlin, Eddie overdosed. Plain and simple. It wasn't a retaliation murder by the guy he turned in two years ago, or the Pack. They don't bother with kids, except to use the street gangs as a training ground."

"He may have overdosed, but somebody did it to him. He wasn't using!"

Her voice rose on the last words, and Quisto lowered his gaze from her face. There wasn't much to say in the face of such stubbornness. He'd seen it before, in people like Caitlin, do-gooders who had a lamentable tendency never to see what was right beneath their noses.

"Never mind," she said, dumping what remained in her glass into the old, stained sink behind the bar, as if it had lost its flavor. "You don't believe me, Gage didn't believe me, nobody does. Everybody just wants to write Eddie off as another kid who fell victim to his own weakness, another casualty of the streets. Well, he wasn't. I don't care what any of you say."

"Caitlin—"

"Especially you," she snapped, glaring at him. This was the woman who had slapped him. "You had no business letting Eddie get involved with this kind of thing. He couldn't have known how dangerous it was, not really."

"I told you—"

"I know what you told me. And I know what Eddie told me. And I'm not a fool, contrary to what you seem to think. I know that the truth is somewhere in the middle. But no matter what, Eddie was still a child. More so than most fourteen-year-olds around here. You should have made sure he stayed safe."

Quisto knew she was reacting out of grief, but still, it stung. "What was I supposed to do? Follow him around twenty-four hours a day? Maybe move in with him?"

"Did you tell him you couldn't have made those arrests without him? Did you tell him he'd been instrumental in stopping the Pack from getting a foothold in Marina del Mar?"

Quisto shifted uncomfortably on the stool. "Well...yes, but it was true, and he deserved to know that."

"And I suppose it never occurred to you that you were pumping up that boy's dreams, that you were feeding his fantasy of being a hero, something special, special enough to get out of this place? And you never thought that with all that praise you might be encouraging him to do more of the same thing that got him all those pats on the back to begin with?"

"I also warned him. I told him to stay out of it, that we didn't want or need any more from him. I told him he'd taken too big a risk even coming to us the first time, and not to do it again. Contrary to what *you* seem to think, I don't make a habit of using children as informants."

"But you used this one."

Quisto sighed, feeling a bit battered. He'd undergone cross-examinations that were less wearying. "He'd already come to us. That damage was done."

"So you stopped the Pack, kept them out of your peaceful little enclave, probably got your own pats on the back, then tossed Eddie back into the cesspool, is that it?"

Quisto's temper sparked, but he'd learned long ago to rein it in when dealing with people who were upset. Still, there was an edge in his voice when he spoke; something about Caitlin Murphy got to him in a way he wasn't used to at all.

"I checked on him every few weeks. And I told him if he ever felt like he was in danger, to call me. He even had my home number, for God's sake. What else could I have done?"

Caitlin wrapped her arms around herself and stepped back from the bar. She leaned against the low counter behind her, lowered her head and shook it sadly. Her hair fell forward, masking her face.

"I don't know," she said, her voice tight, as if she were fighting tears. "Order up a miracle, I suppose."

"I'm sorry, Caitlin," he said gently, "but miracles are the first thing a cop loses faith in."

Chapter 4

Quisto sat idly tapping the end of a pen on his desk. There were many things he should be doing. He felt like doing none of them. But anything would be better than what he'd been doing for the past two days, walking around seemingly in a fog, only sharpening to attention at a glimpse of red-gold hair. And spending far too much time wondering about the woman who had brought that particular shade of strawberry blonde to his attention.

With Chance on vacation, he was at loose ends, clearing up paperwork and reports that had backed up during their last undercover operation. That it might indeed have been their last one together was not something he wanted to think about. Chance had become more than a partner, he'd become a friend, more of a friend than Quisto had ever expected to find in the legendary detective. It had taken time. Chance had been very closed off after the death of his wife and unborn son and the suicide of his former partner, but eventually he'd let Quisto get past his formidable walls.

And when he was going through hell, falling in love with a woman everyone else considered a suspect in the biggest money-laundering operation Marina del Mar had ever seen, it had been Quisto Chance had turned to for help. And he *had* helped him, because that was what partners did. It had broken down Chance's last reservations; the bond between the two men was unshakable now.

And he himself, Quisto thought with a soft smile, now had a namesake and godson in Sean Rafael Buckner, who, at a mere year and a half old, had everyone in his family— and Quisto's—wrapped around his tiny finger.

The phone sitting at his elbow rang, and he grabbed it quickly, gratefully, hoping for something sufficiently distracting.

"Romero."

"Gage Butler," the voice on the other end supplied succinctly. "Got something here I think you might be interested in."

Quisto straightened. "What?"

"That kid, the OD?"

"Eddie."

"Yeah. Salazar. I got the analysis on the contents of the syringe back this morning."

"Already?"

"I have a friend at the lab."

"Useful," Quisto said.

"Often," Butler agreed.

"So what was it? Heroin? Coke?"

"Neither. That's just it. It wasn't anything like that. It was procaine."

Quisto's brows furrowed. "What?"

"Procaine. It's a commonly used local anesthetic. Like lidocaine. My source tells me rapid intravenous injection would most likely cause a complete cardiac arrest. And that it wouldn't take much."

"Damn."

"Exactly. Looks like maybe Caitlin was right, after all. Not much chance the kid did it himself. Somebody either did it to him, or fooled him into thinking he was shooting up something else."

"Damn," Quisto said again.

"Kind of thought you'd feel that way. That's why I wanted to let you know."

Quisto's jaw tightened. Murdered. Eddie really had been murdered. That silly, eager kid. He felt the slow heat of anger starting to build.

"I'll have to turn this over to our felony unit now," Butler said. "I'll let you know who lands it."

"I'd appreciate that," Quisto said. "Anything else in his system?"

"Don't know. Won't, until the toxicology reports are in, and you know how long that takes. But I thought you might want to hear about this right away."

"Yes. Thanks. Will you let me know about the blood analysis?"

"As soon as I get it."

"Thanks, Detective."

"Gage."

"Quisto."

"You got it. Later."

Perhaps, Quisto thought as he hung up, he hadn't given Gage Butler enough credit. He'd been misled by the youthful appearance. Or those all-American blond good looks. It had happened before; he'd had his doubts about Chance, too, at first. But he'd soon written them off to a gut-level reaction he'd thought he'd beaten long ago, when he'd come to terms with the fact that he would never be one of the fair-haired boys of America, in more ways than one. He *had* beaten it long ago. He didn't know why he was thinking about it now, but apparently he needed to work on it a little more, if it was throwing off his judgment.

So Caitlin had been right. It had been murder. Perhaps she'd even been right about Eddie being clean, as well. He wondered if Gage had called her, too. Probably, he thought rather morosely. If the man was serious about wanting to know her better, he wouldn't pass up a chance to score some points with the lovely and stubborn Ms. Murphy.

Well, let him, Quisto thought. He had other things to do than worry about than Caitlin Murphy. Like worrying about who had killed Eddie. And why.

Not that he really had much doubt about the latter. The way Eddie had died had *message* written all over it; it had been an execution. Somebody had found out that the boy had cooperated with the police.

He sat there for a long moment. The anger within him was building. Eddie had been a kid—tougher than most of the fourteen-year-olds in Marina del Mar, yes, but not as hardened as many in Marina Heights. He'd still had a chance to come out right.

He thought again of Caitlin's wall, of all those young faces. Of Eddie's face, added to that grim parade of death. He threw down his pen, grabbed his jacket from the back of his chair and walked up to the front of the detective division office. He flipped the switch on the light next to his name on the display board, turning it from green to red, and scribbled Unknown on the chalkboard for his return time, then Out of the City for his destination. Then he headed for Lieutenant Morgan's office.

Morgan was a quiet man in his late forties, a calming influence on the varied personalities in the Marina del Mar detective division. Quisto had always respected the man, but his respect had turned to a genuine liking after Morgan's actions during the lengthy investigation that had thrown Chance and Shea together. And especially after the tragic shooting that had almost torn them apart again.

"Got a second, Lieutenant?"

Morgan looked up from what appeared to be another in a seemingly endless stream of departmental updates on ever-changing case law.

"Anything to get away from this," he said, putting the memo down. "Come on in."

Quisto entered, but didn't sit in the chair Morgan pointed. "Remember Eddie Salazar?"

Morgan's forehead creased, then cleared. "The kid who came to you with the info on that shipload coming in for the Pack?"

Quisto nodded. "He's dead. Murdered. Set up to look like an OD."

"Damn. He was only about sixteen, wasn't he?"

"Worse. Fourteen. Look, Lieutenant, I'd like to check into this a bit, if you don't mind."

"Is Trinity West on it?"

"They will be. Their Juvie detective got the case as a straight overdose. He just found out it wasn't and called me. He'll be turning it over to their felony unit. But you know how loaded down they are. With Chance gone, I've got some time. I'd like to see what I can find."

Morgan looked at him silently for a moment. "Feeling responsible?"

Quisto let out a compressed breath. Morgan knew his men well, and there was little point in trying to deny it. "Yes," he admitted.

"All right. Just make sure you check in over there. I don't want you stepping on any toes."

"No problem."

Those words were, he realized an hour later, far too optimistic.

"That's all I can tell you," the man across the desk said, leaning back in his rather pretentious leather chair with a condescending smile.

Quisto stared at the long carved name plaque on the desk. Lieutenant Ken Robards, Commander, Detective Division, it proclaimed grandly in gilt letters. As soon as he identified himself, Quisto had been directed here by an uncomfortable-seeming detective sergeant whose felony unit desk plaque simply read—in plain white letters—Sgt. Cruz Gregerson.

And he'd run into Gage on the way into the lieutenant's office, and he didn't think he'd imagined the young detective's edginess, either. All of a sudden, the Trinity West detectives were a nervous bunch.

"Good luck," Gage had said wryly, nodding toward the closed office door. "He's... kind of a pain. He's the last holdover from the old days, and he acts it. A dinosaur. He won't go out of his way to help you."

And now, as he sat looking across at the older man, with his buzz-cut blond hair and his heavy jowls, Quisto thought perhaps Gage had understated the facts just slightly. The fat stub of a rather nasty-looking cigar sagged in the ashtray on Robards's desk—unusual in itself in these days of no smoking in public buildings—and his teeth had the yellowed look of someone who indulged in that particular vice regularly.

"That's all you can tell me?" Quisto repeated, not bothering to hide his disbelief. "An informant of mine is murdered, and you just say, 'Stay out of it'?"

"It's our case, Detective Romero. We'll handle it. And we'll handle it without any help from you fancy types in Marina del Mar."

"I never implied that you needed any help. I have a personal interest in this case—"

"So you said. And I said forget it. It's our jurisdiction. Go home, Romero."

Cruz Gregerson, an apologetic expression on his face, was waiting for him when he walked out of the office.

"Sorry about this," the young sergeant said. "Look, I don't know what the deal is, but I know it wasn't his—" he motioned with a thumb toward the office Quisto had just left, in a gesture that fell somewhat short of respectful "—decision. Not that he's ever been much on interagency cooperation. He's old-school, from back when it was all more like competition than teamwork. But this... it came down from higher up."

Quisto studied the other man for a moment, seeing the paradox in his name mirrored in his dark, nearly black hair and bright blue eyes. "The chief?"

Gregerson shrugged. "I don't know. Possibly. He's not like most brass, he keeps his hand in—on the day-to-day street level, I mean."

"Unusual," Quisto observed.

"Chief de los Reyes is an unusual man."

"So I've heard." Quisto rubbed a hand over his jaw. "If not him, who?"

"Captain Mallery, maybe. V and I runs out of his office, and they handle the Pack. But the only word I got was to keep you out of it."

Unusual, Quisto thought, to have a captain in charge of Vice and Intelligence. But he'd already gotten the impression that Trinity West was an unusual place.

"Who's going to be handling the case here?" he asked.

"That's the weird part. I don't know. Not yet. Robards says he's considering who to assign the case to—V and I, since the Pack may be involved, or the Felony Unit."

"While it gets cold?"

"Colder by the minute." Gregerson shook his head. "Like I said, I don't get it. But I'd highly recommend staying out of Robards's way. He's a vindictive old bastard."

"Thanks for the warning."

"Anytime."

Quisto headed for the door, then turned to go past the desk where he'd sat talking to Gage yesterday. He was there, on the phone, that rebellious shock of pale hair falling over his forehead as he talked. Quisto stopped.

"...strictly an LOPC booking, Mrs. Wagner. Yes, it does stand for Lack of Parental Control."

Gage glanced up, saw Quisto standing there and rolled his eyes expressively as he listened. Quisto couldn't help grinning back.

"No, Mrs. Wagner," Gage said into the phone, "it's not meant to imply that you're not a good parent, it's only because that's the way the section is worded."

When at last Gage hung up, he was shaking his head. "The kids I can deal with," he said with a wry smile. "It's the parents who make me nuts."

Quisto smiled sympathetically; the juvenile/sex crimes detail had never been an assignment he'd coveted. "Maybe you need a change."

Gage's smile faded, and something Quisto could only have described as a shadow flickered in his eyes. "No. I have too much to do here," he said quietly.

Quisto sensed he was talking about something much more and much deeper than placating parents who were more concerned about what their child's problems said about them than about the child. But as soon as he noticed it, the shadow vanished, and Gage was smiling again.

"How'd it go with the old . . . man?"

Quisto smiled at the hesitation, easily able to fill in the word Gage had changed at the last minute. Apparently there was more than a little tension among the men having to deal with the Trinity West detective commander. Lieutenant Morgan was looking even better than usual.

"He told me to butt out. Jurisdiction and all that crap. Any idea what's going on?" he asked.

Gage shook his head. "All I know is I had to turn over my file and all my notes to Robards this morning. He told me whatever I knew was to be considered confidential, especially to you." Gage's mouth quirked wryly. "Of course, I'd already told you all I knew. But I didn't tell him that."

"Thanks."

Gage looked at him for a moment. "Why do I get the feeling you're not going to butt out?"

Quisto grinned, but shook his head. "You're probably better off if I don't answer that."

"I had that feeling, too."

A few minutes later, Quisto was back in his car—his own small red coupe, instead of the luxurious black BMW he and Chance used on undercover assignments, courtesy of the federal asset-forfeiture Statutes—and tapping his finger restlessly on the steering wheel as he sat waiting to pull out of the department parking lot into the heavy lunch-hour traffic on Trinity Street West.

He didn't understand this. He didn't understand it at all. He'd been completely stonewalled. It was natural for a department to be wary of others meddling in their jurisdiction, but not like this. Besides, they knew he had a personal

nterest in this, and that should have gotten him a quick go-
ahead.

He opened the center console between the front bucket
eats and took out a small cellular phone. He flipped it
pen, turned it on and dialed quickly. Lieutenant Morgan
nswered on the second ring, and Quisto quickly told him
vhat had happened. There was a long moment of silence on
he line, long enough to make Quisto nervous.

"Lieutenant?"

"I'm sorry, Quisto. I have to withdraw my permission for
ou to get involved in this."

"What?" Quisto was stunned; Morgan never wavered in
acking his men.

"I have no choice. And I can't explain, either, so don't
sk me to. You have no official go-ahead. I'm sorry."

He didn't have to explain, Quisto thought as he said only
hat he understood and disconnected. Obviously Lieuten-
nt Robards had picked up his phone the moment Quisto
valked out of his office. And although Morgan's wording
ould be interpreted as meaning that what he did on his own
vas his business, it also told him that Morgan didn't want
o know about it. And effectively cut him off from any de-
artment support.

He spotted an opening in the steady stream of traffic and
lived into it, just in time to hit the red light at the corner. He
at there for a moment, tapping his finger again. Then he
icked up the phone and dialed again, a different number.
A familiar female voice answered.

"Detective Division."

"Hola, querida," he said. *"¿Como estás?"*

"I'm not your darling, and I'm fine in spite of it," came
he laughing answer.

"Ah, Elena, you wound me."

"You'll recover, Romero. What can I do for you?"

For once, he wasn't ready with a quick, racy suggestion
n answer. You're losing it, Romero, he thought as he asked
uickly, "Put me down for a vacation day, will you? Some-
hing's come up."

"Are you all right?"

The instant concern in the detective secretary's voice mad
him smile; Elena Colfax might be a martinet of sorts whe
it came to her job, but she was the first one there if some
one was in trouble.

"I'm fine. There's just something I need to do, and it'
personal. Better put me down for tomorrow, too."

"All right. The lieutenant knows?"

Quisto hesitated. He knew Morgan would easily gues
what he was up to, and he didn't want Elena to get int
trouble. So he gave her something she could say that was, i
fact, true. "He suggested himself that I take some time whil
Chance is on vacation. Something about my having tw
months' worth of time on the books."

Elena laughed. "All right. I'll put you down."

He disconnected just as the light changed. He'd made th
turn before he realized that, instead of heading back tc
ward Marina del Mar, he'd turned the other way on Trinit
Street West, heading to where the street changed to Trinit
Street East—and straight toward the Neutral Zone.

He nearly turned right back around. He even change
lanes, getting ready to do just that. Then he realized wha
he was doing. And changed right back again. He'd b
damned if he'd run like a scalded puppy just because Cait
lin Murphy didn't think much of him.

At least he assumed she didn't. Over and above her ai
ger at him for what had happened to Eddie. She had, afte
all, called him...a bit dramatic. And he was reasonably sur
she hadn't meant it as a compliment. He'd been called man
things by many women, some complimentary and some nc
so, but *dramatic* wasn't one of them. Not in so many word:
anyway.

Women, Quisto thought. Now that was an area he neede
to pay some attention to. For a guy who'd once had th
busiest social life in the department, there had been a deart
of feminine presence in his life of late. He couldn't reall
remember when it had started, but he had a sneaking su:

picion it had begun somewhere around the time Chance and Shea blasted his illusions about love to bits.

Just watching the hell they'd gone through for each other had rattled him; their happiness since they'd been married had made him wonder if he should do some reassessing. He'd managed to shrug off the relatively happy marriages of his siblings by falling back on the quite truthful fact that none of them were married to cops, who had one of the highest divorce rates of any profession. And if his aversion to involvement went any deeper that that, he'd managed to ignore it.

But Chance had been the worst kind of cop for any woman to get involved with—deeply wounded, hanging on day by day, full of guilt and despair—and Shea had fallen in love with him anyway. And her love had been Chance's salvation; the walled-off, taciturn man Quisto had met four years ago bore little resemblance to the Chance Buckner of today, secure in his wife's love and a doting father to Quisto's godson.

And that kind of change was as frightening as it was amazing. As much as he had come to like Shea, the amount of power she had over Chance made Quisto wary. He didn't like the idea of anyone having that much power over him, although it certainly didn't seem to bother Chance any. And if he was honest, Quisto had to admit it went both ways; nothing in life mattered more to Shea than Chance, and now their son. And he wasn't sure he liked the idea of having that much power over someone else's happiness any better.

But on days when he was feeling particularly sappy, which seemed to be coming more often of late, he began to question his own certainty that such a life was not for him. He'd told Chance once that he left the fireworks and trumpets to the serious guys, that he believed in pure recreation. He'd never figured back then that someday the game might get boring.

Nor had he ever figured he'd be spending time lost in introspective contemplation, a habit he'd never had before and didn't care for now. If he was going to contemplate anything, it should be Eddie Salazar's death. And what he was going to do about it. Because no matter what the brass at Trinity West said, he was involved in this.

He was a lot more concerned about what Lieutenant Morgan had said. He both liked and respected the man. But he also knew that, regardless of what orders Morgan had been given, he would understand why Quisto couldn't follow them. He had to do this. He had to find out who had murdered a fourteen-year-old boy to make a point.

And there was one very obvious place for him to start. And he wasn't going to avoid it, just to stay out of Caitlin Murphy's way.

Chapter 5

"You've got to stop leaving that back door open."

Caitlin stifled a yelp as she whirled around. "My God, you startled me!"

"Exactly. And I wasn't even trying. Anybody off the street could wander in here."

For a moment, she just stared at Quisto Romero, thinking it quite unfair that any one man had those looks *and* that much flair and charm. He was lounging negligently against the doorjamb, dressed today in a pair of dark blue pants and a pale blue knit shirt that set off his dark coloring and golden-brown skin and made her reconsider her earlier assessment of him. He might be a couple of inches shorter than his over-six-foot partner, and more wiry than bulky, but he was no slouch in the muscularity department.

Eddie had said he was *un gran galante,* a real ladies' man, and she believed it. She was accustomed to Hispanic good looks; many of her kids here and at school were gorgeous, with lovely skin and huge brown eyes that could melt the hardest of hearts. But this man was ... amazing. He looked as if he'd stepped out of some bas-relief on an ancient temple. With those intense dark eyes, softened by long, thick lashes, and that thick, raven-black hair, combed back from his forehead in a neatly feathered cut, she'd be willing to bet there was a string of broken hearts in his wake that would stretch from here back to his police station in Marina del Mar.

"You really should keep that door shut," he said, shoving off with his shoulder and walking toward her. "And locked when you're here alone."

"I don't have air-conditioning in here," she explained. "With that door closed, it gets far too warm."

"Better warm than dead."

She grimaced. "I'm perfectly safe here."

"Then why did you jump a foot just now?"

"I told you. You startled me."

"And it could just have easily been somebody with less generous intentions."

There was no use arguing with him, Caitlin thought. He was a cop, and cops looked for trouble around every corner. And they seemed convinced that every kid in a neighborhood like this was trouble looking for a place to happen. At least, everyone she'd ever talked to seemed convinced.

"Generous intentions?" she asked instead.

Quisto grinned. White, even teeth flashed, and, amazingly, a dimple creased his left cheek. Lord, she thought, she'd underestimated. That string of broken hearts would march all the way to the sea.

"Lunch," he said, lifting a large bag she hadn't even noticed he was holding. "Hope you like Chinese."

"I love Chinese," she said, surprised that he'd bothered, and puzzled as to why he had. Perhaps a peace offering. Their parting yesterday hadn't been of the friendliest sort. If it was, she was willing to accept; peace was, after all, what the Neutral Zone was all about. "Thank you."

"My pleasure." He shrugged. "I was in the neighborhood."

She watched as he set out several of the familiar square white boxes, sets of chopsticks and backup plastic forks, the requisite bag of almond cookies, and the fortune cookies that had become traditional, despite their non-Chinese origin. Caitlin saw that the name on the bag was that of her own favorite source for Chinese food, a small family-run place farther out on the east side.

"The Jade Dragon is a long way from Marina del Mar," she said.

"But the best takeout for miles around."

"Yes, it is. Not many people outside Marina Heights know that."

He paused in setting down a small stack of napkins and looked at her. "I heard about the place from a guy from Marina Heights I arrested once."

"Oh." She should have known, Caitlin thought.

Quisto gave her a wry look. "Actually, my brother told me about it. He eats there all the time. But that's not what you wanted to hear, was it?"

Caught, Caitlin blushed.

"You expected just what I told you, because you're convinced the only thing I'd ever have to do with somebody from Marina Heights would be to arrest them."

She couldn't deny it, not after what she'd so smugly thought when he dangled that bait in front of her. "I'm sorry," she said simply. "I did assume that."

As if he were a little taken aback by her easy admission and apology, he blinked. Without comment, he went back to taking boxes of food out of the bag, until there were half a dozen of them sitting on the bar.

"Is that your brother the doctor?" she asked after a moment, uncomfortable with the silence after being caught in something she rarely did—making assumptions without knowing the facts. That she had accused him of the same thing only made her more embarrassed.

"No," Quisto said absently as he dug out a couple of paper plates. "The contractor." He set the plates down. "My sister goes there, too, though. She likes their rice."

"That's the lawyer?"

"No," he repeated, still absently, as he separated the plates, set them down and turned to opening the boxes. "The account executive. She works for a big ad agency in Marina del Mar and stops at the Jade Dragon on the way home a couple of times a week."

Caitlin hesitated, then asked. "Er...how many of you are there?"

"Hmm?" Quisto opened the last box, then turned his attention to her.

"Brothers and sisters."

"Oh. Eight, altogether."

"Eight?" Caitlin's eyes widened; she was an only child herself, and the thought of that many siblings seemed overwhelming.

"Five brothers, two sisters. All married, with at least two kids apiece."

"My God. Where are you?"

"On the food chain, you mean?" He grinned at her again, and its impact was no less than before. "Alas, the very bottom. I'm the baby Romero. You got a spoon?"

She walked around the bar, pulled open a drawer and handed him a serving spoon.

"Thanks. Anyway," he went on, "it makes for some turmoil when everybody's all together. My partner nearly bailed and ran the first time he came to visit."

"Your partner visits your family?"

"Are you kidding? My mother adopted him the first time she met him." He started to scoop food from the steaming boxes onto the plates: rice, noodles, vegetables, shrimp, chicken and pork. "I think if it had come down to a choice between us, I would have been out the door."

"You're not serious," Caitlin exclaimed.

"I'm dead serious. 'Chance needs me now, you don't,' I think is how she put it."

"Did he?"

Quisto nodded. "He was...going through a really tough time then."

"Didn't you need her?"

He stopped dishing out the food and looked at her. "I always need her. We all do. She's our base, our strength, all the Romeros. She's the reason we're all where we are. But at that time, Chance was barely making it from day to day. He did need her more than I did."

Caitlin swallowed against a sudden tightness in her throat. This man's simple admission of loving emotion, something she never would have expected, moved her nearly to tears. It was a moment before she could speak.

"What about . . . his own parents?"

Quisto shrugged, handing her a well-filled plate. "They're good, loving people. But except for occasional visits, they're a long way away, and they've had simple, fairly straightforward lives. They don't know about the kind of battle Chance was fighting."

She wanted to ask, wanted to know more, but some undertone of finality in his voice told her that he wasn't going to be telling her any more about what had to be something very private to his partner. It was hard to imagine the man she'd so briefly met, his blue eyes sparkling with laughter as he teased his partner, his face showing his barely contained eagerness to get home to his wife, as the man Quisto had just described.

She sat down on a bar stool and pulled a plate close; the aromas were making her stomach growl. "And your mother does know about that kind of battle?"

He offered her a choice of chopsticks or a plastic fork. She was hungry, so she went for convenience over tradition and took the fork.

"Yes," Quisto said as he took his own plate and sat down on another stool. "She does. She knows about being frightened, about guilt and death. She barely got out of Cuba alive when Castro took over. A lot of her family didn't."

Caitlin's eyes widened. "Really?"

"An uncle of hers had seen the handwriting on the wall. He got out back in fifty-three, three years before Castro started his "Twenty-sixth of July" movement. After Batista fell, he spent the next ten years smuggling out the family that had survived. He hired some Americans with the proper political sympathies, willing to run the risk. My father, my mother and my oldest brother, Hernan, came out in the bilges of a fishing boat he'd bought. She was already pregnant with my sister then. They all nearly died from the heat, but they had to stay there for over ten hours. The boat was searched twice by Castro's patrols.''

"My God," Caitlin breathed. "But they didn't find them?"

Quisto took a bite of the sweet-and-sour pork, shaking his head as he chewed. "No," he said after he swallowed. "My uncle had rigged up slings below decks that the people he was smuggling would lie in. When you opened the hatch to the bilge, and looked with a flashlight, you wouldn't see them unless you got down on your hands and knees and practically climbed into the bilge yourself. And he made sure that area was always nice and dirty, so they weren't very eager to do it."

"My God," Caitlin said again. "It sounds like something out of a movie."

"I assure you, it was very, very real to my mother. And my brother." He smiled at her then, as if to purposely lighten the mood. "That's the doctor. He was inspired by the man who took care of them after they arrived in Florida. My sister was born two days after they landed."

"What about your father?"

The lighter mood vanished. "I never knew my father," he said, his voice tight. "Eat. Before it gets cold."

Sensing that she had inadvertently hit on a very sore subject, Caitlin suppressed her inborn aversion to being given orders, and ate. The food was up to the Jade Dragon's usual standards, and she made quick work of the full plate Quisto had given her, casting an occasional glance at him, wondering if he was still upset over what had seemed to her a natural question.

After they finished, he held out a hand with the two sealed-in-plastic fortune cookies lying on his palm, and she judged by his grin that he'd gotten over it.

"Take your pick," he said.

"Doesn't matter, as long as they taste the same."

His grin widened. "I take it you don't believe in the future-forecasting abilities of the fortune cookie?"

She reached out and took one of the bent-crescent cookies. "I think we make our own futures, to the extent that life allows us to."

"Wise," Quisto said. "So don't read, just eat."

Caitlin sighed. "Do you really know anyone who can toss away a fortune without reading it?"

He laughed as he tore open the wrapper of the cookie she'd left him. "I thought perhaps I'd met the first one."

"'Fraid not." She tore open her own wrapper as he cracked open his cookie.

"Hmmm..." he said as he retrieved the narrow strip of paper and read it. "Inscrutable, rather ominous and, as usual, able to be interpreted in a number of ways."

Caitlin chuckled. "What does it say?"

"'The mistakes of the past may overwhelm the joy of the future.'"

"Whew," she said. "Heavy stuff. And kind of grim. I think I'd prefer it the other way around."

"The mistakes of the future may overwhelm the joy of the past?" Quisto asked solemnly.

"No," Caitlin exclaimed. "I meant the joy of the future may overwhelm the mistakes of the past."

"Ah. And therein lies the difference between us, Caitlin Murphy. The pessimist and the optimist."

She saw the corners of his mouth twitch and knew she'd been had. "You did that on purpose," she said accusingly.

"I merely dangled the bait, *querida*. You're the one who bit."

Her sense of humor won out. "And hard," she agreed, laughing.

"So, what does yours say?"

She broke the cookie open and plucked out the strip of paper. "Well, here's some wisdom for you. 'Things are not always as they seem.' No kidding."

"Hey, they stole that," Quisto said, his voice raised in obviously mock outrage.

"Stole what? From who?"

"From Sergeant Decker. He teaches at the L.A. academy. That's his first rule of investigation."

She laughed. "Oh, and he made it up, is that it?"

"He said he did," Quisto said plaintively.

For a moment, Caitlin wondered if he was taking a swipe at her belief in Eddie. But there was nothing but teasing amusement in his eyes, and she decided he wasn't, and laughed again.

"Unfortunately," Quisto said, his expression suddenly serious, "that's a rule I seem to have forgotten. And I owe you an apology because of it."

Caitlin gaped at him. An apology? "What?"

"About Eddie."

"I . . . What do you mean?"

His dark brows lowered. "Didn't Gage call you?"

"Well, yes, he left a message on the machine to call him, but I haven't done it yet." Her mouth twisted downward at one corner. "I didn't want to talk about Eddie anymore. It seems pointless, when nobody—"

"You were right, Caitlin."

"...believes me. I—" She stopped, blinking, as what he'd said registered. "What?"

"You were right. Eddie was murdered."

She stared, not certain she'd really heard him say it.

"I'm sorry," he added. "I assumed you had talked to Gage by now and knew."

"I . . . No."

"It wasn't narcotics in the syringe. At least, not that kind. It was a local anesthetic. For what it's worth, it wouldn't have been . . . painful."

She felt an odd lassitude, when she should, she supposed, be feeling triumph that she'd been right all along.

"Are you all right?" he asked.

"I . . . should feel vindicated, I guess. But I don't. Eddie's still dead. Nothing can change that."

"No," Quisto said, very quietly, "but it can change whether or not whoever did it gets away with it."

"But we know who did it," she said.

Quisto shook his head. "We're guessing."

"But it's the Pack. Isn't it?"

"They're the most likely," he agreed.

"They're who Eddie informed on. It *has* to be them."

Quisto's mouth twisted wryly. "That's not enough to succeed in court. We have no proof."

"But if they found out Eddie talked to you and your partner . . ."

"We don't even know that."

"What do you mean?"

"We don't know if they even know exactly who Eddie talked to. There were a lot of cops, local and federal, involved in that raid. Any one of them could have been Eddie's contact, for all the Pack knows. Unless . . ."

"Unless what?" she asked when he stopped.

"Unless Eddie gave me up."

"No. No, he would never have done that. You were a hero to him. He would have died before—"

She broke off suddenly when she realized that Eddie might have done exactly that. Quisto reached out and laid a hand over hers. His skin was warm, his touch gentle, and she took an unexpected comfort in the contact.

"I know. But there are ways to get information—" He broke off, and abruptly changed direction. "But I don't think he did. The Pack doesn't waste any time, and if they'd learned two days ago I was Eddie's contact, they would have tried for me by now."

"You think they really would? Kill a cop?"

He let out a humorless chuckle. "They killed your chief," he pointed out.

She'd heard that rumor, but the papers had always added a disclaimer saying the Pack was only suspected in the shooting.

"They said in the news that that was...retaliation."

"For our bust," Quisto said, nodding. "Our chief was out of town, so they took out yours. So we heard on the street. And Big Charlie was bragging it up that way."

She knew that was the street nickname of the man who had been the Pack's leader at the time, the man who had been arrested along with several of his followers. "He's still in jail, isn't he?"

Quisto nodded. "And will be for the foreseeable future. But that hasn't slowed them down any. It was always the Pack's policy that the right-hand man stay behind, just in case. So Alarico was right there, ready to step into Charlie's shoes when he didn't come home."

She'd heard that name, as well, from the kids. "'Rules all,'" she murmured.

"Yes. Appropriate name, isn't it?"

"I hear he brags about it. That that's what his name means, and no one had better forget it."

"Sounds like our boy. He's even more dangerous than Charlie was, because he doesn't have Charlie's restraint."

She looked at him, startled by the word. "Restraint?"

"Yes, believe it or not. Charlie picked his targets carefully. And if the risk outweighed the gain, he was like any good military commander—he dropped back and waited until the balance shifted."

"But...Alarico's not like that?"

"Not from everything I've heard. He's impulsive, and that's always dangerous. He doesn't think things through. Although," Quisto added, looking thoughtful, "he hasn't cut loose like we expected him to. We expected things to change right away after he took over, expected the Pack to get more reckless, to act without Charlie's caution. But something's holding Alarico back. We thought for a while Charlie was running them from prison, but there's no evidence of that."

Something struck her suddenly, and she leaned back on her stool as she studied him. "Isn't this...confidential information? Why are you telling me all this?"

He smiled and gave her a look she was sure would have melted the iceberg that sank the *Titanic,* and no amount of telling herself she wasn't susceptible to such practiced charm could make her completely immune.

"By way of apology?" he suggested. "I wasn't very gracious about rejecting your theory about Eddie."

"No," she said, her voice a little sharp, as she fought the unexpected effects of that smiling look. "You weren't. You were determined to think Eddie had come to an end you saw as inevitable."

"Caitlin—"

"He was just a boy. He was as innocent as anybody who lives here could be. He—"

"Was no angel," Quisto said.

"I never said he was. But he wasn't a bad kid. None of them are, not really."

Quisto groaned audibly. "Caitlin, open your eyes. These aren't innocent kids."

She slid to her feet. "Because they've never had the chance to be."

"That's probably true. But it doesn't change the facts. I'll bet half the kids who hang out in here have records as long as your arm."

She put her hands on her hips and glared at him. "Of course you'd bet on it, because that's what you think about *all* of them."

He stood up, eyeing her warily, as if wondering whether she was going to haul off and clobber him again. The memory of that still made her cringe inwardly in shame.

"And I'm rarely disappointed," he said pointedly.

"Somebody once said, if you look for the bad in people, you'll surely find it," Caitlin snapped.

Exasperation rang in his voice. "And somebody else once said there's a sucker born every minute."

Caitlin flushed.

Quisto let out a breath, like a man trying to rein in his temper. "Look, I didn't mean to be—"

"Never mind," Caitlin said, cutting him off. "I'm sure you were just expressing an honest opinion. And you're not the first one to say it, either."

"It's just that if you think even Eddie was an utter innocent, you're kidding yourself."

"While you just assume the worst. Especially about street kids. Why is that, Detective?"

"I don't meet many who aren't, as you put it, trouble looking for a place to happen."

"So if you meet one you don't know at all, you assume he's one of those?"

"I have to."

Caitlin's gaze narrowed. "What?"

"When I meet these kids, they've already done something suspicious, or I wouldn't be talking to them in the first place."

"What happened to 'innocent until proven guilty'?"

"That's for the court system." Quisto looked at her for a moment before he added quietly, "If you're wrong, in most cases the only thing hurt is your feelings. If I'm wrong, people can get killed."

She had no answer for that. Nothing but a heartfelt emotion that she wasn't certain she was feeling for herself, the kids she cared so much about . . . or Quisto Romero.

"It's a rotten way to have to live," she whispered.

"Yes," he said, in a voice that made it seem as if he knew all the ways she'd meant it, "it can be."

They stood there for a long moment, just looking at each other. It seemed there was nothing more to say.

"I have to open up," she said at last, turning to gather up the leftovers from their meal.

"You want me to leave?"

She glanced back over her shoulder at him. "That's up to you. But if you stay, you're not a cop. Not here."

"Fair enough. Unless somebody on our ten-most-wanted list wanders in, I'm just here for a root beer float."

He flashed a smile at her, and she couldn't help smiling back. When he wasn't being a stubborn, bull-headed on-the-job cop, Quisto really could be charming, she thought. If only she could be certain he was off the job when he said he was.

Chapter 6

The afternoon was an education in itself, Quisto thought. Not so much about the decaying neighborhood, or even the dynamics of the groups of kids that came and went. Most of them were the young teenagers and preteens he'd been told she catered to, and he was grateful for that; there was a far greater chance he might have had contact with some of the older ones from the surrounding streets.

No, most of all it was an education in the amazing personality of Caitlin Murphy. She seemed to have an uncanny knack, a knowledge of how to approach each new arrival, changing her demeanor, even her body language, as she greeted each individual or group. Some of the younger ones got hugs, some of the older ones a rapid, slangy greeting that made them laugh, some just a nod and a quiet hello.

But they all had one thing in common, and that was the smile that broke out on their young faces the moment they came through the door and saw her. He heard the words *pelo rojo* tossed out a few times, and grinned at the tenacious Ms. Murphy being called *redhead* so familiarly; it had clearly become a nickname among the kids who came here.

And many did. He had to admit, he hadn't expected the steady stream that seemed to flow in and out of the Neutral Zone.

He watched as she worked the crowd—there was no other expression for it, he thought—and saw how they all accepted her. And when she jokingly waved him off as a forlorn, lost tourist she'd taken in, he managed to merely grimace at the laughter and the hoots aimed at him. But he also noticed that the kids kept a wary distance from him; in this neighborhood, any new face was looked upon with suspicion.

Twice during the afternoon, she disappeared through a door in the yellow wall into what appeared to be a small office. The first time, it was to hand a large manila envelope to a slightly older boy who looked quite pleased with whatever she said to him. The second time, she came out with a small white package that she handed to a frightened-looking little girl of about eleven. She knelt beside the child, spoke to her in soft tones. Quisto heard her say, *"No te preocupes, Alicia,"* saw the girl nod and give Caitlin an unsteady smile, and wondered what she was telling the child not to worry about.

The rest of the time, he watched her fill glasses, hand out snacks and, under the guise of joining in, supervise games of darts and a tournament that seemed to be in progress on the single video game that sat against the side wall, away from the street. The kids were noisy, shouting and laughing, and except for the language being a little cruder, it could have been a kids' party anywhere.

And that, he realized, was her goal. That was what she wanted for these kids, just a brief respite, a few moments of normalcy in a world that would most likely turn ugly for these children far too soon. It was the kind of goal he should be admiring, he thought with chagrin, not sniping away at. Maybe she was foolish and naive, but she was trying, and that was more than many would do.

It was a long time before she finally took a moment's break and sat down on a stool beside him. The clientele had changed slightly, he had noticed as the afternoon wore on; the younger children left, to be replaced by some older ones, kids with a bit more hardness in their faces, a bit more harsh wisdom in their eyes.

But the atmosphere remained calm, although the looks he got were much more speculative than before, tinged with a sexual awareness that had been lacking in the younger kids, as the new arrivals cast furtive glances at him and Caitlin. He could almost feel them assessing, calculating, wondering who he was and what he was doing there, with her. He was doing a little wondering along those lines himself.

"Quite a place you run here," he said.

She studied him silently, as if she were trying to see whether there'd been any sarcasm in his words.

He tried again. "The kids all seem to be having a good time."

"That's what I'm here for. To give them a chance at that. A simple, innocent good time is not something they're very familiar with."

"What's wrong with Alicia?" She drew back, and he saw suspicion flare in her eyes. He shrugged. "I heard you tell her not to worry. About what?"

"Is this the cop asking?"

His mouth lifted wryly at one corner. "I'm not a cop this afternoon, remember?"

"Yes. I just wasn't sure you did."

"It is pretty ingrained," he said solemnly, "but I find I can turn it off occasionally. For instance, when my nephew persists in assaulting me with his slingshot. Or when Mrs. Weybridge, my charming little old neighbor, insists on taking a shopping cart home with her. It is a tremendous effort on my part, of course, but . . ." He ended with a dramatically expressive shrug.

Her smile when she realized he was teasing her was worth much more effort than he'd put into getting it.

"Her father is ill. That was some medication I picked up for him, because he can't get out."

He studied her for a moment before asking softly, "And who paid for it?" She colored, and he had his answer. "That's what I thought."

"He can't go to work, so they can't afford his medicine. They'll pay me back."

He doubted that, but he didn't comment. He made a gesture that took in the entire room. "And the rest of this, Caitlin? Who pays for it?"

"A lot of it is donated. The video game, the dart board, the sodas. The furniture and the bar are mostly old junk we fixed up. I get some small donations, when some of the parents can afford it. And the Corderos, who own the little grocery store on the corner, they donate the cookies, chips and—" she grinned and pointed at his drained glass "—the ice cream."

"You know," he said conversationally, "I've heard it said that some teachers actually take time off in the summer. To take trips, relax, regroup, recoup their energies for another year of keeping up with the little . . . scamps."

Caitlin smiled, waving at the roomful of kids. "This is where my energy comes from," she said, her voice quiet but echoing with dedication. "As long as I can see just a tiny bit of good being done here, I can keep going."

That it was only that, a tiny bit, was something Quisto managed to refrain from pointing out to her. If a tenth of these kids stayed away from the gangs, he'd be amazed. The culture was too entrenched, too accepted. He'd bet the majority of these kids still wound up in gangs before they hit sixteen, some a lot sooner. And of those, half would be dead, or so strung out on drugs that they might as well be dead, inside of two years. A lot of them would be in jail, and the rest would fight it out among themselves, until the few survivors got old enough to be absorbed by the Pack.

Or killed by the Pack; the chances were, it seemed, about even on that score.

"You don't believe in any of this, do you?" she asked, as if she'd read his thoughts.

Quisto chose his words carefully. "I believe you have the best of intentions."

Her mouth twisted wryly. "You sound like my father. He thinks it's hopeless."

He wasn't sure he liked that comparison, but he couldn't deny that he tended to agree with the sentiment. "He doesn't like what you're doing?"

"He says he appreciates what I'm trying to do, but he doesn't think it will work." She grimaced again. "He and my mother would both be happier if I would just come home and be their little girl again."

"That's...understandable. This isn't the safest place for you to be."

She looked at him for a moment. "You think it's useless, too, don't you?"

"I think the odds are against you having much success, yes," he said.

Her mouth quirked. "At least you're honest."

"I will try never to lie to you, *querida.*"

Faint spots of color tinged her cheeks again. Quisto smiled, pleased out of all proportion by this evidence that she wasn't quite as cool and indifferent to him as she tried to appear. But she didn't react to the endearment; she just, Caitlin-like, got back to the subject.

"But isn't any success at all worth it? Isn't one kid who walks away from the gangs, one kid who succeeds in getting out, worth any effort?"

Quisto considered pointing out to her that walking away from the gangs in this neighborhood was as likely to get you killed as joining one was. But the earnestness of her expression forestalled him; he'd done enough today to try to make her face reality.

"I suppose, as long as you have the energy," he said. "But it will eat you alive if you let it, Caitlin."

She seemed surprised at even that much of a concession from him. Apparently to cover her disconcertedness, she hastened around to the back of the bar.

"Want another float?"

He shook his head, smiling. "My mouth says yes, but my waistline says no. With Chance on vacation, I'm being far too lazy."

"Lazy?"

"No racquetball."

"Oh. You two play a lot?"

"Not as much as we used to before he got married." He grinned at her then. "So now we play harder."

She smiled back at him, and again he was startled by how pleased that simple fact made him.

"Who wins?"

"We are, shall we say, about even. He's bigger, but I'm faster."

She laughed, and he felt his own smile widen until he felt like one of the kids, delighted by her attention.

"So, what was in the envelope?" he asked, trying to shake the ridiculous feeling.

"Envelope?"

"The one you gave the other kid. The older one."

Suspicion flared in her eyes again. Quisto sighed. "Talk about assuming," he muttered.

"I'm never sure when a cop stops being a cop. If ever."

"Some don't," he said, "but I was just curious. Not cop-curious, just normal-person curious. He looked quite happy about it, whatever it was."

She hesitated, then accepted his explanation. "It was his homework."

Quisto blinked. "What?"

"You heard me. He had to write an essay for school. I read it over for him. Neither of his parents write English, so I offered to help."

"Oh." Then his forehead creased. "But it's summer."

"And Pedro is in summer school. To improve his English, so he can get a job after school to help his parents." She gave him a pointed look. "He's one of the ones who can escape. He's bright, he's working hard, and he's determined. He'll make it."

If he lives long enough, Quisto thought. But he didn't say it. He just asked, "Where did you learn your Spanish?"

"I took years of it in school, but I don't think I ever really learned it until I got here. Keeping up with the kids, with how fast some of them talk, really teaches you in a hurry."

"I'll bet," he said with a smile.

He watched as a new wave of kids—more older ones, he noticed—hit the bar, laughingly demanding drinks, and making some disdainful comments about the lack of alcohol. This was a rowdier bunch, and Quisto kept a wary eye on them. He frowned when he saw a couple of familiar faces. He turned on his bar stool to survey the room again. A few more older kids had arrived while he and Caitlin were talking, and he recognized two more faces. A knot began to form in his stomach. Because he knew where he'd seen them before. Not in person, but in photographs.

Mug shots. In a crime-warning flyer they'd gotten from Trinity West.

He had to sneak in and out of the station, since he was officially on a vacation day and didn't want to explain to anyone what he was doing, but he managed to surreptitiously make some copies on the machine in the administrative division, deserted at this late hour. Then he used the computer terminal there to pull up the Marina del Mar local files, then the county juvenile files, and came up with about what he'd expected. He copied that, as well.

After a bare ten minutes, he was done, having managed to avoid seeing anyone except the janitor, who was hardly going to report his presence to anyone. He opened the outer door for the man, held it for him as he wheeled his cleaning cart through, and smilingly asked him how he was.

"Hola, José. ¿Como le va?"

"Bien, Señor Romero, bien. Gracias. ¿Y usted?"

He answered with a thumbs-up, then hurried out before anyone else spotted him. He was behind the wheel of his car before the short exchange with José reminded him of Caitlin talking about where she'd really learned Spanish. His mouth twisted into a rueful grimace. Everything lately seemed to remind him of something to do with Caitlin.

And Caitlin, he thought, wasn't going to be happy with what he'd found out tonight. His expression became grim as he started the car. He pulled out into the street, thankful that traffic was light after eleven o'clock.

He'd had to do it, he told himself. If she didn't know what she was dealing with, she could wind up in danger. She had to be more careful. At least careful enough to keep that damned back door shut when she was in there alone. And to get her to do that, he had to convince her that the kids who came to the Zone weren't the harmless innocents she kept insisting they were. Hell, if one of them strolled in with a gun, she'd probably insist it was a toy, right up until he shot her with it.

The image slammed into him with the force of a large-caliber bullet. He hit the brakes, then glanced around, in some part of his mind aware that he'd been lucky no one was behind him. Then he pulled to the side of the road, stunned by the impact the brutal vision of Caitlin lying dead in a spreading pool of her own blood had had on him.

He sat there, trying to slow the slamming of his heart while he tried not to think about why the image had hit him so hard. It had been like that instant on the case where Chance had met Shea, that moment when he burst through a door to see Chance down, blood spreading beneath him. It hadn't been his, but the moment before he'd known that was etched on Quisto's mind with gut-wrenching clarity. Nothing had ever jolted him like that, before or since. Until now. And this wasn't even real, just his imagination gone haywire.

He ran a hand over his face, feeling the stubble on his jaw. He'd meant to go home, to figure out the best way to approach her with knowledge she wasn't going to want to hear. He'd meant to work out a tactful approach, a way to tell her what she was dealing with without making her mad at him, if that was possible. He'd meant to go back in the morning, maybe take her to breakfast, and discuss it calmly.

But there was nothing calming about what had just flashed through his mind, nothing calming about picturing the glorious red-gold of her hair matted with blood, nothing calming about the thought of bright blue eyes gone glassy and lifeless, vacant of everything, including the trust that had killed her.

He couldn't wait. He *wouldn't* wait. And he didn't care if she got angry at him. If he hurried, he might still catch her at the club. She didn't close up until eleven, and she'd said she had some paperwork to clear up, something about the city council and a complaint about her use of the building. As if it really mattered in this neighborhood, where the Neutral Zone was one of only three places open for an entire city block.

He drove hurriedly, pulling into the alley behind the Neutral Zone when he arrived. The door was closed, he saw, but when he walked up to it he found it unlocked. He pulled it open without knocking, and saw a shaft of light spilling out across the floor from the open office doorway.

He should, he told himself, sneak up on her and scare the daylights out of her. Maybe that would teach her to lock that blasted door. But the memory of that painful, bloody picture of her was too fresh, and his nerves were too raw. He couldn't do it. So instead, he called out her name.

Seconds later, she appeared in the office doorway. She was still wearing her paint-flecked jeans, and those absurdly small white high-top tennis shoes on her feet, but she'd pulled a heavy sweatshirt over her T-shirt. The pale yellow sweatshirt was decorated simply with the logo of the Marina Heights Middle School. She had pulled her hair back into a ponytail with a yellow cloth band of some kind. She looked young, effervescent, energetic even at this hour... and very much alive.

"Quisto? What are you doing back here?"

"I just...wanted to talk to you. But I can wait until you're done."

"I was just wrapping up. Come on into the office."

He followed her into the lit room, which was bigger than he'd expected, a long rectangle about seven by twelve feet. At the end nearest the door, beneath an old schoolroom-style clock, was a desk, rather cluttered with a basic single-line desk phone atop an ancient-looking answering machine, a battered-looking rotary card file, some file folders, several loose scraps of paper, and a framed photograph of what appeared to be a slightly younger Caitlin and a good-looking young man with eyes nearly as blue as her own and a mop of hair nearly as blond as Gage Butler's. Perhaps Gage was wrong in thinking he wasn't Caitlin's type, Quisto thought sourly.

She sat in the battered desk chair and began to put the file folders into a drawer. Quisto glanced around the rest of the office.

A file cabinet sat beside the desk at a right angle, and next to that a narrow, four-foot-long table was placed against the long side wall. It held a coffee maker, a small radio, a partial roll of paper towels, and a large stack of worn-looking books. At the other end of the office, opposite the desk, were a sofa and a small lamp table that barely fit along the narrower wall. On one arm of the sofa sat a pillow and a neatly folded blanket that made him twitchy; surely she didn't sleep here?

Quisto had to stop himself from constantly looking back at the framed photo on the desk, wanting and not wanting to know who the man was at the same time. His irritation with himself put an edge in his voice.

"You left the back door unlocked."

She shrugged. "Sometimes one of the kids comes by after I close up the front."

"So, naturally, you leave it open."

"Don't worry, I lock it when I leave."

"When you leave?" he yelped, that bloody image still too vivid in his mind. "Damn it, Caitlin, it's *you* you should be worried about protecting, not this...this..." For once in his life, words failed him, and he waved rather vaguely at their surroundings.

She leaned back in her chair. "I've done it that way for a year, long before you ever wandered down here."

"You've been lucky."

She sighed audibly. "Are we going to fight about this again?"

"We don't have to fight about anything, if you'll just see reason."

"Meaning your way of looking at things? I don't think I'd like that."

He raised one leg to sit on the edge of her desk, looking at her with an earnestness that wasn't at all feigned. "Then how about some plain common sense? Caitlin, you're here for the exact reason you should be more careful. Because this is a rough neighborhood. If it wasn't, there'd be no need for a place like the Neutral Zone."

To him, the logic was infallible, but he was still a little surprised when she nodded in agreement.

"Exactly. But if those kids think I'm afraid of them, then any chance I have to accomplish anything here practically vanishes."

"And not being afraid of them could get you killed."

It came out so tight, so hoarse it startled him. It seemed to surprise her, as well, because she started to speak, then stopped, as if reconsidering a sharp retort. It was a moment before she did speak. Softly.

"Have you ever heard the phrase *self-fulfilling prophecy,* Quisto?"

He hesitated, afraid of not having his voice under control, then finally risked a simple "Of course."

"If the world thinks you're rotten, you might as well be rotten, since you're going to get blamed for it anyway. And if these kids know I don't trust them, then there is a proven tendency for them to live up to that distrust."

"Theories are fine, when you're a psychologist in an ivory tower somewhere," Quisto said, his voice steadier now, as anger at her disregard for her own safety began to build again. "But you're down here, in the gutter, where kids like Eddie get murdered just to make a point."

Caitlin paled, but she didn't waver. "That was the Pack, not my kids."

"Where do you think the Pack comes from? Those kids you're so devoted to are the minor leagues, Caitlin. The Pack's own personal training ground. And those that survive, the ones that are tough enough and nasty enough to live through it, make it to the Pack as adults."

She leaned forward. "Don't you see? That's what I'm trying to stop. My kids are still young. If I can just show them another way..."

"I'll grant you that some of them may be salvageable. Some of the really young ones. But—"

"I know they are, Quisto," she exclaimed. "Why, do you know, eight months ago Pedro, the boy whose paper I looked at, could barely read?" She gestured toward the stack of books on the table behind her. "And now he's read every one of those books I brought in for him. When everyone else was out in the big room, he hid back here and read, like a starving person who's eating for the first time in days. From *Huckleberry Finn* to *Don Quixote,* he read them all."

Her enthusiasm, the pure joy in her eyes, was infectious. If she'd chosen to be a revolutionary, she could have inspired fighting in the streets. And perhaps she had done just that, he thought. But that joy, that light in her eyes, only made him even more vividly aware of what she was risking. He chose his words carefully, speaking as gently as he could, still battling that image of her lying dead on this very floor.

"All I'm asking is that you be a little more careful about your own safety, Caitlin. Any kid who lives around here is going to understand you locking the doors at night. They're not fools."

"Neither am I. I know better than to think a locked door is going to stop someone who really wants in."

He drew back a little. She'd surprised him again with that sound judgment. She was such a strange mix of naiveté and wisdom, he never quite knew what to expect from her. She seemed to recognize his quandary, and pressed her point.

"Besides, I don't know that what little I'd gain in security would be worth what I might lose in trust. The kids might see locking the door now, after nearly a year of not doing it, as a sign that I'm giving up on them."

Exasperation was growing, along with his anger, both fueled by his fear for her. "Don't make this a symbolic thing you end up dying for."

"My kids would never hurt me. They're—"

"Thieves," he said, his voice turning cold in the face of her stubborn faith. "Burglars. Oh, and a purse snatcher who specializes in taking off little old ladies the day they get their social security checks."

Caitlin stared at him. "What?"

He yanked some folded sheets of paper out of his back pocket. He shouldn't be showing them to a civilian, but he couldn't think of any other way to convince her. Besides, Gage had put the bulletin out, and he didn't think he would really mind. In fact, he was a little surprised the Trinity West detective hadn't done it himself.

He opened the stapled pages to the photographs, and held them out to her. Beneath each stark but clearly recognizable photograph was a list of offenses, most starting with petty theft, then escalating, one of them as far as assault with a deadly weapon on a shopkeeper who had had the nerve to ask for ID when the boy tried to purchase alcohol.

"Six of Marina Heights' finest problem children," he said. "Real high on Trinity West's list of kids to be watched. And three of them were in here last night."

She stared at the pages for a long, silent moment. Then, in a hollow voice, she said, "You weren't supposed to be a cop last night."

"I wasn't, Caitlin. If I had been, if I hadn't promised you, I would have nabbed ol' Frank there. He's got an outstanding warrant for burglary. Broke into his own grandmother's house and stole her heirloom silverware." He sat back and folded his arms across his chest. "So if you think you're safe because a lot of these kids like you, think again."

With slow, painfully precise movements, she refolded the documents. She handed them back to him without looking at him. She got to her feet, wrapped her arms around herself and walked a few feet toward the back of the office, as if she couldn't stand to be close to him.

"What did you hope to accomplish with that?" she asked, in that same hollow-sounding voice.

"I hoped," he said, "that you'd listen. That you'd be more careful. That you'd see some of these kids for who and what they are, and not wind up dead because you persist in wearing rose-colored glasses."

She turned and looked at him then, and what he saw in her eyes made his stomach knot. Pain, sadness and awareness combined there to give her a look of somber wisdom far beyond her years. He'd meant to shock her into realizing the truth; he'd never meant to utterly tear down her defenses. She kept walking, then turned and sank down on the couch.

"I know they're not angels," she said once more. "I've always known that. And I never expected them to magically become angels just because I'm trying to help."

"Caitlin," he began, remorse welling up inside him, making him wish he'd never done this to her. She kept on, as if he hadn't spoken at all.

"All I can ask of them is that they behave here, on my terms. And pray that some of them see the good side of... playing by the rules. They can't choose a better path if they don't know or believe it exists. And I'm not naive enough to believe I can make them choose a better path." She lowered her eyes, staring at her hands, which were clenched into fists on her knees. "I just want them to know there *is* another way."

Quisto didn't know what to do. He felt slightly ill, as if he'd purposely destroyed something beautiful in his effort to make it fit into a mold it wasn't made for. The most he'd ever felt before, when dealing with a woman, was a slight discomfort if she refused to accept his efforts to keep things light and on the surface. But this feeling, this sickening combination of guilt and remorse, was something completely different, something he'd never encountered before. And he didn't know how to deal with it. Or the fact that he'd severely underestimated her; what he'd thought was naiveté was simply a fiercely determined optimism in the face of ugliness.

"Caitlin..." he said softly. She didn't look up. He crossed the room, half expecting her to dodge away from him. She didn't. He sat down beside her. "Caitlin, I'm sorry. I never meant to... hurt you like this."

She made a tiny sound he couldn't have labeled. "The truth hurts, isn't that what they say?"

He swore inwardly. Barely realizing what he was doing, he put an arm around her shoulders. She stiffened, but then let him pull her against him. He still didn't know what to do, or say; he didn't get into emotional conversations with women. That was opening the door to a closeness he wanted no part of.

But he couldn't deny that he badly wanted to undo some of the damage he'd done tonight.

"You *are* doing good here, Caitlin. Really. It's just that... sometimes I..." He took a deep breath, searching for words. "I see so much of the bad sometimes, I forget there's just as much good."

She moved; it was a tiny motion that could have been a shrug or merely a deep breath. He resisted pulling her more fully into his arms; he didn't think Caitlin Murphy was a woman who would respond to his more usual methods of comforting distressed females. But she seemed to be listening, and that was more than he'd hoped for at first. And when he spoke again, he was shocked to hear himself pouring out what had brought him racing over here tonight.

"And I've only been pushing you because I'm afraid something might happen to you if you're not more careful. I don't ever want to come over here and find you... a victim of your own trust."

She leaned back then, looking up at him. "Is this how you... charm your ladies? Express a little sincere concern about their welfare, and then... what? Offer to protect them? To be the big, bad cop and chase away the bogeyman?''

He winced, for once more ashamed of his reputation than laughingly amused by it. "Did I say you were too trusting?"

"Among other things."

"Trusting of everyone but me, it seems."

"Maybe with good reason."

He didn't want to know what those reasons were. He'd never worried much about what other people thought of him; he was who he was, and they could either take it or leave it. It was an attitude he'd reached long ago, when he came to terms with his life, his history, his family. But this woman made him question things he'd long taken for granted. She made him question himself, and that was something he didn't much care for.

"Maybe," he said at last, on a long, weary exhalation. "But I wish you would believe that I really didn't mean to hurt you tonight."

"You just meant to rub a little reality in my face."

He sighed, closing his eyes. "Yes."

"And now that you have?"

His eyes snapped open. She was looking at him, whatever she was feeling for once hidden by a neutral expression.

"I wish I hadn't," he admitted. "At least, not like this."

"Then why did you?"

He grimaced. "If I told you, you'd think I was loco."

"Tell me anyway."

He couldn't. He knew he couldn't. There was no way he could tell her about that ugly, bloody vision. And then, before he could stop himself, he was doing it. The words were coming in spite of his efforts to stop, coming in short, choppy bursts.

"I ... had this ... thought about ... something happening to you. About finding you ... on the floor here, bleeding ... dying ... because you left that door open once too often ... It was so damned real, I ..."

He finally managed to stop, shaking his head, wondering what the hell had gotten into him, talking like this.

She didn't speak. Beyond a slight widening of her eyes, she didn't even react. But she leaned toward him once more and, without a word, let her head rest against his shoulder.

And he felt as if he'd been given a medal.

Chapter 7

"He must have turned it over to V and I, because nobody in Detectives has it. Haven't heard a thing since the day they warned you off."

Quisto frowned as he changed lanes, then spoke into the cellular phone again. "Can't you check with your vice guys, see if it landed on them?"

Gage laughed. "Only if you can find them. Those guys take their superspy stuff real serious."

"Great," Quisto muttered, squinting as another turn headed him directly into the morning sun.

"If I hear anything— Yes, sir, that's right. Your son was given a bicycle citation for riding on the sidewalk."

Quisto blinked, then chuckled. "Lieutenant Robards passing by?"

"Absolutely."

"So the gag's really on?"

"And you might want to buy him a lock for that bike, sir."

"That tight, huh?"

"Yes, sir."

"Damn." Quisto eased into the left-turn pocket and came to a halt at a red light. "Listen, thanks for your help."

"No problem. I know exactly how you feel."

Quisto didn't know the young detective beyond their two meetings and a couple of phone calls, but he sensed the man meant exactly what he said. However young he might be, Gage Butler knew what it was like to be personally involved in a case and to have roadblocks thrown in front of you at every turn.

"Someday you'll have to tell me why you know."

"Someday I will. Okay, it's all clear now, Robards is headed for the can. With any luck, he'll be gone for half an hour."

Quisto laughed. "Gage, my friend, how long have you been a cop?"

He heard a rueful chuckle. "Don't you mean how old am I?"

"Ah. You've been asked before."

"Constantly."

"So?"

"Don't let the baby face fool you. I'm twenty-eight, buddy. And aging fast."

Only a little younger than he was himself, Quisto thought. It must be that he was just feeling old lately. "The job will do it," he said.

"Yeah. Listen, if I do hear anything else, I'll call you."

"Thanks." Quisto meant it; he knew that if the other detective was caught passing on information on a case both of them had been ordered to leave alone, they'd both go down in flames. "Better take my home number, though. And my pager. I'm . . . taking a couple of days off."

"Oh, really?" Gage's tone was dry. "Somehow that doesn't surprise me."

"Sure it does. Because I didn't tell you that. You haven't even talked to me."

"No, I haven't, have I? But in case I should want to, say, call you about a lateral transfer to the upper crust, give me those numbers."

Quisto chuckled, and gave him the numbers. "Don't get yourself in a bind over this, though."

Gage laughed. "Been there, done that. If Robards isn't mad at me, I figure I'm not doing my job."

Quisto laughed again, really beginning to like the man. As he hung up, he wondered why Caitlin had apparently rebuffed his interest. Perhaps because of the man in that photograph on her desk. He wondered why she kept it there, instead of at home. Perhaps she had another one there.

But most of all, he wondered who the lucky guy was.

"Gage won't tell me anything, either." Caitlin kept pacing her narrow office, as she'd been doing since Quisto had arrived and told her things were in limbo.

"He can't tell you what he doesn't know. He doesn't even know who's got the case anymore."

Caitlin turned to Quisto and gave him a baleful look. "Probably because nobody has it. They're not doing a thing, are they? They've just written Eddie off as another street kid who won't grow up to give them problems as an adult, haven't they? They're probably glad about it—"

"Caitlin, stop. You know that's not true."

"Do I?"

She knew her voice was rising, but she couldn't help it. Eddie was dead, and nobody seemed to care. Nobody seemed the least bit interested. Not even Gage, and she'd thought he was different. And then she had hoped, when Quisto had seemed so shaken about Eddie's death and had even gone so far as to apologize to her when he found out she'd been right and it truly was murder, that he would take some action. But that hope had apparently been unfounded, as well.

"So that's it? It's all over? Gage does nothing, you do nothing..."

"I told you, I can't do anything. It's out of my—"

"Jurisdiction. Yes, so you said. What a joke. If somebody robs a bank in Marina del Mar, do you stop chasing him at the city limits?"

"Sure," Quisto said, sounding weary of the whole thing. "And we all hang out at doughnut shops all the time, too. And harass taxpaying citizens with traffic tickets instead of catching criminals. Or any one of a dozen other old stereotypes about cops you'd like to drag out."

He said it in the way of a man who had heard such accusations far too many times. She looked at him thoughtfully for a moment; she'd never thought of it that way, that cops were on the receiving end of such stereotyping as much as anyone else. And it probably wasn't any more true than the assumptions people made about her kids.

As if he'd read her thoughts, he went on, his tone more level now. "Why don't you go teach a class at Marina del Mar High next semester?"

Caitlin frowned in puzzlement for a split second before his intent registered. "Because I don't work there," she said wryly. "Which is your point, I suppose."

"Do it anyway."

She sighed. "I'd be in big trouble. I get the point, Quisto."

"I've been ordered off, Caitlin. So has Gage. It's up to whoever's handling it now."

"And we don't even know who that is."

"No. Not yet."

She sat down on the couch, weary of pacing, weary of thinking, weary of everything. "I talked to Eddie's mother. They won't even let her . . . have him."

"It's a murder case now. That means a full autopsy, and a lot of other details."

"She's very worried. She wants to see him properly buried, but she's afraid she can't afford it."

Quisto sat beside her, and for a moment she was deluged with memories of last night, when he'd held her so gently, when she'd sensed his genuine remorse at having so bluntly forced her to let down the resolute optimism that was her only shield against the misery she saw every day. She'd felt comforted in a way she never would have expected, and she'd begun to question her assessment of this man.

"Does she blame me, too?" he asked.

Her gaze shot to his face. He hadn't sounded hurt, or upset, but as if he were merely asking for routine information. But another memory, of her own emotional outburst to Rosa Salazar, castigating the then unknown Detective Romero for getting Eddie killed, rang in her mind, making her uncomfortable now that she knew he hadn't intentionally done any such thing. She looked away, staring at her hands in her lap.

"Why do you ask?"

"I would like to go and see her, speak to her. But not if my presence is going to upset her."

She felt even worse now, in the face of his gentlemanly concern for Eddie's grieving mother.

"I . . . don't know how she feels now. She was very upset at first. And I . . ." She made herself look at him. "I didn't help much, I'm afraid. I was very angry at you."

"I noticed."

A ghost of a smile flitted across his face, and his mouth quirked at one corner. The left corner, she realized, where her slap had landed. She flushed, and looked away again.

"I'm still sorry about that. I abhor the use of violence, and then I go and do something like that."

"Maybe it's good that we're reminded of the power of rage and grief now and then," Quisto said softly. "It helps us understand why people sometimes do things they normally wouldn't."

She lifted her head to look at him again, this time in nothing short of amazement. Was this the same man who had come here last night, intent on shattering what he thought were her foolish illusions about the kids who frequented the Zone? Was this gentle wisdom coming from the cop who had called her a sucker for believing in those kids?

Perhaps this was not the cop, she thought, but the man. Perhaps this was the man who let his voice echo with unembarrassed pride in his own mother's courage. The man who had understood when his partner needed that woman's courage more than her own son did for a time. The man who had been so struck by some kind of mental image of Caitlin, hurt and bleeding, that he came back here late at night, on his own time, in an effort to warn her. There were, it seemed, many layers to Quisto Romero.

"That was—" she hesitated, looking for the right words "—a most eloquent acceptance of my apology. Thank you."

"You're welcome." He gave her that crooked grin that, despite her knowing it had probably been one of the main weapons in his arsenal of charm for years, still made her smile back. "But next time, if you please, warn me? So I can duck? You have a wicked right."

"There won't be a next time," she promised fervently. "I feel badly enough about this one."

"Thank you, *querida.* I feel safer now."

His tone was light, teasing, and she laughed. But even as she did so, she became very much aware of the scant few inches between them on the couch. He seemed so close, much closer than he actually was, and she didn't understand why she was feeling so tense. Hastily she stood up, with an unsubtle look at the clock on the wall above her desk.

"Nearly time to open," she said briskly.

He rose, looking at her as if he'd sensed her haste—and the reason for it. "Do you get a bigger crowd on Fridays?"

She nodded as she pulled open the center desk drawer. "Usually. Not as big as Saturday night, but bigger than during the week."

"Rowdier?"

"A little." She reached into the drawer, then paused, looking back at him. "But just weekend high spirits. They don't get nasty, if that's what you mean."

"And the occasional stoned or drunk kid doesn't wander in off the street?"

Caitlin sighed; he was back to thinking she was a fool. As soon as the exasperated sound escaped her, Quisto's hands came up in a gesture of denial.

"That was not an . . . attack on your common sense. I'm truly curious. Maintaining such peace in what is, in some respects, a war zone is an amazing feat."

Mollified, Caitlin answered him as she plucked the door keys out of the drawer. "Of course they wander in now and then. But the kids and I wander them right back out again."

"And they just . . . let you?"

"They know I'll call the police if I have to. And the other kids don't want the Neutral Zone shut down, which could happen if the police can show we're a nuisance, so they help keep things under control."

"So you get them to act in their own best interests, is that it?"

She smiled at him. "Exactly."

He was silent, watching her, for a moment. Then he said slowly, "And you're hoping it will sink in that if they can keep this little corner of their world under control, they can do it elsewhere, as well?"

Caitlin's breath caught. He understood. The tough, cynical Detective Quisto Romero understood.

"Exactly," she repeated, her voice almost a whisper. "If I can just get them to realize they don't have to give in to the violence, the scare tactics, then they have a chance."

"I wish you luck, Caitlin Murphy."

He said it solemnly, almost like a benediction. There was no doubting his sincerity, and she felt a sudden tightness in her chest. Her fingers tightened around the keys. She had to turn away, afraid he might see the sudden sheen of moisture in her eyes. She didn't understand why or how this man's approval had become so important to her, but it had.

She closed the drawer, saying, more as a distraction than anything else, "I'm hoping I get some of the older kids tonight, like I usually do on Fridays. I want to talk to a couple of them. I might be able to find something out."

"Find something out?"

His voice had changed somehow, but she couldn't quite pin down the difference. She walked out of the office, toward the front door, looking back over her shoulder to see that he was coming after her.

"A couple of them knew Eddie," she explained. "He was kind of at that in-between stage, you know? Too old to be with the young ones, but not old enough for the older group." She reached the door, slid the key into the lock and turned it. "But he was always trying to hang out with the older kids, so some of them might know something—"

"Caitlin—"

"And I know at least one of them has been making noises about knowing somebody in the Pack. If I—"

"Caitlin, stop!"

She gave him a startled look as he gently but firmly grasped her shoulders, turning her away from the door. Then he reached over and turned the key in the opposite direction, locking the door again.

"What's wrong?"

"What's wrong?" He stared at her. "You're talking about poking around in a murder, probably committed by a group that accepts only the toughest of the street-gang survivors, and you're asking what's wrong?"

"I'm just going to ask some questions."

"And how long do you think it would take before the Pack got word you were poking that cute little nose of yours into their business?"

She felt heat rise in her cheeks, and told herself it was due to anger at his arrogant interference, not the reference to her looks.

"I wasn't going to come right out and ask them about the Pack," she said. "I'm not stupid."

"I never said you were. But this isn't helping a kid with his homework."

Her hands went to her hips, and she glared at him, indignation rolling off her in almost palpable waves. "So the little lady should stick to her schoolwork, is that it?"

To her amazement, he grinned. "You're not going to have any luck proving me a sexist, Caitlin. Not with my mother. She thumped that out of us boys very early in life."

She didn't know which took the wind so thoroughly out of her sails—that blasted grin, or the easy amusement and pride in his words.

"Oh. What did you mean, then?"

"I just meant," he said, "you should leave the investigating to the police. Just like we leave the teaching to you."

"I'd be happy to leave the investigating to the police. If I had any idea who to leave it to. If I had any faith at all that anybody was really doing anything."

"Somebody will be working on it."

"Somebody? A fourteen-year-old boy is dead, and that's the best you can do—*somebody* will be working on it?"

Quisto expelled a long breath. "I think it only fair to warn you, *querida,* you are in danger of proving an old, tired cliché true."

"What cliché?" she asked, eyeing him warily.

"That red hair signifies a temper to match."

"My temper has nothing to do with it," she said sharply, although she could feel her grip on it falter. When she went on, the words came in a rush. "Eddie's dead, no one would believe he'd been murdered, and now that they do, his poor mother can't even bury the child. You and Gage both tell me you don't know a thing, can't find out a thing and don't even know who's assigned to the case, and no one seems to give a damn. I have a right to be angry!"

She turned her back on him and unlocked the door. She pulled it open and saw a small group of kids clustered outside on the sidewalk. Regulars, some of the youngest, waiting for her to open.

"Caitlin," Quisto said as the kids—three boys and two girls—headed toward the door, "I mean it. Stay out of this. It's far too dangerous."

She stubbornly didn't answer him. Nor did she look at him, for fear that he would see the determination in her eyes.

"Caitlin..." he said warningly.

"I heard you," she muttered, acknowledging him but promising nothing. Then she raised her voice to a normal tone, calling out to the kids cheerfully, "Hi, Matt! Sandra, you look great, I like your hair that way. *Ah, Carlito, ven aquí.* Mr. Cordero sent over a box of those cookies you like."

She sensed, rather than saw, Quisto moving away. More kids arrived on the heels of the first, then more still, and when she finally had time to look around, he was gone.

When the boy she'd been waiting for finally arrived, a couple of hours later, Quisto's warning played back in her mind. She hesitated, but she couldn't just let it go. Quisto's hands had been tied, and no one at Trinity West seemed to be pushing for any answers. Eddie's mother was shattered, beyond even asking the police what was being done about her son's murder, even if she'd been the sort to do so in the first place. No one else seemed to care except her.

But she would be careful, she thought. She didn't want another lecture from Quisto; she'd already had quite enough of his opinions on her life and the way she ran it. Although, she had to admit, it gave her a warm feeling that he had bothered, that he had seemed genuinely worried about her. He'd even left her his card, with his home number scrawled on the back, and a pager number in case that didn't work. He'd been the very picture of honest concern. Her mouth twisted wryly; it was no doubt part of his reportedly legendary polished charm, giving women that feeling.

But there hadn't seemed anything polished about his tense description of the grim, bloody image that had driven him back to the Neutral Zone last night. And little of conscious charm, and everything of warmth and honesty, in the way he'd held her afterward.

When she finally talked to the boy, Quisto's concern and her own intentions seemed wasted; he merely stared at her with wide eyes, seemingly stunned that Eddie's death had been a murder. Perhaps all his talk about the Pack had been just that, she thought, talk.

She tried a couple of the other older boys, but got the same reaction. The rumor that Eddie had overdosed had apparently been easily acceptable to these kids, who lived with that kind of occurrence on a daily basis.

She was wondering what to do next when she was approached by Sandra, one of the quieter and more reserved of the older girls, who came in only occasionally.

"You're crazy, asking questions like that," Sandra said, looking over her shoulder nervously, as if looking for anyone who might overhear them.

"That seems to be the consensus," Caitlin muttered under her breath.

Sandra pushed her sandy-blond hair back behind her right ear. "Alarico, he doesn't like anybody asking questions about the Pack," she warned.

Caitlin froze, then tried to cover the reaction by reaching for the girl's empty glass. She hadn't said a word about the Pack, she'd only asked if anyone knew what had really happened to Eddie.

"I'm sure he doesn't," she said after a moment, when she had her expression schooled to neutrality. "And he's a big man on the streets, isn't he? Head of the Pack now?"

"You'd better be careful, Caitlin." Sandra leaned forward, whispering now, fear echoing in her voice. "My boyfriend, he...sort of hangs out with the Pack. He says there's one of them, a big Indian guy, he said, who's very scary. He takes care of things for Alarico, you know?"

"Things?" Caitlin asked. Like maybe a kid who talked to the police?

Sandra nodded vehemently. "He's nobody you want to mess with."

"All I want to know is if anybody knows anything about what really happened to Eddie."

"Let it go," Sandra urged her.

"I can't," Caitlin said. "Somebody has to care."

"Hey, we all liked Eddie. But you can't help him now. And he liked you a lot, Caitlin. He wouldn't want something to happen to you on account of him."

"What's going to happen to me?"

"Who knows, if you keep asking questions like this and it gets back to Alarico? And it will. He knows everything that goes on."

"How?"

Sandra glanced around again, the fear in her eyes growing. "He just does. He may hang out over on Steele Street, but he's got people everywhere, not just on the east side, you know?"

Steele Street. The east side. Where they'd found Eddie, propped against a Dumpster, like so much garbage.

"I gotta go," Sandra said, her fear finally winning out. "You just stop, okay?" The girl was nearly running by the time she reached the door.

Everyone, it seemed, was determined to scare her off. First Quisto, now the kids. And all she'd done was ask a couple of simple questions. She hadn't even mentioned the Pack. But it was obvious that Sandra, at least, assumed that the Pack was behind Eddie's death. Had the girl already known it was murder? Had she heard something from her boyfriend? And what was his connection with that band of adult thugs, who could teach even the most vicious youth gangs lessons in savagery?

She thought about it for the rest of the evening, and she was still thinking about it when at last she locked up and headed home. She knew she was right; even Quisto had admitted it was probably the Pack. But one girl's scared warning hardly constituted proof. And that was what she needed—proof. Something concrete, something she could take to the Marina Heights police station on Trinity West and wave in their face, something that would force them to get serious about this. Maybe Eddie had only been a kid, and maybe he hadn't meant much to anyone except his mother and her, but he deserved better than to have his death swept under the carpet like a dustball.

She slept little that night. By morning, she was tired, angry and frustrated, wondering if there was any fairness at all in this world. It was no mood in which to be calling Eddie's bereaved mother, but she'd promised. Rosa was still heart-sore, and Caitlin listened to her wail, her Spanish failing her at some of the more intense moments. She had hoped that when Rosa learned her boy had been murdered, not died in that awful way, she would become angry enough to overcome her grief, but obviously the woman had not yet reached that point.

That's okay, Caitlin thought. Soothing words of comfort were all she could offer for the moment as she said goodbye and hung up, thinking, *I'm furious enough for both of us.*

And she was. Furious enough that when she left her small apartment—small because it was all she could afford, with the expenses of keeping the Neutral Zone open—instead of heading for the club, she turned her battered little blue compact toward the east side. And Steele Street.

He was going to stay away, Quisto told himself. And he was going to stop sitting here in his darkened apartment overlooking the marina, thinking about Caitlin Murphy. She was far too unsettling, and he didn't like being unsettled. He didn't know why or how she managed to do it, but she did. And, he admitted rather grimly, time and distance didn't seem to be helping much.

He hadn't seen her since yesterday afternoon, when he'd walked out of the Neutral Zone, shaking his head in exasperation over the woman who couldn't see that she was swimming in shark-filled waters. He couldn't tell her that he wasn't giving up, especially when he was working not only without authorization, but actually against a direct order. He'd had to pretend he was doing nothing, and she'd come up with this half-baked plan of hers.

He'd called Gage and asked him to have the uniforms go by the club a little more often than usual. He himself, on the other hand, would be keeping his distance.

"Something wrong?" Gage had asked, concern in his voice.

"Just a lady who can't take orders."

There had been a pause before Gage said, "I know a cop or two like that."

Quisto knew what the man was asking, and guessed from Gage's guarded language that he was being monitored somehow. "You pick up some . . . fleas or something?"

"One-sided ones," Gage said, indicating that he didn't think his phone was tapped, only that he was being listened to on his end.

"Great," Quisto muttered. "Just have Patrol keep an eye on the place, will you? I know they can't sit there, but I'm afraid she's going to be drawing some attention to herself with some questions she'd be better off not asking."

Gage let out a low whistle. "Damn."

"Exactly. I told her not to, but I get the idea the lady's not much for orders."

"No, she's not." There was a pause before Gage added, "You seem to be . . . spending a lot of time with her. There something going on there, Quisto?"

"She's just driving me crazy," Quisto said wryly.

"You want to define that for me?"

Something in Gage's voice made Quisto remember his statement that he didn't know Caitlin as well as he'd like to. "Got her staked out already?"

"No." Gage's tone was surprisingly flat. "I don't have . . . any room for that in my life right now."

Quisto sensed there was a great deal behind those words, in the same way he'd once sensed that behind Chance Buckner's unflappable exterior was a haunted man. And he also sensed that Gage Butler was about as likely to talk about it as Chance had been.

"But that doesn't mean I want to see her get hurt," Gage added.

"Was that a warning?" Quisto asked, mildly curious.

"Let's just say I've heard some stories recently about a certain Marina del Mar cop's success with the ladies."

"My reputation precedeth me, is that it?"

"Something like that."

"Well, don't worry about it. There hasn't been much room for that in my life lately, either."

He had hung up then, feeling more than a little embarrassed by the reputation he'd once been amused by, and perhaps even the tiniest bit proud of. He'd always told himself he wasn't hurting anyone, that he never kept it a secret that he played the field, never made any promises of exclusivity to any of the many women he saw on a casual or sometimes more serious basis. He'd been open and generous to them all, and he'd heard little in the way of complaints.

Except, of course, from those who wanted more than he was willing to give.

And if there had seemed something lacking in those effortless relationships of late, it was simply that he'd been preoccupied, busy, involved in some complex cases. It wasn't that his outlook had changed. It wasn't that his partner was a living, breathing example that something more existed, that it was possible to be absolutely crazy in love with somebody and have it returned.

None of which explained why he was still sitting here in the dark on a Saturday night, when he would normally have been out on the town, contemplating the reflection of the lights on the water of the marina outside his window. Not that he hadn't done this before—more often lately, it seemed—but it had never been with this vague sense of dissatisfaction. Somehow the sight of row upon row of boats, from small runabouts to luxurious yachts that cost more to keep up than he earned in a year, was more than just an ironic comment on people's priorities. He kept thinking of the wall at the Neutral Zone. All those faces, kids who would never have kids of their own. Kids the people who owned these boats would look at warily, and no doubt lock their doors against.

He could have been one of them. Easily. Had his mother not possessed an unquenchable courage and determination, he could have been one of them. But she'd worked long hours, ruled her children with an iron hand, and made certain every one of them got an education, which she saw as a fighting chance to make it.

And she'd done it alone for the past twenty-nine years.

He took a sip from the still-full shot glass of tequila he held; it burned all the way down his throat. That was an old, worn pathway that he refused to tread right now. He had enough to think about without dwelling on useless, galling things he could do nothing about.

He had to think about Eddie, and what he was going to do. He'd put out some careful feelers to some people on the street today, knowing he was walking a fine line; technically, the department couldn't control what he did on his off time, but when it came to disobeying a direct order, they did more than frown. He'd be up on insubordination charges faster than he could write down the word.

But he couldn't just walk away. If Gage had still been handling the case, Quisto might have let it go and trusted him to do the job right. Even if Trinity West's much-vaunted felony unit had landed the case, he might have left well enough alone; Cruz Gregerson seemed sharp enough to deserve the reputation his unit had earned throughout the county. But something was happening with this case, something odd, and it gave him that twitchy feeling he'd learned early on in his career never to ignore.

With a disgusted sigh, he stood up. He yanked the drapes closed, shutting out the view of the marina. He picked up his glass and walked to the bar, dumping what was left down the aluminum sink. Even his favorite tequila had lost its appeal.

He went to bed still disgruntled, trying to write his uncharacteristic mood off to what was—or wasn't—going on with Eddie's murder, but feeling it was more than that. And wondering where all this questioning of his own feelings had come from; he'd never been much given to a great deal of introspection.

Surprisingly, he slept. Fitfully, but more than he had for the past couple of nights. And when the phone rang just after dawn, he was so soundly asleep it took him several fumbling moments to find the thing.

"'Lo?"

"Quisto?"

His grogginess vanished at the sound of her voice, at the undertone that made every nerve, every trained instinct, go instantly on alert. "Caitlin?"

"Yes. I..."

He sat up straight, wide awake now. "What's wrong?"

"I'm sorry, I know it's early—"

"Caitlin, what's wrong? Are you hurt?"

"No, no, I'm not... It's just... I found..." He heard her take a deep, shaky breath before going on. "Could you...come over here? To the Zone?"

What was she doing there on Sunday morning? She didn't even open on Sundays. He opened his mouth to ask, and to demand that she tell him what had her so shaken, but suddenly the phone was a remote, distant thing. She'd said she wasn't hurt, but he wanted to see for himself.

"I'll be right there."

He was grateful for the lack of traffic so early on a Sunday morning; thanks to the deserted streets, he was there in less than fifteen minutes. He hadn't bothered to shave, eat or even grab a cup of badly needed coffee, and he'd combed his hair with his fingers as he drove; nothing seemed more important than getting to her.

When he arrived, he nearly sprained his wrist yanking at the back door. It was locked. And the fact that she had at last taken his advice scared him even more than the sound of her voice had. He pounded loudly, calling her name.

She was there quickly, pulling the heavy door open. He took one look at her face, at her wide, horror-filled blue eyes, and pulled her, none too gently, into his arms.

"God, what is it? What happened? Is somebody hurt?"

She sagged against him, and he heard her make a gulping noise that sounded as if she were fighting back tears. She seemed, as she'd said, unhurt, but he wasn't sure seeing the dauntless Caitlin Murphy like this, frightened and shaking, wasn't worse than a physical injury he knew how to deal with.

"Caitlin, honey, what's wrong?"

The endearment, one in English that he couldn't ever remember using before, slipped out without his thinking about it, but she didn't seem to notice. He heard her take a deep breath, and felt her draw herself up straight, steadying herself with an effort that was visible. She turned out of his hold, and walked into the Neutral Zone and across to the front door.

Mutely she gestured toward the door, seemingly beyond words. He looked, but saw nothing unusual. He noticed that the key was in the lock; she'd apparently already had it open this morning. He reached out and turned the knob. The door swung inward.

The smell of blood hit his nose in the instant after his eyes registered the viscous red-brown puddle on her doorstep. And on the door itself, in large, bloody letters was scrawled the word *curiosity*.

Chapter 8

"'Curiosity killed the cat,'" Caitlin said. "I suppose that's the message?"

"The Pack has never been known for its subtlety."

Quisto felt her tremble. They were sitting on the couch in her office, Caitlin with her knees drawn up in front of her, leaning against his side as he kept his arm around her. She seemed to take comfort from it, and was calm now, but he knew the bloody mess he'd just cleaned off her doorstep was still vivid in her mind. It was in his, and he was a lot more used to such things than she was.

Then she looked up at him, her wide blue eyes troubled. "I'm sorry I bothered you, but—"

"That doesn't matter now. Just tell me what happened."

"I know you think I should have called the police, but... I'm already fighting with the city to stay open, and if they got hold of this... The cops are always very nice about it, but I know they'd rather see me gone...."

She let her voice trail off with a helpless shrug. He refrained from pointing out that she had, in essence, called the police. Or that she had put him in a difficult position; he should report this to the locals himself. They needed to know what kind of trouble was possibly brewing on their doorstep. But he already knew he wasn't going to do it. She'd trusted him, and he wasn't going to let her down.

"Never mind that, either, right now," he said. "What happened?"

"I heard a noise at the main door, just after daylight. I got up, went out . . . and found just what you saw."

"What kind of noise?"

"I . . . don't know, really. A thump or something."

He let out a relieved breath. She hadn't heard them kill the animal, then; judging from the amount of blood, he had to assume it had been done right there at her door, but he certainly wasn't about to point that out to her, either.

Then something she'd said struck him. "You got up?"

She nodded slightly; he felt, more than saw, the movement.

"Got up, as in...woke up?" he asked carefully. The tiny movement came again. Quisto nearly bit his tongue in his effort to keep his voice even. "You slept here?"

"This couch folds out into a bed. It's comfortable, really, and—"

"Caitlin, are you out of your mind? Sleeping here?"

"I've done it before, lots of times. Sometimes I'm just too tired to drive home."

"Lots of times," he echoed, groaning. He tried to rein in his temper, but his roiling stomach wasn't making the task particularly easy. "Tell me you at least lock the back door then?"

"Of course I do. That's why it was locked when you got here."

Somewhat mollified, he felt his stomach go back to merely being a large, painful knot.

"So you couldn't resist poking around, could you?"

She wrapped her arms around her upraised knees. "I told you, I couldn't just let it go," she said.

"Caitlin, I know how you feel, I really do, but you're in way over your head. You know that now, don't you?"

She looked up at him again, puzzlement clear on her face this time. "That's what I don't understand," she said. "I didn't find out anything. None of the kids knew anything, not really."

"Not really?"

"One of the girls said I should stop asking questions about the Pack, when I hadn't even mentioned them at all. So I think she knows it was them, but we already know it was, so that wasn't worth much. And Sandra never would have told anyone I was asking. She warned me, in fact, just like you did, about asking questions."

"And you listened to her just as well as you listened to me," Quisto said dryly.

"I know you're angry, and I suppose you have every right to be, after I woke you up so early on a Sunday."

"Caitlin, I told you, it's all right."

She took a deep breath, then let it out in a sigh. "Thank you for... cleaning that up. And scrubbing the door. You didn't have to do that."

"No point in leaving it for the world to see. Although I'm sure the Pack would have preferred it that way."

"Why?" she asked. "Why bother? It only gave them away, because if they didn't kill Eddie, why would they care if I was asking questions about him?"

"Because they don't like anybody asking questions about anything to do with them."

"But I didn't find out anything. So why warn me?"

"You may know your kids, Caitlin, but you have a lot to learn about the mentality of the Pack. If they let you get away with poking around, they've lost some of their power to intimidate. And that's what their power base is built on."

"Well, they certainly have Steele Street intimidated. No one would even talk to me. They just laughed."

Quisto froze. "What?"

"They laughed. They didn't even bother to threaten me, just laughed and walked away."

"You went to Steele Street?" It took everything he had not to shout it.

"I just wanted to—"

"You went to Steele Street?" he repeated, his grip on his rage slipping by the second.

"Well, that's where they found Eddie, and I thought if—"

"You thought?" He lost his battle abruptly. He leaped to his feet, turning to stare down at her. "Like hell, you thought! My God, Caitlin, are you crazy? I know you're not stupid, so you have to be just plain out of your mind!"

She winced, but she met his gaze. "Okay, maybe it wasn't the smartest thing—"

"Maybe? You go poking around in the Pack's turf, practically hammering on their front door, and *maybe* it wasn't the smartest thing?"

She stood up then. "I had to do something! Eddie's dead, and nobody's doing anything, and—" She stopped, blinking rapidly, and Quisto saw the moisture pooling in her eyes. She bit her lower lip so fiercely, he was amazed it didn't bleed. And he was more amazed at the fact that he almost felt the pain himself.

"Caitlin—"

"Somebody has to care," she said, her voice a hoarse, strained whisper, as she lowered her brimming eyes. And she was shaking. Not over what had been done to her, he knew, not over the gruesome discovery she had made, but over the simple fact that a boy had been murdered and, from what she could see, no one seemed to care. Her efforts were useless, and she had to know it, deep down, but she was fighting anyway. The only way she knew how.

His anger evaporated as something hot and painful and vaguely familiar stirred inside him. He felt the way he had as a child, when his big brother had crawled home bloody and beaten by the very street gang he'd refused to join. Or when his so-strong sister had quietly wept after losing out on a promotion simply because there was an equally but not better qualified candidate who had the advantage of being male.

He didn't stop to analyze the feeling; he wanted only one thing right now—Caitlin out of here.

"Get your things," he said gruffly.

Her head came up. "What?"

"Get your things together. We're getting out of here."

"What?" she repeated, staring at him.

"You heard me."

"But I have things to do—"

"Not here, and not now. You have other clothes here?"

"Yes, some. Why—"

"Good. Change. You've got blood on those."

"I need a shower—"

"You'll get one. How about a toothbrush?"

"In the bathroom, but—"

"I'll get it. Change. Grab anything you want to take. You've got five minutes," he said.

"Quisto, I appreciate your help—"

"Then show it. For once, just do as I ask and don't argue, will you?"

He turned on his heel and strode out of the office, walked through the main room, hearing his footsteps echo in the high-ceilinged emptiness. He went into the small bathroom, saw a toothbrush and a small tube of toothpaste on the sink and a hair dryer and hairbrush on the tiny counter, along with a small cosmetics bag. He saw a plastic grocery bag looped over the door handle, and lifted it free. He grabbed everything and dumped it into the bag, then walked quickly back to the office, wondering if she was going to cooperate or be stubborn about this.

To his surprise, she had already changed into fresh jeans and a silky-looking black shirt that made her hair look like a summer sunset at its most brilliant moment.

"Thank you," he said, relieved that he wasn't going to have to fight her.

"For once," she said.

He looked at her, puzzled. "What?"

"You said for once do as you said without arguing. Okay, I will, because I'm sorry I dragged you out here so early. I'm just reminding you this is only for once."

A smile tugged at the corners of his mouth, but he stopped it; he didn't think she'd appreciate it. And he could never explain that he was smiling not because he found her funny, but because he found her...what? Admirable? Brave? Courageously honest? Or simply dangerously attractive?

All of the above, he muttered silently. "And after this it's back to fighting me tooth and nail every step of the way?"

"If necessary."

Quisto let out a sigh, but inwardly he was acknowledging that he'd expected nothing less. Caitlin Murphy was not a woman who gave up. Ever. Even if it meant putting herself at risk.

Which meant it was up to him to keep her out of harm's way. The question was, where? Under normal circumstances, he would have had any number of options, any number of places he could take her. But now he was running alone, and if he used any of his usual resources, he would only make things worse if things caved in on him.

If Chance had been around, he would have called for help, but he and Shea weren't due back until tomorrow. They were probably still lounging in the sun somewhere right now; Chance had been more than a little secretive about where they were going. So it was more likely, Quisto thought wryly, knowing those two, that they were still making mad, passionate love somewhere, and hadn't even seen the sun yet.

Caitlin moved, picking up her purse and leaning over to switch on the answering machine. The silky blouse clung to her, and the nipped-in waist of her jeans set off the soft, feminine curve of her hip. Heat blasted through Quisto, a barrage of sensation that nearly staggered him. Barely able to breathe, he stared as she tidied a few things on the desk, wondering what on earth had hit him.

He knew what physical attraction felt like, had on more than one occasion been hit by—and sometimes acted upon—a bolt of pure, unadulterated lust. But this...this was something different. This wasn't a tickle that made him think of scratching, but a demand, fierce and seething and beyond anything he'd ever known, that made all his experience seem useless. He felt like a man in what he thought was a familiar place who finds that all the road signs have been changed.

She straightened and turned to look at him, and he made a desperate effort to pull himself together. He was going to have to move that attention to his libido up on the priority list, he thought ruefully, if this was what a woman so far from his usual type, a woman who didn't even like him much, did to him just by moving a certain way. He'd get Caitlin settled, and then he'd attend to that.

The question was, get Caitlin settled where? He had no more choices now than he'd had before he was hit by that freight train of hot, clawing need. Her place, which she'd told him was only a few blocks away, was far too close to the center of this hurricane she'd stirred up. Even his place was too close, and besides, despite her seeming compliance, he didn't trust her to stay put for very long if he left her alone while he did what he had to do.

There was only one place he could think of. And as he led her out to his car, past her worse-for-wear compact, he winced at the thought. He put the bag with her things in the back seat, then held the door for her, contemplating all the while. He knew what would happen, knew what taking her there would mean, the heat he would take afterward, but he had no choice right now. He was on his own, out-of-bounds as far as the department was concerned. Which meant he had nobody to depend on except the people he had always depended on.

With a sigh, he got into the driver's seat.

After about twenty minutes, they left Marina Heights for the county area that bordered it. Quisto made several turns, and they entered an older but well-kept neighborhood of small stucco houses, most of them coolly shaded by large trees. Caitlin thought it peacefully inviting, but wondered where they were headed; Quisto hadn't said much since they'd left the Neutral Zone.

Quisto slowed as they turned first onto a narrow side street, then into a short cul-de-sac. He slowed further when they saw a group of children playing some sort of combination of soccer and hockey with a soccer ball and some sticks. Caitlin heard the slap of wood on the leather ball, and the shrill yelling and laughter of childish voices. It all seemed so very normal, and the ugliness of this morning seemed to recede a little.

"¡Tío Quisto!"

One of the bigger children, who looked about eight or nine, yelled out at the sight of the car, and Quisto waved. Uncle? Caitlin wondered. He'd brought her to one of his brothers' or sisters' houses?

She looked at him, surprised. But before she could ask, they were surrounded by chattering children, some speaking Spanish, some English, and a couple a fractured combination of both that made Caitlin smile. But it came from all of them at once, so rapidly and so loudly that she quickly gave up trying to understand it all. Besides, she already knew by their grins and excitement the thing that she found most interesting; whoever these kids were, they knew and adored Quisto Romero.

He answered them laughingly, reaching out to tousle the hair of the one who had called him uncle.

"Will you play a game with us?" the boy asked eagerly. "You can be on our team again."

"Lo siento, Chico. Not this time. Besides, you guys are too tough for me."

The boy looked disappointed, but then he shrugged. "That's okay. You don't have to be sorry. We're ahead by ten goals, anyway."

Quisto laughed. "Don't get too confident, *mi hijo.* That's when they sneak up on you."

"Okay," the boy agreed easily. Then he looked at Caitlin. "Who's she?"

"A friend."

"Oh. How come you brought her here? You never bring ladies here."

Caitlin glanced at Quisto and saw, to her amazement, that he was blushing. "Never mind," he told the boy, avoiding looking at her.

Chico studied her for a moment. "Are you a detective, too, like Uncle Quisto and Uncle Chance?"

Caitlin blinked, surprised. "No. I'm a teacher."

"Oh." The boy made a face. "Yuck."

"Chico..." Quisto said warningly.

"Sorry," the boy said quickly. "Teachers are okay. Just not in summer."

Caitlin laughed. "I'll go along with that."

Chico looked surprised in turn, then grinned. "I wouldn't mind having you for a teacher. You're pretty, and you have a nice laugh."

"Thank you," Caitlin said. She flicked her gaze back to Quisto. "The Romeros learn young, it seems."

He muttered something she couldn't hear, then told the boy, "Go back to your game. I'll see you later."

He drove carefully past them, and Caitlin heard the mysterious game resume behind them as soon as the car passed. So Quisto Romero played with kids in the street, she thought. That was something she never would have expected. She gave him a sideways glance; he was watching the kids in the mirror, smiling.

At the end of the block, the car slowed again, in front of the house at the end of the turning circle. Caitlin looked at the tidy little house and the front yard, which was a wonderland of plants, flowers and birdhouses, and appeared to be a haven for scattered toys. Then she looked at Quisto, who shrugged, his lips twisting into a wry expression as he eased the car into the driveway.

"Which sibling lives here?" she asked.

"None of them. Anymore, that is."

"Oh. I thought because . . . that was your nephew, wasn't it?"

"One of them, yes."

"Then who does live here?"

Quisto opened the car door, put one foot out onto the concrete of the driveway, then looked back at her.

"My mother," he said, and got out.

Caitlin sat motionless, completely taken aback. His mother? He'd brought her to his mother's house?

How come you brought her here? You never bring ladies here.

Chico's words came back to her vividly. Was it true? Of all the women he was reputed to have dated, had he really brought none of them here? And if it *was* true, why her?

Because, she told herself wryly, he's not dating you.

But Chico hadn't said girlfriends, just ladies. Did that mean—

"Are you going to get out?"

Caitlin blushed; she hadn't even realized he'd come around and opened her door. She scrambled out of the car.

"Why bring me here?" she asked, more bluntly than she'd meant to.

"My mother will take good care of you."

Caitlin frowned. "Take care of me?"

Quisto shook his head, as if regretting his choice of words. "Just come inside, will you?"

She did, without protest, not because she needed taking care of, but because she was immensely curious about this woman. Both because of her amazing personal history, and because she was the mother of one of the most exasperating, bothersome men Caitlin had ever met. If all the Romero brothers were like this one, she wanted to meet the woman who apparently managed to keep them all in line.

And it had nothing at all to do with the fact that she was more fascinated by Quisto Romero than by any man she'd ever met.

The first thing that struck her was how tiny Celeste Romero was. The second was how much her youngest son resembled her. The same quick, lustrous dark eyes, the same thick dark hair, the same finely drawn features. She was a beautiful woman, just as her son was a beautiful man.

Mrs. Romero greeted her effusively, and welcomed her into her home with a courtly grace that also reminded Caitlin of her son. No sooner was she supplied with a cup of perfectly brewed coffee than Quisto took his mother aside and spoke to her rapidly. Caitlin was tempted to try to eavesdrop, since the woman's glances her way indicated that they were talking about her, but she resisted the urge, and wandered over to look at a long wall that was covered with photographs.

Unlike the somber wall at the Zone, this wall was covered with the remembrances and milestones of a large family, school photos, parties, graduations, weddings, babies. She found herself smiling when she was able to pick the irrepressible Quisto at various ages out of the group photographs, and grinning at the serious expression he'd worn in his high school graduation photo. She read the diploma beside the picture. Rafael. Yes, it was, as he'd said, a bit dramatic, she thought. But, as she'd replied, so was he. Just a bit. Just enough to get all the feminine attention he seemed to attract so naturally.

By comparison, the photo of him at his police-academy graduation was a joyous thing, that flashing, devastating smile betraying his elation as he'd achieved a dream. She knew just by looking at him that that was what it was; it was clear from his expression that it was something he'd wanted very, very much. And he looked impressive in the dark blue uniform, although even the formality of the hat pulled low over his forehead couldn't detract from the sheer exuberance the image portrayed.

Caitlin found herself blinking rapidly as she backed up a step and looked at the entire expanse of pictures. It was a wall of joy, as opposed to a wall of grim reminder, and in that moment Caitlin decided that this was what the yellow wall would become, that there had to be a place for the good, that the kids needed that as much as, if not more

than, they needed the reminders of what could happen.
Good tests from school, she thought. Graduations. Birthdays. Yes, there should be a birthday section, celebrating
another year, to counterbalance the years never to be lived.
And she'd add—

"I'll be back in the morning," Quisto said, close to her
left ear.

"Mmm..." she said, still looking at the wall. Then, as his
words sank in, her head snapped around and she stared at
him. "What?"

"I have some things I have to do, but Mom will take good
care of you. I'll be back to get you tomorrow."

"Excuse me? You can't have said what I think you said."

Quisto looked like a man facing a battle he'd expected but
hoped to avoid. "Caitlin, please—"

"You don't really expect me to just stay here, do you? I
have things to do, a life—"

"And I'm trying to make sure you keep it," he said, his
voice grim.

"You just drop me here and take off, and I'm supposed
to sit quietly and wait for you to come back? You can't be
serious."

"I am," he said, reaching out to grasp her shoulders and
turn her to face him. "Deadly serious."

She stared up into his face, her brows lowered, a dozen
furious protests on her lips. But something in his eyes stayed
her tongue; he *was* serious. There was more than worry in
his eyes. There was fear. Fear, and it was genuine. And for
her. The thought rattled her, that this man she'd thought so
uncaring just a week ago was now so concerned about her
safety that he'd brought her to his own mother's home.
Where he'd never brought a woman before.

"Just until things settle down a little," he said. "Until
we're sure that . . . mess this morning was the extent of their
message, and not just the beginning."

She wavered, remembering the awful nausea that had
swept her when she opened the door to that bloody scene.
Maybe he was right. A day away wouldn't hurt, not really.

And she would like to talk to his mother. Just because she'd led such an interesting life, of course.

"Besides," Quisto said, his voice changing, as if he'd sensed her thoughts, "if you leave now, you'll hurt my mother's feelings, and I'll be hearing about it for weeks."

"That alone might be worth it," she said, thinking she'd dearly love to see the smooth, charming Quisto Romero being chewed out by his tiny mother.

"Ah, *querida,* no, have mercy," he said, his voice taking on the inflection that she realized came whenever he said anything in Spanish, as if he were thinking in the structure of the other language. The formal structure, not the rough-and-tumble street Spanish most of her kids spoke, although she guessed he spoke that, as well.

And she wondered why the Spanish endearment didn't have the effect on her that that one brief "Caitlin, honey" he'd spoken had had. Perhaps because the *querida* seemed just something he said, part of that Latin charm that no doubt fascinated the ladies.

Or perhaps just because she was kidding herself into thinking it had meant something.

"Have mercy?" she asked, shoving her silly thoughts aside.

"You have not seen my mother in action. If you had, you would take pity on me and save me from such a fate."

She almost laughed. And when Celeste Romero appeared to announce that she had fixed breakfast for them both, and stifled her son's protest with a stern "Be quiet and eat, Rafael. You don't take care of yourself properly," she couldn't resist. She would stay, she thought. Not because she was afraid, or even because of Quisto, but out of sheer curiosity.

And if there was anyone willing to satisfy her curiosity, she thought a few hours later, it was Celeste Romero. Quisto had apparently told her only that Caitlin was a teacher dealing with the unpleasant death of a young friend. After expressing condolences and empathy rather than sympathy, she accepted Caitlin's desire to talk about something else. When she realized she had a genuinely interested audience, Celeste began a string of reminiscences that held Caitlin rapt for hours. It was a tale of lives torn apart by revolution, of brushes with death and narrow escapes, of a once wealthy aristocratic family beginning again with nothing in a new country and, despite all the adversities, forming bonds that could never be broken.

Except, apparently, for one. One that was conspicuously absent, except for a brief mention now and then. And when the mentions did come, it was as if they were of someone bigger than life, legendary, in the same tone people used when they spoke of presidents and revolutionaries.

I never knew my father.

"Quisto's father..." Caitlin began, but stopped, not sure what she wanted to ask, or even if she wanted an answer.

"Ah, Esteban," Celeste said, a look of sadness mingled with pride in her dark eyes. "Our pride, and our cross to this day. Rafael, he has never forgiven his father."

Caitlin felt as if she were prying, but she was driven by a need to know, a need she didn't quite understand. "You and your husband... you're divorced?"

"No. Esteban is my husband, and it will always be so."

The older woman's voice matched the look Caitlin had seen in her eyes, sadness and pride combined.

"Quisto said... he never knew his father."

Celeste looked at her curiously. "He told you this?" When Caitlin nodded, she seemed surprised. "He does not usually speak of his father, not even to us, his family."

"Why? What has he never forgiven him for?"

"For not being here. He has been gone since before Rafael was born."

"Gone? Where is he?"

"He is in Cuba."

Caitlin blinked. "But... Quisto said he came out when you and his brother did, on that boat..."

Celeste's eyes widened. *"Dios mío,"* she breathed. "Even this he told you?"

Caitlin nodded. And, unexpectedly, Celeste smiled. Widely. Taken aback, Caitlin could only shake her head in confusion.

"I don't understand. Quisto's father...he went back to Cuba?"

"He has been there since before Rafael was born."

"Why?"

"Esteban, he is a...passionate man. And he has one passion that overshadows all else. He has never given it up. He never will. He lives to see our home one day free again."

"You mean...he went back to...to what?"

"To organize. To lead. To fight. And if necessary, to die." Celeste smiled. "It is...ironic, is it not? Rafael is very much like his father, although they have never known each other."

Celeste looked at her hands, and for the first time Caitlin really noticed the simple gold wedding band on her left hand, thin now with age and wear. "I did not know I was carrying Rafael when my husband left us."

"He never came back?"

"No, *mi hija*," Celeste said gently. "He could not."

Caitlin barely noticed the affectionate term. "Why?"

"Because, the day after he reached Cuba in my brother's boat, he was captured by Castro's soldiers."

Caitlin's breath caught. Celeste nodded.

"He is...what they call a political prisoner. He has been for all these years. He is allowed no letters, no communication, because they fear him, fear the people will rally to him if he is able to spread his words. He does not even know Rafael exists."

Chapter 9

Caitlin yawned, stretched and sat up, a little surprised that she had slept at all. But after a fascinating—and very illuminating—day and evening spent talking with Celeste Romero, she had been unexpectedly relaxed, and had slept deeply. Quisto's mother had seemed determined to lighten the mood after the grim story of Esteban Romero's fate, so Caitlin had heard many tales of Quisto's youth, some that had made her smile, some that had made her cry.

And when Dr. Hernan Romero, Quisto's distinguished-looking oldest brother, arrived to pick up his son, Chico, he had contributed a story about a disaster with a barbecue at a family picnic, involving a fire engine and a couple of disgusted fire fighters, that made her grin.

And when he followed that up with the story of how the nickname Quisto had grown out of Chico's inability to pronounce the title already given to the youngest Romero son by the rest of the family—*conquistador*—she had laughed out loud, even as she realized it was probably more appropriate than she would like to believe. With his looks and his charm, and those old-world manners he could ex-

ercise when he chose to, she was sure Quisto could have any
woman he wanted under his spell.

After Hernan and Chico left, Mrs. Romero had insisted
she eat what was to her a huge dinner, and long before her
usual time, Caitlin had been yawning. She had taken a
longed-for shower and toppled, half-asleep, into the bed in
the guest room Celeste had shown her to.

"Thank you, Mrs. Romero," she'd said.

"Call me *Mamá*," the woman said, a gleam Caitlin didn't
understand in her eyes. "Everyone in the family does."

Her last waking thought had been that if this was the
welcome total strangers got, it was no wonder Quisto's
partner had found comfort here.

And now, as the morning sun streamed through cheerful
red-and-white curtains, she felt more rested than she had
since the day she had received the phone call about Eddie.
Quisto had been right; she'd needed this. She would even,
she thought ruefully, admit that she had needed his mother's pampering and fussing. How many strays, she wondered, had Quisto brought home for his mother's tender
care?

She shrugged out of the T-shirt she'd slept in, and dressed
quickly in her jeans and shirt from yesterday. Still bare-
foot, she wandered toward the kitchen, smelling the entic-
ing aroma of coffee and more than ready for a cup of Mrs.
Romero's—*Mamá*'s—delicious brew.

She stopped in her tracks when she realized *Mamá* had
company, three people gathered around the dining room
table. A man she'd seen once before, and a beautiful woman
with thick dark hair and enormous soft gray eyes, holding
a baby she was feeding something orange-colored out of a
small jar. The Buckners, it seemed, were back from their
vacation.

"Well, well..."

The man leaned back in his chair, grinning at her. Caitlin
stared at Quisto's partner, her face flaming as she remembered the last—and only—time she'd ever seen him. Quisto's mother began introductions, but got no further than

Caitlin's name before Chance Buckner interrupted her with a raised hand and a laugh.

"We've met, *Mamá*. So to speak." He stood up, and offered his hand. "Nice to see you again, Ms Murphy." He looked at the woman sitting beside him. Quiet pride tinged his voice when he said, "This is my wife, Shea. And my son."

The woman looked at Caitlin with interest. "Forgive me for not getting up," she said, her voice lovely and melodic, "but getting Sean to eat is always an adventure, and I don't want to interrupt the process."

"Oh, no, don't, not on my account," Caitlin said quickly, watching as Shea sneaked a spoonful into the baby's mouth while he looked at the newcomer with interest. The boy, who looked somewhere between one and two, had his father's bright blue eyes and his mother's thick, dark hair, a striking combination.

Mamá Romero bustled about, pouring Caitlin a cup of coffee and then departing to the kitchen, insisting she needed a nice breakfast, ignoring Caitlin's demurral and refusing her offer of assistance.

"So where did you two meet?" Shea asked as she wiped her son's chin.

Caitlin flushed anew, and Chance laughed.

"Remember the redhead with the mean right hook I told you about?" he said to his wife.

Shea's eyes widened. "Really?"

Caitlin groaned with embarrassment, but the feeling faded when Shea looked at her, her gray eyes alight with lively amusement. "Darn. I would have loved to have seen that. I miss all the good stuff."

Despite her discomfiture, Caitlin couldn't help smiling back. "I'm so embarrassed," she said. "It's just not like me to do anything like that."

"I understand, Caitlin," Chance said softly. "I heard about Eddie." Her gaze went to his face. His eyes were warm with understanding, and when he spoke again, his voice was quiet and oddly comforting. "We all do things out of character sometimes, under stress."

"Yes," Shea agreed softly. "We know that better than most, I think."

Caitlin looked at them, at the quiet contentment and unmistakable love that glowed in their eyes, and wondered what awful battle they'd had to fight to get to where they were. But there was knowledge there, too, and she knew they meant what they'd said. And that they would understand.

"I feel even worse," she admitted, "now that I know I was wrong."

"Wrong?"

"About Quisto."

Shea looked at her assessingly. "Many people underestimate him, in many ways. Some see only the surface charm, some see only the cop."

"And some never look any farther," Chance added.

Caitlin's gaze flicked to the big man; had that been aimed at her?

"There's a lot more to Quisto than meets the eye," Shea said. "That's why he's Sean's godfather. And Sean is his namesake."

Caitlin blinked. "He is?"

Chance nodded. "Sean Rafael Buckner."

"Because," Shea put in quietly, "if not for Quisto, Sean might not be here at all. And Chance and I . . ."

She let her words trail off, looking up at her husband with a love so pure glowing in her face that Caitlin felt her throat tighten unbearably.

"I was working undercover on a case when we met," Chance said quietly.

"And I was a suspect," Shea said wryly.

"To everyone but me," Chance said. "And Quisto, because he took my word."

"But when I found out Chance was an undercover cop, I thought everything we'd shared was a lie. If Quisto hadn't come to me and convinced me otherwise . . ."

Both Chance and Shea looked down lovingly at their son, who was playing with a shiny lock of his mother's hair, trying his best to smear his breakfast into it. Sean Rafael Buckner. There were more facets to Quisto Romero than she ever would have imagined, Caitlin thought. She had, just as Shea had said, underestimated him.

There was no way around it, Quisto thought resignedly. He'd spent all day and most of the night talking to every cop he knew and could trust to keep his mouth shut, and every contact he had on the street, and he'd gotten exactly nowhere. He'd known, probably from the start, that there was only one way he was going to be able to get this done, but he'd hesitated, knowing how much trouble he was letting himself in for if something went wrong. Against orders, out of his jurisdiction, using department-owned property, on a case being hushed up at a high level . . . there couldn't be a more volatile recipe for disaster. Or any more potent reasons to simply stay out of it.

And on the other side there was only one reason to get involved in it. The death of one skinny fourteen-year-old street kid who had trusted him.

He sat up on the edge of his bed, running a hand over his stubbled jaw, then yawning once more. He'd only had about four hours of sleep, but it would have to do. He needed to get over to his mother's and pick up Caitlin.

Caitlin.

Perhaps there was another reason to get involved.

He shook his head sharply, then got up and headed for the shower. For the first time in a long time, he felt the need to take a cold one. His mouth twisted wryly; Quisto Romero didn't have to take cold showers. But then, he didn't react to women the way he reacted to Caitlin Murphy, either. He was cool, controlled, and most of the time relatively uninvolved, even in the most intimate of moments. He liked it that way.

And if he wanted to keep it that way, he'd better quit thinking about a certain strawberry blonde, he told himself. But how he was going to do that, when she was smack in the middle of all this, he didn't know. He still couldn't tell her what he was doing, couldn't risk it. So how was he going to keep her from poking around even more, and perhaps earning herself more than just a grim, bloody warning? That warning might slow her down, might make her a bit more cautious, but he doubted very much that it would stop her.

So, he thought as he let the water roll over him, he'd just have to move fast. He would call in and take the next couple of weeks off, maybe more. He had the time coming, and although it was unusual to take it like this, it wasn't unheard-of. Lieutenant Morgan would no doubt have his suspicions about what he was up to, but hopefully he would look the other way long enough for Quisto to get the job done. He would make some calls to some people he trusted to set up what he needed, and make sure that the few members of the Pack who could recognize him were still locked away. Then he'd come back here and change cars; the BMW was much more in keeping with the hasty cover he'd worked out.

But first he would pick up Caitlin and deliver her safely to the Neutral Zone. He would prefer to take her home and tell her to stay there, locked up and safe, but he had a fairly good idea what kind of reaction that would get.

And he'd have to stay away from her. He couldn't concentrate as intently as he would have to to pull this off if he was thinking about her all the time. And the more he saw of her, the harder it became to chase her out of his mind. She always seemed to be there, taunting him, tantalizing him, giving rise to images that left him aching in a way he'd never known.

And there he was, thinking about her again. He shut off the water with a sharp movement, but still stood there for a moment, thinking.

He'd never given much deep thought to the way he conducted the social side of his life. He'd often been teased about his supposed string of conquests, but it had never bothered him much. Yes, he played the field, but he'd never pretended not to. And he made the rules clear up front; if a woman thought she could convince him to change them, she was welcome to try, but he refused to feel guilty when she failed.

His family—with his mother being the most vocal—had been nagging at him for years to find some nice girl and settle down. To "grow up," his oldest sister said. He had laughed them off, feeling no urge to join them in marital bliss. He was different, he told himself; he wasn't cut out to be tied down. He'd been convinced cops shouldn't, anyway, not when every day they walked out the door there was the chance they might not come back.

At least he'd been convinced until Chance and Shea. They, and his godson, were the ones who had made him wonder. When Chance had one day told him he wasn't tied down, he'd been set free, Quisto had looked at his partner's once-haunted eyes and known it was the truth. And when he looked at Shea's, he knew she counted it well worth the risk.

That was it, he thought firmly as he got out of the shower, toweled himself dry and dressed; it was the Buckners who had upset his equilibrium. Not Caitlin Murphy. And by the time he reached his mother's street, he had the strawberry blonde neatly tucked back into the category where she belonged, that of a concerned and somewhat unruly citizen who had gotten too caught up in a case. She needed protection, and to learn a little caution, but it wasn't up to him to take care of it.

It lasted until he turned the corner.

In the middle of the street were the same group of kids, minus Chico, playing the same game. And in the middle of them, her hair a fiery beacon in the morning sun, was Caitlin. She had a stick in her hand, and her eyes were fastened on the black-and-white ball with the fierce intensity she brought to everything. She was yelling and cheering as loudly as the kids, running as fast, spinning, turning, and when she blocked a goal—a goal being a hit off the fire hydrant at the exact end of the cul-de-sac—the kids cheered her raucously.

He felt like doing the same thing. And then he felt like plucking her out of that group of cheering children and spiriting her off somewhere private to explore the crazy feelings she caused in him. For a very long time.

He shook his head, wishing that was all it would take to shake off these feelings. The task he'd set for himself was going to be tricky enough without that kind of distraction. He made quick work of his greetings to his mother, and Caitlin surrendered her stick to the smallest boy with a flourish. She was ready to go, anxious to get back to the Neutral Zone in time to open.

"I don't want them to think they've scared me off" was all she said before lapsing into silence for the rest of the ride. Quisto ruefully acknowledged the accuracy of his earlier thought; no way would she just go home and stay there until this was over, one way or another.

Quisto was grateful for her silence—he didn't feel up to small talk this morning—but he was edgy at the same time, wondering why she was so quiet. And why she kept glancing at him like that. Perhaps leaving her with his mother hadn't been such a great idea; who knew what kind of crazy things his mother had told her?

But he hadn't had to worry about her last night, and that alone was worth a great deal. Just because he hadn't accomplished what he hoped to, it didn't change that.

She gave him a rather puzzled look when he just dropped her off in back of the Zone.

"I checked the building before I came to get you," he said. "Everything looks fine. I don't think they've been back."

"Oh." She seemed to accept his explanation, and she unlocked the door.

"If you need me, you've got my pager number."

Something in her expression changed at his words, but she only nodded as she pulled the door open. He opened his mouth to go on, then shut it again. He started to get back into his car, then stopped.

"Just let it rest for a while, will you? Please? Don't give them any reason to think you need more than a warning."

He'd never pleaded with a woman before, and he didn't like doing it now, but his worry overpowered his pride. He would do, he realized rather grimly, just about anything to keep that brutal vision he'd had of her from coming true.

Unexpectedly, she didn't argue with him. "I'll let it rest. For now."

He was so glad she'd promised, he didn't even mind the qualifier. He'd deal with that when the time came. And if he got lucky, maybe that time wouldn't come at all.

So much for luck, Quisto thought. He'd been walking these streets for two solid days—and now into two nights, he thought, glancing at his watch and seeing that it was after nine—and nothing. He'd gotten a lot of looks, some wary, some speculative, but no one had approached him. No one had asked him who the hell he thought he was, moving through the Pack's territory as if he belonged.

Maybe he'd taken the wrong approach. He started to head back to where he'd parked the BMW, rather blatantly, on a corner near Steele Street, wondering if going in as a typical gangster who'd had to leave his home turf for new environs would have been a better idea. Maybe he should be in baggy clothes and walking with that homeboy swagger.

But he'd gone with his gut feel on this, the feel that the Pack saw far too many of those to want another one. And that he was a bit too old to carry it off without arousing suspicion; any gangster who survived to his age usually had his own niche carved out, and would die before leaving his neighborhood. So here he was, wearing carefully chosen clothes that stopped just short of being too flashy, topped with a black canvas duster-length coat that was too warm for summer weather, but made the impression he wanted. His hair was slicked back with gel, and although he hated the feel of it, he wanted to be recognizable. Noticeable. And he *was* getting noticed; it just wasn't having the results he wanted.

He turned the corner and immediately changed his mind. Four men were waiting for him beside the Beemer.

Two of them he'd never seen before, but the other two he recognized immediately; he'd seen mug shots of them when he and Chance began investigating Eddie's information that the Pack was looking to set up shop in Marina del Mar, and were going to start with a boatload of narcotics coming into the marina.

The group, two Hispanics, a black and a Caucasian, were typical of the Pack's membership, looking hardened, tough and merciless. And right now, they weren't looking at him like they wanted to invite him for tea. He looked at each one assessingly. No visible weapons, but he had little doubt they carried them, concealed in any number of inventive ways. Although he'd forgone his pistol, he had a few weapons of his own tucked away here and there; a man would be a fool to walk these streets without them. Especially when his intention was to leap into the lion's den.

"Alarico wants to see you."

He turned his attention to the tall, gaunt man who'd spoken, one of the Hispanic men, whose eyes looked unnaturally wide and dark, and whose skin looked damp; Quisto wondered what he was on.

"How nice. Let me just give you my card, and he can call for an appointment."

The man's eyes flicked quickly to his companions, then back to Quisto in disbelief. He took a swipe at his runny nose. "He don't call punks like you. You go to him."

"Not if that's the best he can do in the way of a gracious invitation," Quisto said.

He heard a chuckle, and glanced at the source. The muscular black man's mouth was quirked upward at one corner. "Perhaps you should explain to our guest the honor he is being given by not being simply slaughtered right here."

The man's voice was beautiful, low and pleasantly modulated, his words enunciated with a precision that was

clearly natural and not studied. It made the threat somehow even more believable than any crude street language
would have.

"Shut up, Carny," the tall man said sharply. Then, back
to Quisto: "Move it, pretty boy. The boss doesn't like to be
kept waiting."

"And I imagine it doesn't happen often, with this kind of
charming escort."

"Muévete, pendejo," the man snapped.

Quisto wasn't sure he cared for the change from *pretty
boy* to the untranslatable but far more insulting *pendejo,* but
he chose not to dwell on the matter, or the order to move it.

"Ah, *amigo,* when you ask so sweetly, how can I refuse?"

The black man chuckled again, earning himself another
dirty look from the tall one, which seemed not to faze him
at all.

They fell into a formation around him, two in front and
two behind, and Quisto knew from the wordless efficiency
with which it happened that this was not new to them. Perhaps this truly was Alarico's official welcoming party. He
allowed himself a small bit of satisfaction; he'd obviously
piqued the leader's curiosity, or he would have sent this
band out to run him out of town, rather than bring him in.
Or, as Carny had said, simply slaughter him where he stood.
He knew the Pack's record well enough to know that that
wasn't at all out of the realm of possibility.

He didn't know exactly what he'd expected, but he knew
the Pack's headquarters wasn't it. He hadn't been surprised when they turned onto Steele Street and led him toward a large warehouse, but he'd been beyond startled when
he stepped inside and found what looked for all the world
like a modern office.

And a lot, he realized with a wry amusement, like a police station. A few desks, a couple of file cabinets, maps on
the walls marked with colored pushpins, and several phones.
Off in one corner was an entertainment center, where a big-

screen television faced a couple of comfortable-looking couches.

"Nice," Quisto said. "Who says crime doesn't pay?"

"Shut up," the tall, thin man said as he planted a hand on Quisto's back and shoved him toward an open door that led to what had apparently once been a private office.

Quisto whirled, crouched, and came up hard and fast with a fist into the thin man's belly. He heard the air whoosh out of the man's lungs in the same instant he heard the unmistakable sound of automatic weapons being readied. The thin man yowled as he stumbled backward, then fell. Quisto didn't look at any of the three other men he was sure had drawn down on him. He kept his eyes fastened on the thin man, who was clutching his belly, shrieking his rage. Quisto stood and straightened his coat.

"Don't ever," he said coldly, "touch me again."

He turned his back on the man, knowing what would happen. It did; he heard the scrambling as the man regained his feet.

"Don't try it, *pendejo*," Quisto said without turning around, "or I'll paint this pretty place with your blood."

He heard a curse, low and exceedingly profane. He braced himself, ready to dive, gauging his room, wondering if the man would just shoot or, as he'd been counting on, feel the need to kill him with his bare hands.

"Carlos! Enough!"

The order, short and sharp, came from the doorway. The thin man stopped; Quisto heard the slight slipping of his feet as Carlos's run at his back came to an abrupt halt.

"You'll have your chance later," the same voice said. "Now go."

Quisto turned slowly, and gave the man in the doorway a slow once-over. About his own height, with a pockmarked face and a pair of brown eyes that were oddly pale, he wasn't overly impressive, but his aura of power was evident.

"Alarico, I presume?" Quisto said.

The man nodded, as if pleased he had known. Proud, Quisto thought, filing the knowledge away as a possible weak spot.

"And you . . . do you have a name?"

Quisto hesitated just long enough for the thought that he wasn't going to answer to form before he said easily, "Rafael will do."

Alarico frowned. "Just Rafael?"

"That's all you need for now. Unless you're going to write me a check."

Alarico looked startled. Then he laughed. Quisto wished he could be a little more certain it was out of amusement, rather than malevolent intent.

"Come in and sit down . . . Rafael." Alarico gestured toward the inner office. "We have . . . things to discuss."

"Do we?"

"Yes, we do."

The words were cold, harsh, and Quisto knew the fun was over. He stepped obligingly into the room, wondering as Alarico followed and closed the door behind him if he would ever get out.

That thought was quickly erased by the surprise of seeing another man in the small room, a man leaning back so far in a plain wooden chair that the front legs were at least ten inches off the floor. His feet were up on the corner of the desk that took up much of the room's space. In his right hand was a large knife with an intricately carved wooden handle, and in his left hand something Quisto couldn't see. The man barely glanced up as they stepped into the room. And he was a man who had apparently been in here during the entire scuffle outside and had never moved.

And that made Quisto both curious and nervous.

The man looked nearly Chance's height, and was just as strongly muscled. But there the resemblance ended. No blond and blue-eyed good looks here. Bronzed, chiseled features, obsidian eyes, and a mane of straight black hair that fell well past his shoulders, held by a black bandanna tied around his head, this man couldn't be much more

Chance's opposite. Then Quisto nearly smiled at the irony of it. Chance had always been teased about his all-American good looks, but it was this man who truly fit that description. There was little doubt that his ancestors were the original Americans, who had walked this land long before Chance's fair-skinned forefathers, or even Quisto's own Spanish ones, arrived.

And there was little doubt of something else, as well. Whoever he was, this man who was so cool he never moved at the sound of a fight and the cocking of multiple weapons a bare ten feet away, he had the coldest eyes Quisto had ever seen.

And he had the gut-level feeling that he'd just met the wild card in this game.

Chapter 10

"So you moved for your health, is that it?"

Quisto grinned at Alarico. "Climate, actually. I needed someplace a little . . . cooler."

"And just what was making it so hot?"

Quisto shrugged. He glanced up at the map on the wall behind Alarico's desk, studded, as were the others outside, with various colored pushpins. He wasn't sure what it depicted, but the pins covered an area that was disturbingly large. Marina del Mar was the one mostly blank spot, he noted with satisfaction. *Not bad for us "fancy types,"* he thought.

"I ask questions, I expect answers," Alarico said.

Quisto shifted his gaze back to the man behind the desk. He'd been grilling him for a couple of hours now. Quisto had fed him the story he'd prepared, in bits and pieces, hoping the man would buy it before he ran out of things he'd been able to prepare for on such short notice and without many of his usual resources. He hadn't gotten the warning he'd been expecting, that no one did anything in

Pack territory without their permission, and that encouraged him. A little.

"One damn cop had it in for me. Wouldn't let it drop."

Alarico lifted one scraggly eyebrow. "Why didn't you just take care of him?"

"Kill a cop? No thanks. That earns you a coffin."

"So you let one cop run you out of Sacramento?"

"Better to move here than into Folsom," Quisto retorted. "I've done time once, and I don't ever intend to again."

Quisto saw Alarico look at his hands, his neck, his face. He knew the man was looking for what was usually considered proof of time served, and gave a snort of disgust. "Tattoos are a kid's game. You can't do what I do with your rap sheet inked across your chest."

Alarico flushed angrily, and Quisto guessed there was a permanent record or two of his own time inside on the man's body somewhere.

"He's right."

It was the first time the man Alarico had referred to only as Ryan had spoken. His voice was as big as he was, but low and controlled. And utterly inflectionless. He never looked up, merely concentrated on apparently destroying a tiny piece of wood with that six-inch knife blade.

"What?" Alarico said, seeming as startled as if the chair the man was in—still having never moved—had spoken.

"Marks that advertise you're a con are for fools. If you wish to walk between worlds, you must blend into both."

Alarico said nothing to the man, just turned his gaze to Quisto again. "Is that what you do? Walk in two worlds?"

Interesting, Quisto thought. Whoever Ryan was, his words were taken seriously, even by the leader of the Pack. He nodded in answer.

"And I do it well."

"And you plan to do this here?"

Quisto laughed. "Hardly. No offense, my friend, but you don't have my kind of targets in this town. But your friends to the west, in that lovely, rich town of Marina del Mar, are ripe for the plucking.''

Quisto knew he wasn't imagining the sudden tension in the room. Alarico leaned forward, his gaze suddenly sharper. Ryan, much subtler than the man who thought he was his boss, hadn't moved at all—Quisto was beginning to think it would take something akin to a flash-bang grenade to make him even blink—but Quisto sensed a new tension in his body.

"You may have overestimated your talents," Alarico said slowly. "Marina del Mar is a very tough nut to crack."

Quisto smiled; it was a taunting smile that he risked only because he knew Alarico was intrigued. "Yes. I heard you tried to crack it a while back, and your former leader and his henchmen wound up in the slammer."

Alarico's lip curled into a snarl, but before he could speak, Quisto went on.

"That was stupid. Why bring drugs into a town that already has so much wealth for the picking, without the risk?"

"Those lovely rich people you mention pay a lot of money for their protection."

But not necessarily to their police force, Quisto thought wryly. "Yes. That makes it difficult," he agreed, "but not impossible."

Alarico snorted. "You may not be so cocky once you try."

Quisto lifted a brow. "Ah, but I have not only tried, I have succeeded."

"What?"

"Don't you read the papers? You should, you know. A man in your line of work should know what's going on around him at all times, don't you think?"

"I have other ways of finding out," Alarico said, sounding defensive. Definitely proud, Quisto thought.

"Then you've heard about the two unsolved jewel thefts in the past month," Quisto said easily.

His tone belied his inner tension; this was the biggest part of his gamble. The thefts were real, that they were unsolved was a fact, but he was taking the big chance that nothing would break on the case before he was through here. It was a calculated risk; he knew the burglary detectives had few clues, and that, as professional as the suspect seemed to be, it was unlikely they'd turn up anything very soon.

"The ones for over a quarter of a million in hot rocks?"

"Closer to a half million, actually. There were some very nice pieces. It was a shame to break some of them up."

Alarico stared at him. "You? You're saying you pulled those robberies off? How?"

"Simple. I did my shopping in advance, at a charity ball. Then I er... lifted the guest list, and made a couple of late-night visits."

"A charity ball? What the hell are you talking about?"

"Walking in both worlds," Ryan said softly, speaking for only the second time, his ceaseless movements with the knife halting for a moment. Quisto turned to look at him. He could have sworn there had been a note of near-admiration in the man's deep voice, but, as it had been since Quisto had first laid eyes on him, his face was expressionless.

"Exactly," he said, acknowledging the man's perception.

Alarico's gaze flicked from one man to the other, as if he saw something in them both that made him nervous.

"You're saying you got into some big charity thing in Marina del Mar? How? Did you pass yourself off as a waiter?" he said, snickering.

Quisto looked at him coolly. "Actually, as the son of a former Cuban aristocrat."

Alarico blinked. "A what?"

"A man of distinction, as it were," Quisto said, dropping into the formal inflection that was second nature to him. "Used to the finer things, as are the people of Marina del Mar. They welcomed me. I have become their... token cause. I speak of the loss of human rights in Cuba, and give them a way to show support for a politically correct cause without disturbing their lives overmuch."

He was surprised at the bitterness that rang in his voice; he hadn't realized it was still so...close. But it had made his words, and his sour attitude, even more convincing. He felt Ryan's dark eyes on him, but didn't look. He concentrated on Alarico, waiting. At last what he'd been expecting came.

"What are you doing here?"

"Looking for you," he said nonchalantly.

Alarico's forehead creased. "Why?"

"Because I think we can be of mutual assistance to each other," Quisto said.

Something flickered in the other man's eyes—interest, wariness, both tinged with a distinct flash of greed. Now, Quisto thought, the game really begins.

He laid out the plan for both of them—he had no doubts now that Ryan had nearly as much say in things as Alarico, and suspected he was the new right-hand man—hoping it sounded as reasonable as it had at three yesterday morning.

"So you see? I have the access you do not. But you have the manpower, and the network for...disposal that I do not. I do the scouting, provide the target and the time, keep them distracted...and you do the rest."

"It has...potential," Alarico said.

"It's your chance to move out of the small time here, Alarico."

He could sense that the man wanted to go for it, but he hadn't survived to become head of the Pack by being foolish. "And just how do we know you're who you say you are?"

"Why, you'll check me out, of course," Quisto said. "As I'm sure you intended to do anyway. You know, you really should computerize your operation. It's so much faster, and more efficient."

Alarico frowned. "Computers," he snorted derisively.

Quisto shrugged and stood up. "Rafael Romero. I did my time at Chino. Got out five years ago. And my rap is as blank as your buddy Carlos's mind ever since. I've reformed." He grinned. "Which means I've gotten very, very good."

He knew it would hold up if they checked; that cover had been established when he first went into narcotics. And he doubted they'd have any contacts in the Marina del Mar upper crust to verify his presence at the ball that had taken place at the yacht club at the marina last month, but if they did, he had that covered, as well. The host, James Worthington, a wealthy local stockbroker, had good reason to say whatever Quisto asked him to say; that reason was now twelve years old, and alive only because Quisto had been there to administer CPR when she was pulled from the water after falling off her father's yacht in the marina below his apartment.

He only hoped that would be enough. "You call me and let me know if you think we can do business," he said, scribbling a number on the back of a business card and holding it out to the man. "Oh," he added, turning the card over before Alarico took it, "that's my former parole officer, if you're interested. Call him. He can tell you what a fine, upstanding citizen I've become."

He grinned again. This time, Alarico smiled back. They would check him out, Quisto thought, but he had a feeling the fish had taken the bait. Alarico was letting him leave, and not once had he warned him about Pack territory, or told him to get out of Marina Heights. It seemed almost too easy.

He glanced at Ryan, who was looking at him steadily, calculatingly, with those eyes that were cold enough to give the bravest of men a chill. And never once had he moved, except to carve away at that little piece of wood. Quisto walked out thinking that if still waters ran deep, Ryan was one of those ocean trenches that went halfway to the earth's core.

He was aware that Alarico was following him, at a discreet distance, but the man said nothing, so he kept going. But the moment he stepped outside the warehouse, he knew he should have expected this. It *had* been too easy. Gathered outside in the dark were a half-dozen men, clustered behind the now sneering Carlos. And Alarico had halted in the doorway, no doubt to watch with some amount of glee.

"Let's see how tough you are now, pretty boy!" Carlos exclaimed.

"I'm flattered," Quisto said dryly, as he shifted his weight to the balls of his feet, ready to move in any direction. "It will take seven of you to prove how tough I am?"

"They're just here to make sure you don't run."

The group fanned out, starting to circle. Quisto glanced at Alarico.

"Initiation?" he asked.

The man smiled a not-very-pleasant smile of anticipation. "Only if you survive."

Damn, Quisto thought. He was getting too old for this macho crap. Or too civilized. But he only shrugged and looked back at Carlos.

"You're very sure you want to do this? You're ugly enough already."

Carlos swore at him.

"Original," Quisto said mockingly, but inwardly he was groaning, wishing he'd kept a little more up to date on all that fancy martial arts training the department provided.

Carlos started toward him, wiping at his runny nose in what was clearly a habitual motion.

"Very well," Quisto said with an exaggerated sigh of resignation as he shrugged out of his canvas coat. "Let me just take off my—"

He flipped the duster at Carlos's face. The man jumped back. In the second that gave him, Quisto retreated to a darker part of the street. His night vision, better than most people's, wasn't much of an edge, but that and his quickness were all he had right now. He just hoped he could stay alive long enough for either to be of any help.

The circle closed in. He'd survived worse than this, he told himself. It wasn't much comfort.

It began as if orchestrated. A few feints, jabs and swings that he dodged easily. He knew it meant nothing; they'd done this before, and often, and this was only the beginning. He resigned himself to taking a beating. All he could do was try to keep it as mild as possible.

And, he thought suddenly as he remembered Alarico's smile of anticipation, take as many as he could down with him. If he was judging the man right, that would be the determining factor. And they'd probably be especially hard on him, since he didn't have the street credentials others came in with.

Then he had no more time to think, only to react. At first it was enough. He dodged, ducked and spun away, and the blows that landed on him were only glancing. And he landed a few solid ones of his own. More than a few, if you counted the kick that sent Carlos reeling backward. He saw at least two of the seven go down hard, and another slip and fall when his expected target suddenly wasn't there. It was an elaborate dance, with overtones of ritual that he sensed even though his hands were more than full with the constant onslaught. For a while, he was almost proud of doing better than just holding his own.

But Quisto knew when the tide had turned. He could sense that now they weren't simply testing a newcomer's skill, they were angry. He'd hurt too many of them. Instead of coming one at a time, they came in pairs now. Quisto picked the one he saw the most vulnerability in and attacked. He knew the blows the other delivered were doing damage, his body was screaming in protest, but he concentrated on doing as much damage as he could in return. Time and again they came at him, until his head was spinning and he could barely hear over the ringing in his ears.

But he kept his feet. Despite the pain, the blood he could feel running down his face from a strong punch that connected with his head, the blows that were making it almost impossible to breathe, he stayed on his feet. Somehow he knew that was important, that he stay upright. If nothing else, he had to do that.

It wasn't until he saw the glint of light on a set of metal knuckles that he began to wonder if he'd made them too

angry. Or if Alarico hadn't actually bought a single word of
the story he'd spun.

Because it looked like they were going to kill him right
here.

Caitlin hummed an upbeat, cheerful tune she'd always
liked, thinking the words more than singing them—something about chasing away old ghosts—as she hung another
picture on the yellow wall. The kids hadn't understood at
first when she asked them to bring her some happy pictures. She'd had to explain what she meant, and even then,
they'd been doubtful.

It tugged at her heart, that they had so much trouble understanding about happiness, even the fleeting kind caught
on film. But a few had brought in photos of birthday parties, a couple had brought in Christmas pictures, and one
had, to Caitlin's delight, brought in this shot, an adorable
picture of a batch of lop-eared puppies in a wicker basket.
It was exactly the touch of normalcy she wanted for this
wall, and she prayed that someday it would hold enough to
heal some of the wounds left by the other wall.

She stepped down from her precarious perch on a wobbly bar stool and looked up at her work in satisfaction.
She'd arrived before full light this morning, after yet another restless night of little sleep; it had seemed pointless to
lie there staring at the ceiling, when she had work she could
be doing. Work that just might succeed in distracting her
from the thoughts that kept returning, despite her efforts to
stop them.

She hadn't seen or heard a word from Quisto since he'd
dropped her off here on Monday. And here it was Thurs-
day morning, and she was still thinking about him.

Caitlin Murphy, you are a fool, she chided herself. The
likes of Quisto Romero, with all his dark good looks and his
courtly charm, was not for her. Besides, he was a cop, who
despite saying she was doing good here probably still
thought that she was a fool for trying. A cop who let rules

about things like jurisdiction sweep a boy's murder under the rug.

But he wasn't just a cop. He was Celeste Romero's youngest son, little brother to Hernan and Maria and Enrique and all the others, uncle to Chico and a good twenty or so others, godfather to little Sean . . . and he was the man who had held her so gently that night, here in her office. And he was the man who had come in minutes when she called him Sunday morning, sickened by what she'd found at her door, the man who had quietly and quickly cleaned up the bloody mess so that she wouldn't have to, the man who had taken her to his mother's home, where she would be safe, the man who had practically begged her to be careful, when she knew instinctively that begging was something utterly foreign to his nature.

And he was also the first man in years to make her heart take off on a crazy rampage every time she looked at him. And the first man ever to make her dream scandalous, erotic dreams, dreams about touching and kissing and the kind of driving sex she knew little about, until she woke up moaning, her pillow crushed in her grip, sadly lacking the heat and solidness of the man she was craving.

Craving. Yes, that was the word for it. And it was a word she'd never used in conjunction with a man before. It frightened her even as it excited her.

But she would get over it. She had to, she told herself firmly. Because it was quite obvious that Quisto had no further interest in her, not when he'd dropped out of sight like the anchor on her parents' sailboat hitting murky water. She'd probably been merely a nuisance to him, and only whatever guardian instinct there was ingrained in the cop part of him had made him try to protect her.

Yes, that was all it had been, and the sooner she—

A thud at the front door made her heart and breath stop, as if the sound had been a blow. She spun around, her hand going to her mouth as if to stop a scream she knew she didn't have the breath to make.

Not again. Please, not again, she chanted, as if the words could change reality.

Another thud came, this time fainter. She looked at the phone, picturing herself running to it and dialing 911. But then she pictured the arrival of the police, who had told her more than once that she was crazy for trying to keep this place open. They would be kind, as always, but she would see it in their eyes, that if she would just give up this crazy idea, this kind of thing wouldn't happen to her.

It was quiet now. She glanced at her watch. It was barely six, early for anyone to be stirring in this neighborhood. Except the Pack, she thought grimly.

Steeling her nerve, she tiptoed over to the door. She put her ear up to it and listened. Nothing. She waited. Still nothing. And at last she unlocked the door. She turned the knob. She jumped back instinctively as the door seemed to open inward on its own.

And she choked off a scream as a large, dark shape fell inside, on the floor. Again she saw blood, gleaming wetly in the morning light. This time on a man's face.

It was Quisto.

"Sorry," he muttered. "I didn't mean to come here."

"Hush," Caitlin said, rinsing out the washcloth she'd used in the basin of water once more. It was turning pink; she'd have to change it again in a moment.

"I don't even remember doing it," he said. "I—"

He broke off, sucking in a quick breath as she applied the cloth to the cut over his left eye. Then he winced, and she guessed the deep breath hadn't done much for his bruised ribs.

"You need a doctor," she said for the third time since she'd helped him up from the floor and into the office. She'd quickly opened the couch out to convert it into a sleeper, and he'd nearly fallen onto it, barely staying upright long enough to help her peel off his shirt before he fell back on the pillow. She'd gasped at the sight of his torso, scraped and reddened with angry marks that would surely be grim-looking bruises soon.

"No," he repeated. "I'm fine. No doctor."

"Fine? Quisto, you could have broken ribs—"

"No. I know the feeling."

He closed his eyes. She just looked at him for a moment, worried. He looked pale, his usual color gone.

"Then how about your face?" she asked. "That cut over your eye needs stitches, and—"

"Caitlin, please. It's all right. I just need...to rest a while. No doctor."

She rinsed out the cloth again and went back to wiping away blood and grime, not quite so gently this time. "I should just call the paramedics and have them cart you away."

His eyes came open. They were clouded with pain, but he struggled to sit up. "Don't. I'll leave," he began.

"No, you won't." She pushed him, gently but firmly, back down on the bed. "You scared me to death. I'm allowed to complain a little."

He started to smile, but one side of his mouth was swollen, and he stopped, wincing.

"What happened?"

It was the third time she'd asked that, too, and she supposed she'd get the same nonanswer. She did.

"I got in a fight."

"No kidding." She'd nursed a kid or two through injuries like this; she knew what kind of altercation caused them. She supposed it could have been worse; he hadn't been knifed or shot. "A fight over what?"

"I ran into some guys who didn't like my attitude."

"So they beat up a cop."

He shifted on the bed, as if trying to find a position that didn't hurt. "I didn't exactly tell them. It didn't seem like a good idea, at those odds."

She didn't want to know how many of them there had been. She guessed by his skinned and swollen knuckles that he'd gotten in a lick or two of his own.

"How many of them were still standing?" she asked dryly.

He gave her a wary look. "A couple," he said.

"And they just let you walk away?"

"They got . . . interrupted." His mouth twisted ruefully, and again he winced at the movement. "And by the time I got out of their sight, I was crawling, not walking."

She was surprised he'd admitted it. "Men," she muttered, and got up to go empty the basin and refill it with clean water.

When she came back, his eyes were closed again, and she thought he'd either fallen asleep or passed out. But when she sat down on the edge of the folding mattress, his dark lashes fluttered, then lifted.

"I really didn't mean . . . to bother you. I don't even remember driving here."

Caitlin blinked. "Driving? You drove here? Like this?"

He blinked in turn. "Well . . . yeah . . . At least I think so."

"And you call *me* crazy," she said, shaking her head as she went back to her task. She finished with the cloth, and began to apply antiseptic to the cuts on his face, gingerly, because she knew it would sting.

He bore her ministrations stoically, with only an occasional wince or grimace when she hit a particularly sore spot, and a throttled grunt when she dabbed at the cut over his eye. She concentrated on what she was doing, although with his shirt off it was impossible not to notice that Quisto Romero was nicely put together. Very nicely. Arms that were strong without being overwhelming, a smoothly muscled chest that was broad without making her wonder how many hours he spent a day working out, a flat belly that made her want to press her hand against it, just over his navel . . .

She kept her eyes away from his face, just in case he was watching her as she again picked up the washcloth and cleansed some grit from an ugly-looking graze on his belly. It ran below his belt line, and she hesitated. She saw his stomach muscles contract, and pulled her hands back. And then she knew he had been watching her, because when she looked up his eyes were riveted on her as he moved his hands, fumbling at the buckle of his belt with fingers that had to be sore.

She yanked her gaze away from his face just in time to see him succeed with the buckle and reach for the tab of his zipper. Her face flaming, she moved her eyes quickly to his knees, and the tear in one pant leg that told her he'd gone down hard at least once. She'd study that, she thought. That should be safe enough. And she'd think about something else, like why he was dressed like this in the first place.

Every time she saw him, he'd been dressed nicely, usually in cotton twill pants and a sweater or knit shirt. Being used to mostly jeans, she'd noticed their absence. But what he was wearing now, a pair of expensive-looking black pants of some silk blend, seemed far fancier than his everyday wear. And she was certain the discarded black shirt that was now much worse for wear was pure silk.

She nearly jumped when she felt his fingers closed around her wrist. Her gaze shot back to his face. He watched her steadily as he pulled her hand back to his belly, and the spot she'd been tending to.

"You were about here, I think."

She couldn't meet his eyes any longer, not when he was looking at her so intently that even the scrape on his jaw and the cut over his eye couldn't detract from the intensity of his gaze.

She looked away hurriedly, thinking she would just quickly finish with this and then get herself a safe distance away—perhaps lock herself in the bathroom. Then she realized she was staring at his slightly unzipped pants, and the tantalizing vee of skin that was revealed, bisected by a path of dark hair that thickened as it disappeared behind the fabric.

There was no reason for this, she told herself. No reason for her to be reacting like this. He hadn't done anything inappropriate; he'd undone the zipper just enough for her to reach the part of that angry red weal that she hadn't been able to before. It wasn't like he'd taken his pants off or anything, or even said anything the least bit suggestive. If only he'd stop *looking* at her like that. She knew he was, she could feel it, and it was making her skin tingle in the oddest way.

With a great effort, she managed to finish without visibly shaking. He made no sound when she applied antiseptic to the area of the scrape that had bled slightly, and she breathed an inward sigh of relief that she was done.

"Thank you." His voice was quiet, yet somehow tense.

"You're welcome."

She recapped the bottle of antiseptic and leaned over to set it on the table. She heard him move, and turned back to see that he was pushing himself upright. Slowly, as if it hurt.

"What are you doing?"

"Getting out of your way."

"Quisto, lie down. You need to rest. You said so yourself."

"I didn't mean here—" He broke off, wincing.

"See?" she said. "Now just lie down. It's a perfectly comfortable bed. I've used it a lot of times."

"Not last night, I hope."

She lowered her gaze to her knees. "No. I haven't stayed here since...that morning."

"Thank you," he said again, this time rather fervently. She raised her eyes to look at him again. He was looking at her again in that intense way that was so unsettling, but she saw lines drawn by pain tightening his face.

"Will you please lie down?"

"Join me?"

She drew back, startled, not quite believing what she'd heard. Or that he'd meant it the way it sounded.

"Sorry," he said wryly. "I shouldn't make offers I'm in no condition to make good on."

Caitlin blushed; she had heard him correctly. He smiled, carefully, as if testing how far he could go before it hurt.

"Well," he said, "if I can't have that, I'll settle for this."

He leaned forward then, and before she realized his intent, he was brushing his lips across hers. She didn't know what startled her more, the leap her heart took, or the sudden jolt that shot through her at even this gentle, tentative contact. The memory of touching him, of gently cleaning his face, of running her hands over his fit, strong body, came rushing back to her, sparking further memories of her heated, embarrassingly sensual dreams.

His lips moved coaxingly, and she felt a little ripple of sensation at the feel of them, warm and firm on hers. He tasted like nothing she'd ever known before, hot, exotic, exciting. And the more she remembered, the more all the facets of this complex man swirled in her mind, the more she gave herself up to the incredible knowledge that he was kissing her so sweetly and that she was loving it.

She heard him make a sound then, half pleasure, half pain, and only then realized she was kissing him back, eagerly. Too eagerly, she thought, flushing now with the heat of embarrassment, rather than arousal. She was no doubt hurting his sore mouth, although he didn't pull away. So she did.

"I—I'm sorry."

Was that her? she wondered, her eyes widening at the sound of her own words. That breathless, husky voice?

"Don't be," he said, and he sounded nearly as breathless as she had. "I'm not."

"But your mouth—"

"Never felt better."

He was looking at her like that again. Only this time there was something else in that steady gaze, something deep and sensual and smoky. It sent a ripple of heat through her. Flustered, she quickly stood up.

"I'll get you a couple of aspirin. That should help a little."

"What you just did helped."

What she'd just done? Kissing him? Or her rudimentary first aid? She didn't know. And she couldn't bring herself to ask. Besides, she didn't know which answer would bother her more.

She turned and darted out of the room.

Chapter 11

The man made him very, very nervous.

Quisto studied the man called Ryan, as he'd been doing for the past two weeks, trying to decide whether it was his excessively calm silence or his chilling lack of emotion when he did speak that made him most uneasy. Or perhaps it was the way he looked at everyone with those dark eyes, constantly assessing but never revealing. Or the way he always had that knife in his hands, was always whittling small pieces of wood into seeming nothingness. The only thing Quisto was certain of was that he'd seen that kind of brooding intensity before, and it usually prefaced an explosion of some kind.

The others seemed wary of him, too, and tended to get quiet when he appeared. Quisto wondered what the big man had done to warrant that watchful respect. And to gain his current position as Alarico's right hand. How far had he gone, this seemingly fierce and unyielding man? So far as to kill a child on Alarico's orders? Had this big, powerful man murdered a skinny fourteen-year-old boy?

"We've let him get away with this for too long," Carlos exclaimed.

Quisto ran a hand through his hair—grateful he'd been able to abandon the hair gel, at least, as part of his cover—and smothered a sigh. They'd been arguing over the approach to take with Martin Cordero, the owner of the grocery store down the street from the Neutral Zone. The man refused to pay the protection money the Pack demanded, a fact that made Quisto admire the quiet little man immensely.

"That is true," Alarico agreed. "But he is very stubborn."

"He should be very dead," Carlos said, a vehemence in his words that drew Quisto's attention to his thin face, to his dilated pupils and runny nose. Meth, Quisto thought yet again. The guy was perpetually high on the stuff.

"I'm sure," Carny put in, in those beautifully modulated tones, "your desire for his demise has nothing to do with the fact that he ran you out of his store with a shotgun when you went to collect."

Quisto smothered a grin. Carlos glared at the black man, who merely smiled back. Quisto glanced back at Ryan; the man's expression hadn't changed—it never seemed to—but something in his dark eyes made Quisto think for an instant that the man was feeling the same admiration for wiry old Martin Cordero.

But Ryan still made him nervous. After the first week of testing, of trying to trip him up, trying to find a flaw in his story or catch him in a lie—and a few more confrontations on a more physical level—the others seemed to have accepted him. Especially when Alarico had given him the nod at last; Quisto knew from his contacts that the leader had checked out his story and gotten the answers he was supposed to get. But Ryan kept watching. Assessing. Calculating.

Carlos said nothing to Carny and turned his gaze to Alarico again. "I say we just kill him and get it over with. He's been nothing but trouble."

"And he'll keep on making trouble," another man said warningly, and was greeted with a chorus of assent.

Damn, Quisto thought. He was going to have to stop this. He couldn't let them murder that innocent old man, whose only crime was being tough enough to stand up to these thugs. He just had to figure out how to do it without giving himself away. He'd had to walk a fine line, solidifying his position inside the gang, before they allowed him to even sit in on these little meetings. He'd had to outline a plan to make a big score during James Worthington's big party in three weeks to convince them he was serious. He just hoped he didn't have to really pull it off; Worthington would co-operate, had even offered whatever Quisto needed of his wife's expensive jewelry or his own art collection, with no guarantee of getting it back, but Quisto hoped fervently it never came to that.

"All right," Alarico said at last. "But you will not do it, Carlos."

"What?" The man sounded outraged.

"You heard me. You will be highly visible somewhere else when it is done. Too many witnesses saw Cordero make a fool out of you. You would be the first suspect, and that would lead the cops right back to us."

Quisto cleared his throat, not sure what he was going to say, but knowing he had to do something to halt this assassination. But before he could speak, there was a thud as Ryan's boots hit the floor, and a hush came over the assembled group as the big man got to his feet.

"You have something to say, *amigo?*" Alarico asked, looking up warily.

"Only goodbye."

Alarico blinked. "What?"

"You start taking directions from a fool who's fried what few brain cells he had to begin with, I'm out of here."

It was the longest sentence Quisto had heard from the man. He watched the exchange with interest; little had happened to change his first perception of Ryan as the wild card in this operation.

"Good riddance, Chief," Carlos said, his lip curling into a sneer.

Ryan didn't say a word. But the look he gave Carlos made the man turn as pale as the white bandanna Ryan was wearing around his forehead today.

"Shut up, Carlos," Alarico said, his gaze never leaving Ryan, as if he weren't quite sure of his control over the man. "You have a problem with this?"

Ryan shrugged, as if the topic were nothing more important than a choice on a menu. "It's a mistake."

"Why?"

"You kill the old man, what do you gain? Revenge for a dimwit so stoned on meth he can't even do the simplest of jobs?"

Carlos sputtered, but Alarico shut him up with a sharp motion of his hand. "We send a message to others who might have the same idea, that they can't refuse to pay."

"You send a message, all right," Ryan drawled. "Straight to the cops. Murder of a man like this isn't something they overlook. This is not some homeboy, someone they will be just as glad to see gone. You really want to bring that kind of heat down on us?"

Alarico studied Ryan for a moment. Quisto held his breath. "I know better than to think you've gone soft, *amigo*," Alarico said. "Or that you're afraid of the cops."

Ryan smiled then, a cold-blooded, humorless expression that sent a ripple of cold down Quisto's spine. Wild card, he thought, was an understatement.

"You kill that old man, you know what you've done? You've created a martyr. And a martyr has a lot more power over people than a man who simply sells groceries." Unexpectedly, Ryan looked at Quisto. There was something there in those dark eyes, some hint of speculation, that made Quisto feel even more uneasy. "Ask our new friend Rafael here about martyrs and causes. I suspect he knows all about them."

Quisto drew back slightly, in spite of his efforts to control his reaction to the unexpected perceptiveness of the man. He'd said very little in his cover story that would lead to such conjecture, but the big man was obviously adept at reading between the lines.

He managed a shrug nearly as casual as Ryan's had been. "He is right. My people have great experience with martyrs. And those trying to maintain the status quo know there is nothing more dangerous to them."

"Then what would you suggest?" Alarico asked. His voice was quiet, yet somehow ominous, as if this were yet another test. As, Quisto realized, it probably was. He chose his words carefully, all the while thinking of how he could keep things under control, or at least keep the damage to a minimum. *Gage, buddy, I hope you meant what you said about helping,* he thought.

"I would suggest an end run," he said finally.

"And exactly what does that mean?" Alarico asked.

"It means another way of getting the same results. Without getting tackled by the cops."

"Just how would you accomplish that?"

Alarico seemed to be seriously listening, so Quisto went on, in a tone implying it mattered nothing to him what they did about the small thorn in their side.

"I would simply do a little damage to his property."

Carlos gave a loud, derisive laugh. "That won't convince that old man."

Quisto turned his head slightly, looking at the man as he would look at a mosquito he would swat sooner or later. Then he turned back to Alarico.

"Carlos has a point," Alarico said. "Cordero is a very stubborn man. A little damage would not persuade him to be . . . more responsive."

"Who said anything about persuading him?" Quisto said, shrugging again.

Alarico blinked. "What?"

"You don't have to persuade him. You just have to convince everyone you have."

Alarico's forehead creased in puzzlement.

"Smooth." It was low, and spoken in a voice tinged with appreciation, and it came, surprisingly, from Ryan. "You're good, Romero."

Quisto looked at Ryan, and was startled to see as much of a genuine smile as he'd ever seen from the man barely curving his lips. He found himself smiling back before he could stop it.

"Perhaps you would be so good as to explain what is so smooth, Ryan?" Alarico asked, sounding irritated.

Ryan looked at the man who was supposedly his boss, although Quisto had his doubts about that. "Simple. You do a little highly visible damage. Then you pass the word that Cordero buckled. That he saw the light."

Alarico's frown deepened. "But he will say he has not. And he is an honest man. People will believe him."

"Not," Quisto said, "if you leave him alone."

"Exactly," Ryan agreed. "Everyone knows the Pack's reputation. No one will believe we just backed down. Cordero can talk, but just the simple fact that we leave him alone will convince them otherwise."

Alarico seemed to be struggling with the concept, and Quisto carefully maintained his appearance of unconcern. After a moment of chatter among the troops, who couldn't quite seem to follow the logic in the plan, either, Quisto spoke again.

"And I'd suggest you visit his store regularly, just as you do all your...clients. Very visibly. And when there are no customers present."

Alarico got it then. "So people will think we're collecting."

Quisto nodded. "Even if you're just buying...cookies."

He let a fleeting memory of Caitlin and a fortune cookie into his mind, just for an instant. He'd had to fight so hard to keep her out of his mind, but he couldn't resist this one sweet, tempting image, just for a moment. Then he would shut her out again, so that he could stay focused, concentrate on what he had to do, and not on the brilliant sheen of her hair, the deep blue of her eyes, the softness of her mouth....

"I see. It could work," Alarico said slowly.

"It would," Ryan said. "No martyrs to inspire the masses, and no cops down our necks. But everyone gets the message anyway. And thinks Cordero's just an old man too proud to admit he gave in."

"A bargain," Quisto said, "for very little effort."

When Alarico finally nodded, Quisto let out a relieved breath that he did his best to hide.

"It is decided," Alarico said.

"What?" Carlos yelped in astonishment. "You're just gonna let that old man skate, and not pay?"

Alarico spun on the thin man. "It is decided. Do not forget what my name means."

"But—"

"Ryan is right," he said coldly. "You are becoming a liability, Carlos. You can't see past your next fix. Or your petty desire for revenge for an insult you brought upon yourself. Be careful that I do not run out of patience with you. I have had people killed for less."

Fear glittered, fever-bright, in Carlos's eyes, and he subsided into silence. Alarico turned his gaze back to Ryan questioningly. The man said nothing, just nodded and sat down, resuming his usual position and seemingly ready to lapse back into his customary silence as he returned his attention to the small piece of wood he pulled out of his pocket. He never sat near the others, but always apart; Quisto had often wondered if it was his choice or theirs.

Alarico looked at Quisto, who met his gaze steadily. "You are new here," the leader said, "but you are wise. Wise enough, I hope, to remember who is in charge."

"Always," Quisto promised, meaning it quite literally.

"Good. I take no disrespect from anyone. And neither years served—" he glanced at Carlos again, making the thin man shift uncomfortably "—nor being new will save you if you offend me." He lifted his eyes to scan the gathered group. "Don't forget the lesson of that foolish boy. He learned the hard way—and permanently—that Alarico is not to be disrespected."

Quisto went very still. "Only a fool would insult a man in your position. I am not a fool," he said, his mind racing as he spoke.

It had to be Eddie. He knew from Gage that there had been no other suspicious deaths of juveniles, or at least none that qualified as "message" murders. But Alarico's words put a whole different spin on things. Was it possible? Had the man ordered Eddie killed for no more reason than that, in street parlance, he'd "dissed" him? Had Eddie let his mouth once more get him in trouble, this time with the wrong man? Did the Pack really have no idea that the boy had informed on them?

"No," Alarico agreed, "I don't believe you are a fool."

With that, the man turned back to business, demanding reports on the protection money they had collected from others in the area who weren't as obstinate as Martin Cordero, and the status of the hunt for a particular car they had apparently been trying to steal for a specific customer.

Quisto wasn't listening. He was still turning everything he'd heard over in his mind, wondering. Had his entire theory been wrong? Had Eddie's death merely been a way for Alarico to maintain his power, and not a message at all? Had the boy's tendency to have a smart mouth gotten him killed? Had—

A scuffle near the door, followed by a male howl of pain and a female exclamation, brought him sharply out of his contemplation.

"I told you I'd kick you again if you didn't ease up!"

For the second time in a very short while, Quisto went utterly still. That voice was familiar. Painfully familiar. A voice he hadn't heard for two weeks, but one that was etched into his memory as clearly as anything in his life had ever been.

Caitlin.

Damn.

He didn't dare look. He could only wait. And pray that she didn't give him away the first time she laid eyes on him.

"What is going on, Lenny?" Alarico demanded.

The man at the door swore before answering. "Found the bitch nosing around Steele Street. Asking questions, like before. Guess she didn't take the hint."

Damn it, Caitlin, why couldn't you let it be? Quisto muttered inwardly.

But he already knew the answer. It just wasn't in her. As far as she knew, no one cared about Eddie's death but her. So she naturally—naturally for Caitlin, anyway—had to take it upon herself to seek some kind of justice for the boy. That she would most likely get herself killed in the process wouldn't even slow her down, Quisto thought ruefully, let alone stop her. He admired her for it, even as he wanted to throttle her for putting herself at risk.

He heard the shuffling of feet as Lenny pushed her in front of Alarico.

"You are becoming quite an annoyance," the leader said.

"Good," Caitlin said angrily.

Quisto sighed. God, didn't the woman know when to quit? She hadn't seen him yet, and he kept himself turned away from her. That put him face-to-face with Ryan, who was watching him with that steady dark gaze.

"You are trespassing in our territory," Alarico said. "And asking ticklish questions. We warned you what happens to people who are too...curious."

Quisto couldn't see her face, but when she spoke, he knew by the tone of her voice that her chin had come up. "Do you give any more thought to murdering people than you do to animals?"

No, she didn't know when to give up. Quisto grimaced, and turned around. His movement drew Caitlin's gaze, and he saw her eyes widen when she saw him. She opened her mouth, and he spoke quickly, before she could.

"Well, well," he drawled, pouring on the courtly charm, with the intention of distracting Alarico from her reaction, "what have we here? You didn't tell me you dealt with such charming ladies, *amigo.*"

Caitlin frowned, but her mouth snapped closed on whatever she'd been about to blurt out. She was clad in the yellow-specked jeans, and a pale yellow sweater that made the paint spatters look intentional and played up the palest shades of her hair while hugging the soft curves of her breasts far too closely for his equanimity.

"Charming? Hardly," Alarico said with patent irritation. "She is a nuisance. And becoming more of one every day."

"Really, my friend, if you can look at a woman this lovely and think only of the word *nuisance,* you are sadly limited in your view. May I ask for an introduction, please?"

Quisto saw realization dawn in Caitlin's eyes.

"And who are you?" she asked in a biting tone, "The Pack's ambassador of phony goodwill?"

Quisto barely managed to restrain a grin; damn, she was quick. She'd immediately picked up on what he was doing and was playing along like a pro.

He bowed deeply toward her. "My full name, *querida,* would take far too long, and delay our mutual acquaintance. So simply call me Rafael, if you will."

She gave an inelegant snort that wrinkled her nose adorably. Quisto grimaced at his own thought. Adorable? Where had that come from? He should have taken care of that little libido problem before he started this and put himself out of reach of any of his regular ladies. He'd never thought any of *them* adorable for wrinkling their noses.

He turned to Alarico. "So who is this ravishing creature?"

"This," the leader said, with more than a touch of asperity, "is Señorita Murphy. She is a thorn in my side that will soon be removed. Along with that club she insists on trying to run."

"Club?" Quisto said, since it seemed appropriate, but Alarico waved off the query.

"It does not matter. What does matter is that she has ignored my advice to leave our territory, and now she has ignored my warning to stop asking questions about things that are none of her business."

"His name was Eddie. He was a child, not a thing."

God, Caitlin, shut up, Quisto urged silently.

"I have run out of patience with you," Alarico said. "It is time to resolve this problem once and for all. I want you and your 'Neutral Zone' out of my way and out of my life. Permanently." He gestured toward Ryan. "Take Carny with you," Alarico ordered, "and get rid of her."

Carny stepped forward and grabbed her arms, forcing them behind her so sharply that she cried out in pain. Quisto tensed, calculating rapidly, knowing he could do nothing here. Better to follow and intervene then, away from the others. It figured that Alarico would send the two strongest men in the entire Pack. He'd have to—

"Now that's just a rocket-scientist idea," Ryan drawled, never moving, not even lowering his feet from the desk. "That'll really give this town a martyr. Killing Cordero would have been bad enough, but now you want to off some rich white bitch from Marina del Mar, so we can have her family, and the Marina del Mar cops, and God knows who else, on our backs?"

Alarico spun around to look at Ryan. Quisto couldn't see the leader's face, but he could tell from his posture that he was glaring at Ryan. It was all Quisto could do to keep his amazement from showing. Again the man was talking Alarico out of murder. But doing it in an offhand, reasoned, dispassionate way that made it somehow as chilling as the casual order for the actual act. And through it all, Ryan's expression never changed. He could have been discussing the weather.

"You overstep yourself, Ryan," Alarico warned.

The big man shrugged. "Just pointing out that if you thought killing Cordero would put us under scrutiny, you kill her and you'll find out how much heat can really come down. Rumor has it her old man's a judge or something. If you think her murder wouldn't get special treatment, you're a fool."

Quisto risked a glance at Caitlin. She was staring at Alarico, wide-eyed, as if she'd finally realized just how much danger she was in. She didn't look at Quisto, and he thought it might be that she was afraid of what she might betray. She had certainly been quick enough on the uptake to realize he was her only hope right now.

He and, however unlikely it seemed, the man called Ryan.

For a silent moment that seemed agonizingly long to Quisto, Alarico considered. As volatile as the man was, he had been convinced once today that murder wasn't the best solution. Quisto hoped Ryan's cold analysis would win again.

It did.

"Take her back," Alarico snapped at Ryan.

Ryan nodded, glancing at Caitlin. Something flickered in the man's dark gaze, something that distinctly resembled pure male appreciation of a beautiful woman. Quisto grimaced inwardly at the odd feeling, a sensation he couldn't have named, that gripped him.

Quisto glanced at Alarico. Was he really going to let her go? Or was there some unspoken code between the leader and his right hand that meant he would personally take care of the problem called Caitlin Murphy—permanently? Had Ryan's argument and Alarico's agreement only been a ruse, a facade? Was Ryan reserved for those dirty chores that could cause too much trouble? Like Eddie? And now Caitlin?

"You would be wise to stay out of my way," Alarico said, giving Caitlin a gaze of icy warning. "You're on borrowed time. If you don't keep your nose out of my business, that time will run out. And there will be no more warnings."

Quisto sent up the most fervent prayer he could ever remember making. *Please, Caitlin, just be quiet. Don't give him any reason to change his mind. I can't save you if he decides to kill you right here.*

For once, she seemed to see the wisdom in just going meekly. She gave Ryan a wary, almost frightened look as he approached, towering over her. At a nod from the taller man, Carny released her arms. Ryan took her elbow in an almost chivalrous manner and gently began to escort her toward the door.

Quisto wondered if he was watching her walk toward her death.

Chapter 12

Ryan led Caitlin away, still handling her with care, as if she were fragile and he the gentlest of men. As Quisto stood watching them go, that odd sensation he'd noticed before kicked through him again, a strange tightening of his chest, an unfamiliar knotting of his stomach.

It seemed coupled with a rising anger at Ryan, an anger he didn't understand. He should be thankful the man had talked Alarico out of killing her right here and now, not standing there wanting to rip his heart out. It made no sense to feel this growing fury just because Ryan was treating her kindly, not like the tough, dangerous man he was.

The memory of the look of appreciation that had flashed in Ryan's usually unreadable eyes buzzed in Quisto's mind like an insistent hornet. And intensified the crazy feeling tenfold.

What was wrong with him? He'd never felt anything like this. What the hell was it?

And why was he standing here wrestling with this as precious seconds ticked away, seconds that left Caitlin alone with Ryan? He had to get moving, had to get out of here without drawing too much attention to his abrupt departure.

He made a feeble but apparently acceptable excuse, something about meeting with someone who could possibly provide him with a guest list for Worthington's big party before the event, enabling them to hit the homes while the residents were gathered at a known location that could be watched. He was walking out the warehouse door before it hit him.

Jealous.

He was jealous.

He shook his head, nearly laughing out loud at the absurdity of it. Him? Quisto Romero, the *conquistador* himself, jealous? Impossible.

Than why the hell had the sight of Ryan touching Caitlin, even in a perfectly courteous manner, sent him into raging overdrive? Why had he spent every night of the past two weeks wondering what she was doing—and whom she was doing it with? Why was it so damned hard to get her image out of his head? He'd never had to fight anything the way he had to fight her soft, quiet invasion of his mind every waking moment.

And his sleeping moments were better left unrecalled; he'd never before had the kind of dreams he'd been having of late. He'd had the usual sort of arousing dreams as a kid, but never anything this complex, never anything like the combination of erotic and innocent images that had been haunting his nights since he'd last seen her. Hundreds of different visions, the only thing consistent among them the star, a strawberry blonde who took his breath away.

"Caitlin," he whispered.

The moment the name escaped him, he started to run. He didn't trust Ryan. There was more to the man than he let anyone see, and Quisto was very much afraid that what appeared on the surface to be rational logic might just be a mask for the kind of amoral analysis that made for the worst kind of criminal.

His car left rubber skid marks on the streets, and he blasted through a couple of lights that were a little too close to red, but he couldn't slow down. At one corner, he wavered for an instant, wondering if Ryan would have taken her to the Neutral Zone, or home. Assuming, of course, that he hadn't taken her someplace isolated and lonely to carry out some secret command from Alarico to kill her.

His instincts told him it wasn't true, that Alarico had seen the wisdom in Ryan's words. He'd always trusted his instincts before, and rarely had he been wrong. But for the first time in his career—indeed the first time in his life—his instincts weren't enough. Not when Caitlin's life was hanging on them.

He yanked the wheel around and headed for the Neutral Zone. He paused at the end of the block, staring, trying to see whether there was a light on. The sun was hitting the windows, and he couldn't really tell. He opened the special compartment in the driver's door panel, behind the stereo speaker, and pulled out the small 9 mm automatic he kept there. He made a point of not carrying when he was with the Pack; he didn't want them to have any excuse to turn on him. The automatic's deadly weight was comforting when he thought of Caitlin in danger, and he decided then and there that whenever he was in the Neutral Zone, he would go armed.

He sped up and around the corner, pulling into the alley. Her car was there, but he knew that didn't mean anything. He parked a few buildings away, shut the Beemer off and got out, leaving the door unlatched to avoid the noise of it shutting. He made his way quietly to the back door of the Zone, wondering if he'd even be able to hear a thing over the hammering of his own heart. If Ryan had hurt her, he swore, he'd kill him. If he'd even scared her...

The back door was open.

He swore silently. It wasn't propped open for air, as she usually left it, it was open barely a crack. He crept up to it, his back pressed to the wall, the automatic aimed at the sky. He listened intently. At first he heard nothing but the ringing of his own pulse in his ears, driven by a heart that was racing far beyond normal; after all, this was a routine exercise for any street cop, a building with a possible suspect inside. He even had the advantage over most street cops; at least he knew the inside layout. He shouldn't be reacting like this. Hyper, yes, and thrumming with adrenaline, but not like this. On the takedown in Marina del Mar, he'd faced a trio from the Pack armed with MAC-10s and not felt like this. His heart was pounding harder than he could ever remember. And he knew that the difference was Caitlin.

He heard something then, and sucked in a breath and hel˙ it as he leaned toward the open door. Footsteps. Light, smooth, controlled. Light enough that he normally would have assumed they were Caitlin's. But Ryan moved like a panther, with a silence that belied his size and his muscled weight.

Another sound came, and he moved even closer to the door, tilting his head, straining to hear.

Humming. Caitlin was humming. Something bright, bouncy and familiar, though he couldn't put a name to it.

He let out the breath he'd taken what seemed like eons ago. But he kept his weapon at the ready as he nudged the door open with his toe. It obligingly swung back just far enough for him to slip inside. He stopped the moment he was in, listening again. The cheerful humming continued, and he had a sudden vision of her in a room filled with the morning sun, her hair tousled as it caught the light and sent it flying in red-gold sparks, her mouth curved in a soft smile, her lips warm . . . and looking thoroughly kissed.

It was a vision a man could wake up to every day of his life and never get bored, he thought.

And the thought froze him where he stood. What was he doing? Where were these crazy ideas coming from? He didn't think like this, ever. The idea of a life spent with one woman was . . . not his style. Cops left too many widows.

He shook his head sharply; this kind of preoccupation was what got you killed. He still didn't know what was happening inside, only that Caitlin sounded unharmed and unafraid. He edged a little farther inside, around the stub wall that blocked his view of the main room.

She was sitting at the bar, obviously as calm and unhurt as her humming had indicated. An odd smile played over her lips, as if she'd encountered something unexpected but not displeasing. Bemused, he thought. That was how she looked.

She was looking at the yellow wall, but he wasn't sure she was really focused on it. Unlike the last time he'd seen it, now there were photos on the wall. He couldn't make out what they were from here, but he knew instinctively that they weren't the same kind of picture that grimly decorated the opposite wall, that dark, sobering collection of death and young lives cut short. He knew because he knew Caitlin; she had painted that wall a cheery yellow for a reason. And it wasn't to spread the record of violence even farther.

He wasn't wearing a holster, so he slipped the pistol into his waistband at the small of his back, under the black duster. Then he stepped forward, into the room.

"Caitlin?" he said softly, in order not to startle her.

She spun around on the bar stool, quickly, but not in fright, and he got the feeling she'd been expecting him. Her words confirmed his guess.

"I've been wondering if you'd show up." She looked him up and down. "Nice outfit. The undercover uniform of the day?"

Her tone was too bright, and he approached her slowly, a little warily. "Are you all right?"

She held her arms out and looked down at herself. "Do I look all right?"

She looked exquisite, even in jeans, he thought, but he didn't say it; from the glint in her eyes, he didn't think it would go over very well. He sat down on the empty stool beside her.

"He didn't hurt you?"

"Ryan? No. In fact, he was the perfect gentleman."

What the hell did that mean? "Oh?"

She nodded. "I've had dates who were less polite. And less civilized. Despite his rather...intimidating appearance."

Dates. That feeling began to bubble inside him again at the thought of her out with anyone, let alone someone who was less than polite. Damn, he was losing it. Fast.

"Civilized?" he said, fighting for calm. "Interesting choice of words to describe the Pack's right-hand man."

"Is he? I didn't realize. Perhaps I should have. He is a bit...on the edge, isn't he?"

"More than anyone knows, I think."

"An intriguing man," she said.

"Right," Quisto muttered, not liking the look in her eyes. He supposed that, from a female point of view, Ryan could be classified as intriguing. He was certainly exotic enough. And some women liked that dangerous edge; he knew that from personal experience. He just hadn't thought Caitlin was one of them. "Did you invite him back?"

The surly question was out before he could stop it.

Caitlin's brows rose. "As a matter of fact, he asked if he could come back. Very politely."

Damn. His jaw clenched, and his words came out from behind gritted teeth. "And you said?"

"I told him what I tell everyone. Anybody is welcome here, as long as they stick to the rules."

He stared at her. "You told Ryan he had to obey your rules?"

"Yes, I did. You have a problem with that?"

"Didn't he?"

"No. I told you, he was very civilized about it."

"Damn it, Caitlin, he's the second-in-command of the Pack!"

"I told you, I didn't know that."

"You knew he was part of the Pack when you threw out the welcome mat for him!"

"I doubt he'll take me up on it."

Quisto had his own opinion about that; he remembered too clearly the way Ryan had looked at her. "And if he does?"

"I'll deal with it then."

"Well, that'll be a great example for your kids. Have him come in and do a career day, why don't you?"

"What's that supposed to mean?"

"He's dangerous, Caitlin. Don't get tangled up with him."

He knew the words were a mistake the moment he said them. So was his tone; it had come out as an order, and he already knew how she reacted to those. She visibly bristled, and he braced himself.

"Do you really think I'm that stupid? Oh, wait, of course you do."

"I never said—"

"You didn't have to say a word." She gave him a long, steady look, and the angry glint he'd seen in her eyes when he first walked in intensified. "You made your opinion quite clear by not saying a thing. About *anything*."

He'd known this was coming. And he also knew it was too late to try to save it now; she had to know. "I couldn't tell you what I was doing."

"Couldn't? Or wouldn't? Were you afraid I'd blab it around that there was a Marina del Mar cop investigating Eddie's death?"

"No. Never that."

"Then why? Why did you let me go for weeks, thinking nobody gave a damn but me?"

"You could have been in danger. They knew you'd already been asking questions—"

"And all you had to do to stop me was tell me you were going in."

Quisto sighed; this was what he had no real answer for. "I'd hoped you would stop because I asked you to."

"When I thought Eddie's murder was being swept under the rug? Did you really think I could do that?"

"I hoped. After that warning on your doorstep—"

"It's a power thing for you cops, isn't it? You like giving orders, knowing people have to do what you say, and that the average person will do it without question."

"That has nothing to do with this."

"Then why? Why didn't you at least tell me you were working on it? Even that night when you came here...it was them you fought with, wasn't it?"

"Yes." He stopped himself from reflexively touching the spot on his head that was still a little tender, even now. "Caitlin, I couldn't tell you."

"Why? I could have accepted that you couldn't tell me any more, but just to know the police hadn't given up—"

"The number one rule of undercover work is that the fewer people who know what you're doing, the less chance there is for leaks."

"You mean the fewer people you trust."

"In a way, yes."

"Especially when they're not cops."

"It's our job to protect civilians, not involve them."

"And treat them like children? Is that part of the job, too?"

"Sometimes," Quisto said grimly. "When they act that way."

"'They.'" She repeated his word back at him. "It really is that way for you, isn't it? Us and them."

"Sometimes," he repeated grimly. "There are things it's impossible for other people to understand. Until you've had to pull decapitated bodies out of cars, until you've had to see kids twitching on the floor, their brains fried from drugs, until you've had to try and talk to a woman so terrified after a rape that she can't even bear to be in the same room with a man, until you've seen dozens of people so lost they see suicide as their only hope of escape, until you deal with all that day after day, time after time, you can't have a clue what it's like."

Caitlin was staring at him, her eyes wide, the anger in them gone, as if wiped away by the intensity of the words he'd never meant to let out. "Then...why do you do it?"

Why indeed? He'd always thought he knew. But now, looking into Caitlin Murphy's wide, blue eyes, he wasn't certain about much of anything any longer.

"I . . . It was all I ever wanted to do."

"Why?"

He shrugged, embarrassed. He didn't go in much for analyzing his motives. She waited silently, watching him, until he felt compelled to say something. Anything.

"Maybe it's like you said," he said flippantly. "A power thing."

"I didn't really mean that," she said. "I try never to generalize, but I did it then. I'm sorry."

She wasn't going to let him lighten this up, he thought sourly. "No problem."

"Yes, it is. I hate it when I do that. Because I hate it when it's done to me. So why was being a cop all you ever wanted to do?"

He lowered his gaze to the polished wood of the bar. "I . . . I'm not sure. My mother, maybe. She taught all of us kids that the police in this country were to be respected, because they truly were here to protect and serve."

"Respect," Caitlin said quietly. "That's something my kids would understand. It's what they want most, I think. Just some simple respect. Respect enough not to be treated like they're already lost causes, not to be written off before they even have a chance to try."

"Everyone should have that."

"Yes. They should. But so many don't. You were lucky, Quisto. Maybe, if your mother hadn't been so strong, if your family wasn't so strong . . ."

His head came up. "I would have ended up like your kids? Not only not a cop, but . . . lost, in the endless violence of the streets?"

"Or worse."

"Do you think I don't know that?"

"I don't know. Do you?"

He grimaced. "All too well. I learned a long time ago about the limitations this world wanted to put on me because I wasn't one of the fair-haired boys. In all senses of the phrase.''

''You mean because you're Cuban?''

''I didn't even get that distinction. People only cared that I was Hispanic. We were all alike—Cuban, Mexican, South American, it made no difference. It simply meant that other people looked past us instead of at us. It meant we were expected to act a certain way, eat certain foods, work at certain jobs, simply because of our heritage.''

Caitlin nodded. ''My family came here when No Irish Need Apply was the most common sign in any business window. I've heard stories . . .'' She paused, then shook her head. ''But that's different from living it. I've never really had to deal with such things personally.''

''You learn. One day I took a long, hard look at my life. And I made myself see what I had, not what I didn't have. My family, a job, that respect we talked about . . . more than many people I knew had. I have everything I need. You're right. I was lucky. I still am. I tell myself that every day.''

''Why?''

He blinked. ''What?''

''Why do you tell yourself every day? Do you need convincing?''

He stared at her, brows furrowed. ''I . . . don't know.''

''You said you have everything you need.''

''I do.''

''But not everything you want?''

He drew back a little. ''Who does?''

''A rare few, I suppose,'' she said, smiling. ''So what's missing from the life of Quisto Romero?''

He hated this. He'd always avoided this kind of conversation. Especially with women, who seemed prone to this sort of digging into the psyche.

''Well,'' Caitlin drawled, ''I'd say that hit a nerve.''

''I just don't like analyzing everything, all right?''

''Afraid of what you might find?''

He let out a long-held breath. ''Maybe.''

She looked startled. He was a little startled himself; he'd never really let himself think about that occasional nagging feeling he got that something was missing in his life. He'd gone as far as to acknowledge it, but he'd quickly chalked it up to the job, to the all-consuming world of law enforcement that had both widened and narrowed his world.

"No cop is ever completely satisfied," he said.

"Is that what it is?" she asked. "The job?"

He lifted one shoulder in a half shrug. "You see too much of what's wrong with the world, and far too little of what's good. And every day you have to face the fact that there's so little you can do to change the former into the latter."

Caitlin gave him a thoughtful look. "I suppose you spend most of your time seeing people at their worst, don't you?"

His mouth quirked. "Most people don't call the police just to say things are going great."

"It must make you wonder, sometimes, if...people are worth helping."

"Sometimes. But every once in a while, something happens that makes you realize it's all worth it. That child you get to return to its mother, the bad guy you stop before he hurts somebody, the person you meet who really appreciates what you're doing..."

He reached out and put his hand atop hers, not really realizing he was doing it until it was done. She met his gaze, and something in the way she looked at him made his throat a little tight, his voice a little thick when he went on.

"And sometimes you meet somebody who's fighting the same battle, just in a different way. You might not agree with that way, might not even think it works, but it feels darn good to know you're not alone."

She blinked, rapidly, and lowered her eyes. "Thank you," she said, her voice husky.

Something glistened on her cheek, and he looked closer. A tear. Tracing its way down that lovely curve from cheek to chin. He lifted one hand and gently brushed it away with the back of one finger. Her head came up, and he saw the sheen of more tears, yet unshed, in her eyes. Even as he looked down at her, another tear trickled after the first.

"Ah, Caitlin..." he said.

And before he could stop to think about it, he had pulled her into his arms. He lowered his head, driven by some protective, cherishing instinct he hadn't known he had, to kiss away that tiny droplet. It was salty and hot, yet it soothed his lips like the coolest of balms. And the cheek beneath it was satin-smooth and warm and alive, and the feel of her skin beneath his lips sent a wave of heat through him.

He wanted more. He wanted to know every inch of that silken skin, intimately. He wanted to know her, more intimately than he'd ever wanted to know any woman. He wanted to know what thoughts went on behind those lovely eyes, what emotions arose from that tender heart, what her dreams were and whether there was any place for him in them.

In some part of his mind not totally engrossed in the feel of her in his arms and the fact that she hadn't pulled away from him, he was scared. He'd never felt this way, never harbored such solemn thoughts while holding a beautiful woman.

But he'd never held a woman like Caitlin.

And then she tilted her head back, looked at him with those luminous, tear-sheened eyes, and fear was the last thing in his mind. There was no room for it, not when she was so close, not when her lips had parted as if she were feeling the same shortage of air he seemed to feel every time he was close to her.

His mind said give her time to move away; his body screamed at him to hurry. When he moved at last, when he lowered his mouth to hers, he felt a shiver ripple through her. But she didn't pull away, and when his lips met hers she gave a tiny sigh that sounded for all the world like pure welcome.

And she kissed him back. Not with the practiced expertise of others he'd been with, but with an eager, innocent hunger that was somehow much more intoxicating. And arousing. His body came to attention with a fierce suddenness he'd known only with her. In seconds, he was achingly hard and ready. But it was so much more than just that, and he wanted so much more. He wasn't just swamped with physical need, although that was powerful enough; he wanted it all, and he wanted her to want it, too.

That tiny still-functioning part of his brain tried to warn him, told him that he, even with his considerable experience, was rapidly getting in over his head. But there was no way he could stop now. Not when he could taste her lips, not when the honeyed depths of her mouth beckoned, drawing him inexorably.

And when she tentatively, hesitantly, almost shyly, flicked her tongue over his lips, he was lost.

He clutched at her, pulling her hard against him. He felt her arms go up around his neck, felt her hands at his nape, her fingers tangling in his hair. And then he knew nothing but the hot, sweet depths of her mouth as she let him in. He traced the even ridge of her teeth, then plunged forward, no longer able to resist the lure.

He stroked her tongue with his own, groaning when he heard her make a tiny sound of pleasure. When she returned the caress, still with that touch of shy eagerness, he groaned again, unable to stop it. She sagged against him, soft, pliant, warm. With his hands on the gentle curve of her hips, he parted his knees to pull her between them, knowing she would know, the instant she got close enough, that he was thoroughly aroused, and not caring; he wanted her to know what she did to him.

The old, sophisticated, ever-cool man who never let a woman know she was getting to him seemed to have vanished, to have been incinerated, as if in the flames of her hair.

He slid his hands up over her slender rib cage, slowly, stopping just below the soft swell of her breasts. She sighed; it was a whisper of sound against his mouth. He deepened the kiss even more, probing, tasting. And then he withdrew, maintaining only the slightest pressure on her lips with his own. As he'd hoped, she accepted the invitation; when her tongue slid past his lips and hesitantly brushed the soft flesh of his inner lip, his body clenched with a fiercely stabbing need.

He couldn't stop himself—he had to touch her, had to feel that soft, warm flesh. His hands moved to cup her breasts; they nestled into his palms perfectly. Caitlin went very still, and he was afraid for an instant that he'd moved too fast for her.

She isn't one of your casual affairs, he reminded himself. But he couldn't seem to move away. Or slow down. He'd never doubted his control before, but in this, as in everything else, it seemed all rules were off when it came to Caitlin.

And then she moved, sinuously, pressing herself into his hands, as if she'd been longing for him to do just that. He stifled another groan, barely managing to keep himself from grinding his aching flesh against her belly. But as if she'd sensed his restraint and wanted to shatter it, she moved there, as well, shifting her hips in a slow, rubbing caress that nearly made him gasp out loud.

He moved his hands, slowly, sliding his thumbs up over her nipples, thrilled to find them already taut and hard and waiting. He caressed them through the soft sweater, feeling another little shock of stabbing heat when she gasped in unmistakable pleasure.

She moved against him again, as if in response to his touch, her hips moving, catching his rigid flesh between them and increasing his need unbearably with the exquisite friction.

He was rapidly reaching the point of no return, and he knew it. He wrenched his mouth away, only then aware his breath was coming in gasps. He closed his eyes for an agonized moment, wanting more than anything else to sweep her up and carry her to the office and finish this, to ease once and for all the need that had attacked him out of nowhere, unlike anything he'd ever experienced before.

When he opened his eyes, Caitlin was looking at him, her eyes wide and dark, her lips parted, her hands gripping his shoulders tightly, as if she wanted him to do exactly what he'd just been thinking.

"Caitlin?"

It came out only as a hoarse, barely audible whisper, but he saw by the flare of heat in her eyes that she knew what he was asking.

The sudden rattle of the front door, and the raucous shouts of boisterous kids, kept him from learning what her answer would have been; reality had come crashing in.

"I... The kids are here," she said, breathlessly, unnecessarily. "I have to open."

"I know," he nearly growled.

"Quisto—"

"It's all right." It wasn't, he was dying, but he knew he had no choice. The kids were getting louder. But still she hesitated.

"Go," he said, his voice still harsh. "I have to go see if my damn car's still out back, anyway."

Wouldn't that just figure? he thought acidly. He'd have a stolen or stripped BMW to account for, on top of trying to beat his painfully aroused, clamoring body into submission.

When she left his arms and went to open the door, he didn't bother trying to stifle his heartfelt groan.

Chapter 13

"Cordero's Grocery. Tonight. Can't give you a time, except after midnight. You'll just have to get the old man out and be ready for fire. And try not to make it obvious to the outside that you got a tip, all right?"

"All right, buddy. Thanks."

"And you don't know who told you."

"Naturally."

Quisto hung up, knowing Gage would do whatever could be done to keep the feisty old man safe and the damage to a minimum. And feeling grateful that the detective hadn't asked questions Quisto couldn't answer. Like how he'd found out, and what he was doing, and why he didn't want the Pack to know Trinity West had been waiting for them. But then, Gage no doubt knew those were questions he couldn't answer.

And thinking of questions he couldn't answer made him remember the messages he'd found on his machine this morning, from Chance, asking what was going on. He'd called and left a message for his partner that he was okay, but would be out of touch for a while. And trusted that

Chance, too, would know that he couldn't be more specific right now.

It was after that that he'd gone to the warehouse and found plans to firebomb Martin Cordero's store late tonight in full swing. Carny was to be the wheelman, Lenny the primary thrower, while Ryan had been assigned the task of putting together the bombs themselves, which made Quisto wonder yet again exactly who this man was, that his expertise apparently included explosives.

For a few minutes, he'd walked a tightrope, as Carlos rather sullenly suggested Quisto prove himself yet again by coming along, since it was in essence his idea.

"Lo siento, amigo," he had said, his voice as smooth as his gaze was cold. "I have other plans."

Lenny hooted. "You're sorry? Ha! I'll bet. And I'll bet I know what those other plans are, and they involve that hot little redhead who can't keep her nose out of our business."

Instinctively Quisto's eyes flicked to Ryan, who was in his usual chair, and as usual carving a small piece of wood with that wicked-looking blade. The man's movements stilled for a barely perceptible instant, but he never looked up. If he hadn't been watching so intently, Quisto thought, he would have missed it. And he still wasn't sure what it meant.

"So it is true?" Alarico asked, eyeing Quisto. "You are... shall we say, interested in the irritating Miss Murphy?"

Quisto looked at the man for a moment. He read knowledge in the leader's hard eyes. He knew no one had followed him from here, but he guessed it wasn't unlikely that Alarico had someone—perhaps even Ryan, after he'd so chivalrously dropped Caitlin off yesterday—keeping an eye on the Neutral Zone and reporting back to him. He didn't think anyone had been watching him in the alley, but he couldn't be sure. Especially if it had been Ryan, who he sensed had all the instincts of the most dangerous of predators, and who, despite his overpowering presence, could no doubt fade into his surroundings if he had to.

But if he *had* been seen, his actions on entering the back of the Neutral Zone would have been a dead giveaway; he'd gone in like a cop. Or at least like someone with some training. And Alarico gave no sign of knowing that. Quisto decided he had to gamble that he hadn't been seen.

"Let's just say someone should keep an eye on her, and it might as well be me," he said coolly. "I'm not known here, nor am I connected to you."

"She knows you're with us," Lenny pointed out. "And we already know she can't keep her mouth shut."

Quisto merely smiled, not looking at Lenny. Alarico studied him for a moment, then smiled back, luridly.

"I believe Rafael will keep the lady's mouth occupied with other things," he said, and the others let out a chorus of whoops and catcalls. Ryan's feet hit the floor, and without a word the big man shoved his knife back in the sheath at his waist and whatever he'd been carving in his pocket, and walked out.

"Now," Alarico said, rather avidly, "you have news for me?"

Thankful he'd stopped at Worthington's office, Quisto nodded. He produced, with somewhat of a flourish, a mock guest list salted with a few names Alarico would probably recognize as some of the highest of Marina del Mar's high rollers. They were close friends of Worthington's, and had consented to having their names on the list as part of the ruse Quisto hoped he never had to go through with.

Quisto watched the man read the list, saw his eyes narrow at some of the names.

"The host is still the best target by far," Quisto said, plucking an imaginary thread from his sleeve. "His wife has a penchant for pretty stones. Large ones. But there are others of interest, as well. And they will all be at their modest little yacht club for this gala, leaving their homes woefully unguarded. We shall pick and chose for our shopping trip, eh, *amigo?*"

Alarico grinned; it was a greedy, pleased expression. Quisto had counted on that from the beginning, that the man's greed and the urge to move up into a higher class of crime, not to mention the prospect of getting a foothold in Marina del Mar, would silence any lingering doubts he had about the newcomer among them.

And it appeared to have worked; when he'd said he was going to begin to search out the home addresses of the guests, Alarico urged him on with a wave and an eager nod of his head.

He'd been on the car phone to Gage as soon as he was out of sight. He just hoped the Trinity West crew was as tough as they were cracked up to be, and would keep Martin Cordero safe. The old man, Quisto had a feeling, would be more concerned about his store, and he was glad he didn't have to convince him to leave for his own protection.

As for himself, Quisto thought, he would be taking up a position at the Neutral Zone tonight. It would enable him to keep an eye on things. Including, he admitted ruefully, Caitlin. He would make sure she closed up and left at her usual time of eleven, well before the Pack would make its run. He didn't care for the idea of her being there when the Pack was running an operation half a block away. Especially one that could easily turn ugly.

He could just see what she would do—charge right out into the middle of it and probably get herself hurt, or worse. She liked and cared about Mr. Cordero, and he already knew to what lengths Caitlin would go for someone she cared about. God help anybody she loved; he'd spend his life worrying about her.

And it would be worth it.

To somebody who wanted that kind of thing, Quisto told himself, amending the unexpected thought hastily. Which certainly left him out. He had no interest at all in that kind of relationship, with all its ties and restrictions. And dangers.

I haven't been tied down, I've been set free.

His partner's words echoed in his head, and the look of sheer love and joy that had lit his eyes when he said them glowed in Quisto's memory like a taunting beacon. Chance had been even warier of entanglements than he was, Quisto thought, and, he admitted ruefully, with a lot more reason. He'd come through hell, and still he'd found it within himself to risk his heart again, while he, Quisto, had never really risked his at all.

And he liked it that way, Quisto told himself sharply, jerking himself out of this morass of uncharacteristic self-reflection. Maybe he was a coward, but he still didn't like the idea of anyone having the power to make him do things he wouldn't ordinarily do, to change his entire life, to want things he didn't want to want.

And that last phrase, he thought wryly, was symptomatic of his confused state of mind of late. And that kiss this morning hadn't helped any. Nothing like that had ever happened to him before. He'd never been so swamped with heat and sensation and need so swiftly, never felt so recklessly aroused, willing to risk any cost to have her, even emotional cost, even knowing she was not a woman to be taken lightly in any sense. Even knowing she would never, ever play this kind of game by his kind of rules.

If he simply wanted her, as he'd physically wanted any number of women in his somewhat checkered past, it would be easy. He knew how to deny that need if he had to, and he'd done it a lot more often in the past couple of years. But he had always been able to channel that need, had limited himself to women who understood how he played the game, to women who were in it for mutual enjoyment and nothing more. He supposed there had been a few along the way who thought they could change him, or who changed their own minds about what they wanted from him. But with Caitlin, for the first time, he found it was he who was craving more. Maybe because there was so much more to her. Or maybe just because she drove him stark, raving crazy.

He shook his head again; that was a habit he was going to have to break, since it clearly did nothing to straighten out his thought process. Caitlin Murphy had really messed up his thinking. And the sooner this was over and he could get back to his real life, the happier he'd be.

* * *

Caitlin knew it was impossible, but she could have sworn she'd known the exact moment when he walked in. A strange feeling, an odd combination of heat and chill, had rippled down her spine, making her every muscle tense. She'd stood frozen for a long, silent moment, whatever she'd been about to say lost forever. Then she had turned around, and there he was. Watching her.

As she looked at Quisto, a vivid, hot memory of yesterday morning seared through her mind. Unconsciously, she raised her hand, and pressed her fingers to her mouth, remembering the incredible feel of his lips on hers. She saw his eyes widen slightly, saw the sharp rise of his chest, as if he'd taken a sudden deep breath. As if he knew what she'd been remembering, and it did to him what it was doing to her, sending darting little flickers of remembered sensation along nerves that had leaped to life. And knowing that she was a fool, that he was a man whose reputation with women didn't bode well for any female silly enough to lose her head over him, didn't negate the sensation one bit.

Her gaze was fastened on him as he slowly began to cross the morning-lit room toward her. As she watched him approach, moving with that controlled ease that spoke of the power concealed by his at first deceptively wiry build, they could have been alone, for all that anything else registered on her consciousness.

He stopped two feet short of her. She wondered why, when what she wanted more than anything was for him to kiss her again, and she could see in his face, in the way his lips were slightly parted and his jaw was set, that he wanted it, too. But then his gaze shifted, his eyes narrowed, and she suddenly remembered they weren't alone.

"What's he doing here?" Quisto asked her. He didn't sound happy.

Caitlin glanced over her shoulder at the man sitting quietly at the bar. They'd been having a surprisingly pleasant, easy conversation, but now he didn't move, didn't even look up. But when he spoke, his words were clearly directed at Quisto.

"Why don't you ask *him?*" Ryan said.

"Because I don't think I want to hear his answer."

Ryan swung around on the bar stool then, facing them both, a half-full glass of soda in his big hand.

"That's honest enough," he said.

He took a long sip, his quick, dark eyes flicking from Quisto to Caitlin and back. Caitlin sensed the tension between the two men but didn't understand it. It wasn't just that Ryan belonged to the Pack, and Quisto was a cop. This was deeper somehow. Personal. She wondered if they'd clashed since Quisto had gone under cover.

"He stopped by for a soda," she said quickly to Quisto.

Quisto eyed the glass Ryan held, a cynical smile curving his lips. "I doubt that."

"Are you calling the lady a liar?"

"I'm just saying I doubt she serves your drink of choice, so since you're here, it's for something else. And I'd like to know what."

Ryan gave him a long, level look. "No, you wouldn't."

"Excuse me," Caitlin said, interrupting, "but would one of you mind telling me exactly what's going on here?"

"You and I *were* having a nice quiet talk," Ryan said to her. "Weren't we?"

Caitlin sensed Quisto's tension increasing, and again wondered what had happened between these two. "Yes," she said quickly, "we were. It was very..."

Her voice trailed off as Quisto's expression grew even more rigid. "Civilized?" he suggested.

Something in his voice made her think of a circling wolf, waiting for the moment of attack. Ryan made her feel that way, too, despite his quiet courtesy and the surprising easiness of his conversation. She had the sense of something under the surface, something raging and on the edge of violence. And it wasn't very far under the surface, either. She hadn't been comfortable when Ryan showed up, but neither had she been able to summon up the kind of fear she would have expected to feel in his presence, or the distaste she would have expected to have for one of the Pack. She wasn't sure why; all she knew was that, while he made her nervous, he didn't frighten her. And, despite his striking looks and fit, powerful body, he didn't speed up her pulse, either. She could admire him, acknowledge his obvious appeal and exotic attractiveness, but he didn't send her stomach spiraling down an endless drop.

No, that was apparently reserved for one Quisto Romero. And she wasn't sure she was any happier about that than if it had been Ryan who inspired this insanity in her.

"I can be very civilized," Ryan said. "In the right company."

"Just don't get any ideas about becoming a regular."

Ryan smiled, a slow, lazy smile that failed to reach his dark eyes. Caitlin's nervousness increased as she thought of wolves again. Circling. Waiting. Waiting to attack. What was Quisto doing, anyway? Why was he prodding this man? Hadn't he been the one to warn her that Ryan was dangerous? Even she could see the truth of that, that Ryan was more than a little wild, and very close to the edge.

Then she looked at Quisto's face. He was wearing the same kind of expression, one of anticipation, as if he knew there was a battle coming and was looking forward to it. Something dark and fierce glinted in his eyes, and he shifted his weight slightly, to the balls of his feet. She knew then that he was just as wild and on the edge of violence as the man he was facing. They were indeed the two wolves she'd pictured, and they were about to stop circling. They stared at each other, gauging, calculating, as if each were wondering how much damage the other would do, or could take.

This was absurd, Caitlin thought. This couldn't be happening here, in front of her, between two supposedly adult males who right now were acting worse than any of her kids.

And who did Quisto think he was, anyway? So they'd kissed a couple of times. Okay, *really* kissed. That didn't mean he owned her. But that was exactly what he was acting like. Like some undomesticated creature whose territory was being threatened.

It hit her then, the picture they must make, two males on the verge of some kind of knock-down-drag-out fight, and her, the helpless female, standing by and watching.

Like hell.

"All right, that's it! Out. Both of you."

Two dark heads swung around, and both men stared at her, startled.

"Out," she repeated. "I don't know what this silly game you're playing is, but you can go play it somewhere else."

"It's no game," Ryan said softly.

"Oh, I'm sure you have some other name for it. Some clever masculine thing that lets you act like idiots without being called idiots. But take it outside, children."

The two men glanced at each other, then looked back at her.

"I mean it. Out. Take your ridiculous male posturing or bonding or whatever this is out of my club."

She stood firm, crossing her arms across her chest and glaring at each of them in turn. They looked doubtful at first, but then, when she didn't waver, they began to look a little sheepish.

Ryan looked at Quisto. Then at Caitlin. Then at them both, as if he were seeing them together, as if he were seeing once more the moment when Quisto had walked into the room. His mouth twisted, and he let out an audible breath. Then he turned back to Quisto and spoke quietly.

"I've seen you fight, *amigo*. I wouldn't want to try and take you alone."

Quisto looked startled, then rueful. "I've never seen you fight, but I don't have to to feel the same way."

"Fine," Caitlin said in exasperation. "Now you can kiss and make up. But you can do it outside! I have work to do, and I've had enough testosterone for one day."

She stood there, insisting, until at last they seemed to realize she meant it. They walked out, one out the front, one out the back. Caitlin retreated to her office, shaking her head in disgust at men who were sometimes worse than children. And telling herself she'd been right all along, that cops—some cops, anyway—were just overgrown boys who liked the taste of power.

And trying not to acknowledge the perverse little thrill that shot through her at the thought that perhaps, just perhaps, this particular cop might have been the tiniest bit jealous.

Ryan, Quisto thought, was just full of surprises. He hadn't expected the man to have the kind of restraint he'd just shown. But then, he hadn't expected to find the man tamely sipping a soda, chatting casually, as if he were indeed as civilized as Caitlin had said he was.

Nor had he expected to react the way he had. He'd never felt such a violent surge of protectiveness. And, he admitted with grim self-knowledge, possessiveness. There was no way to deny it; he had hated the sight of her with another man. And especially with Ryan, for reasons that had only a little to do with the man's dubious character, and much more to do with his smoldering good looks.

It made no sense. He just wasn't the type to behave this way. He was Quisto Romero, and his name hadn't been derived from the family nickname of *Conquistador* for nothing. He was a love-'em-and-leave-'em type, and he wasn't about to change now. That trumpets-and-fireworks kind of love was for others, not him. People like his family. And his partner.

Chance.

That was who he needed to talk to. Chance would straighten him out. And he'd do it without lecturing, unlike Quisto's family, who nagged him about his bachelor state at every opportunity. Despite his own apparent married bliss, Chance had never lectured Quisto about how he lived his life.

And it might not be a bad idea to have somebody know exactly what he was doing, anyway. Just in case.

He picked up the car phone and dialed quickly, knowing Chance liked to take his lunch early, so he could beat the traffic and make it home to see Shea and the baby.

"Detectives. Buckner."

"Ten-thirty-five, buddy," he said, giving the code for confidential information.

There was a split-second pause before Chance said, "Okay. Go ahead."

"I need..." What? Quisto thought suddenly. Advice? Help? A miracle? "To talk to you," he finally said.

"Where? When?"

"Now."

"Okay," Chance said instantly, and Quisto silently thanked his friend for so quickly understanding what he wasn't saying, that this was something that needed discussing now, and not over the phone.

"Billy's," he said, naming a small restaurant a few blocks from the Marina del Mar police station. Its advantage was a secluded parking lot to the rear, invisible from the street. It was also, ironically, where he and Chance had met when their positions were reversed, when Chance was under cover and falling for a woman in harm's way. Not that he was falling for Caitlin. She just had him in a bit of turmoil, that was all. "I'll even buy lunch."

"For that, I'll be there in ten," Chance said.

"Thanks."

His partner was as good as his word; ten minutes later Quisto saw him pull into the driveway and park out of sight in the rear lot. He leaned back in the isolated booth he'd claimed at the back of the restaurant and waited. Chance found him in short order, no doubt having guessed by his reticence on the phone that he'd be back here, out of sight.

The waitress, new since they'd last been here, took one appreciative look at Chance, at his blond-streaked hair, six-foot frame and dazzling blue eyes, and had their meal to them in amazingly short order. Quisto had seen that dynamic at work many times before, and had long ago become inured to it. Mainly because Chance was so embarrassed by the usual feminine reaction to his looks. And Quisto got his own share of the same, enough that he took a goodly ration of teasing from his partner in turn. But Quisto had learned to use his looks and women's reaction to them; Chance preferred to ignore that particular asset.

Chance waited until they were assured of some privacy, took a couple of bites of his sandwich, then eyed Quisto over the rim of his glass of water.

"Spill it, partner. Where the hell have you been, and what are you doing that has Morgan climbing the walls?"

"Is he?"

Chance gave him sideways look. "He is. I gather it's because he knows more about what you're doing than I do."

"Not really. But I imagine he's doing a lot of guessing." Quisto chewed on a bite of chicken sandwich he didn't really want. "Look, I'm not asking for help. I don't want you in this at all. I just want somebody I trust to know what's going on."

Chance leaned back in the booth, not paying much attention to his sandwich, either. "Eddie Salazar, right?"

"You sure you want to know this? I'm running alone here, buddy. Morgan got orders to pull me in."

"So that explains this sudden need for a month of vacation for the first time in years."

Quisto nodded. "I'm way out there, Chance. If I screw it up, it could go down twisted in a big way. I don't want you to go down with me."

"We're partners, remember?"

"Yeah, but you've got Shea and little Sean to think about now. If you get fired—"

"We'll be fine." Chance grinned. "My wife's a successful songwriter, remember?"

Quisto toyed with a french fry, not really wanting it. His stomach wasn't its usual imperturbable self of late. "You're sure about this?" he asked one last time.

"You should know better than to ask. You were there when my butt was in a sling, buddy. The least I can do is return the favor. Give, Romero."

He gave. And when he'd finished, Chance let out a low whistle. "You take your chances, don't you?"

"It was the best I could do on short notice."

"You need anything?"

"Just a lifeline."

"You know I'll back you. You just holler if you need help."

"I hope it won't come to that."

"Just remember to yell if it does. That's an ugly bunch you're dealing with. Don't try to do it on your own, if it starts to come apart on you."

"Yeah." Quisto picked up another fry, felt how cold it was, and set it back on the plate. "If it does . . . come apart, do something for me, will you?"

"You know I will. What?"

"If I can't . . . you make sure Caitlin's not hurt."

Chance went very still. For a long, silent moment, Quisto felt the steady gaze of those observant eyes.

"So Shea was right," Chance said softly.

"What?" Quisto said, startled.

"She said there was something going on, the moment we met Caitlin at your mother's place."

"There's nothing going on," Quisto said quickly. "Not . . . like that, anyway."

"Oh. So you're just worried about her, is that it?"

"Exactly. She insists on trying to keep that place open, and she's already got the Pack screaming for her blood. She's got more guts than sense, and she's going to get hurt—"

"But you don't feel anything for her."

"I didn't say that."

"Whew." Chance let out a breath of exaggerated relief. "You had me worried. If you didn't feel anything for a woman who looks like that, I'd be checking you for a pulse."

"I just . . . It's not that kind of thing. I mean I haven't . . . We haven't . . ."

Chance grinned. "You haven't? That's some kind of record, for you, isn't it?" Quisto shot his partner a dirty look, but Chance's grin only widened. "So how *do* you feel about the lady?"

Quisto opened his mouth to answer, then shut it. Then opened it again. At last he settled on the truth. "Hell if I know."

"Uh-oh."

"What's that supposed to mean?"

"It means you're in unfamiliar territory."

"You can say that again," Quisto agreed glumly.

"Nah, once is enough."

"Cute."

"You're lucky, though. You've got a partner who's been there."

"Been where?" Quisto asked warily.

"Where you are. That unfamiliar territory."

Quisto's brows lowered as he looked across the table, suppressing the urge to throw a tomato slice at his partner's smug grin.

"What exactly is your point, *amigo?*"

"You mean, what exactly is that territory, don't you?"

Quisto sighed. "All right, if you must. What is it?"

"Easy, Rafael my friend. You're in love."

Chapter 14

It was, without a doubt, the most absurd thing Chance Buckner had ever said. Rascals like Quisto didn't fall in love. They played the field until they were too old to do it gracefully anymore, and then, if they had any style, they retired from the scene with some dignity.

So why was he here, sitting on the edge of Caitlin's desk, watching her every move, analyzing her every word, as if he were searching for something, some sign of how she felt? And why was it that every time she glanced at him, and those spots of high color rose in her cheeks, he felt his heart begin to pound?

He glanced at his watch. Eleven-ten. She was sitting at her desk, showing little sign of being ready to leave. He'd breathed a sigh of relief when she closed up promptly at eleven, shooing the last of the kids out with instructions to go straight home, instructions he was sure only some would follow. But she'd said she had some work to do; she was trying for charitable-organization status, and it was a complex application procedure.

Quisto looked at his watch again, calculating the last possible moment he could let her stay and still maintain his sanity. Eleven-forty, he decided. He knew the plan was to hit Cordero's sometime after midnight, and he wanted her well out of the area by then.

"You don't have to stay, you know," Caitlin said when she caught him looking at his watch a third time. "I'm fine. It's been very quiet."

"For now," he muttered.

"Look, if you have someplace to go—"

"No. I don't. Just . . . hurry a little, will you?"

She gave him a puzzled look. "Is something going on?"

"No." Damn, he felt as if he'd forgotten everything he ever knew about undercover work and keeping a poker face. Hastily, in an effort to divert her, he said, "I saw Chance today. He said to say hello."

Caitlin smiled. "He seems nice. And his wife is lovely."

Smothering a sigh of relief, Quisto nodded. "Yes. To both."

"And your godson is adorable."

Quisto grinned, despite his unease. "Yes, he is."

She looked at him for a moment, then looked away. Her gaze came back to his face, and then darted away again. When he saw her catch her lower lip between her teeth, he was caught between a sudden flash of heat at the sight and the knowledge that he probably wasn't going to like what was coming.

"Chico said you'd never . . . taken a lady to your mother's house before."

He'd been right. "No. No, I haven't."

"Why?" He gaped at the bluntness of it, and she blushed. "I mean, I know it didn't . . . mean anything . . . that you took me there, because I'm not . . . I mean, we're not . . ." Her color deepened, but she kept going. "It's not like that. Not that kind of thing. You know what I mean. But with all the women you've dated, you've really never . . . introduced any of them to your mother?"

Quisto stiffened. He never explained himself to anyone, and he didn't like the urge he was feeling now to do just that. And he wasn't sure he liked the spin she was putting on their relationship, even though he'd used almost those same words with Chance. He especially didn't like the fact that those two feelings weren't particularly compatible.

"No," he said flatly. "I haven't."

"Why?"

"You really want me to answer that?"

"I wouldn't have asked if I didn't."

Quisto grimaced. "I'm no saint, and I have never claimed to be. I've been . . . with a lot of ladies. You already know that."

"So Eddie told me."

Quisto's mouth quirked. "I'll bet." He ran a hand through his hair. "Look, I never intentionally hurt anyone. I've dated a lot of women, but I never lied to any of them. I never told anyone I loved her, never let any of them believe I did. And if they couldn't accept that, I left. Or they did. We all knew what we were doing."

And that, he thought, was the saddest claim to any kind of decency he'd ever heard. He knew it even as he said it. He couldn't even look at her. He just waited. Waited for her to laugh at his rather pitiful attempt to rationalize a lifestyle he'd never allowed himself to really look at before.

She didn't laugh. She asked softly, "Why, Quisto? Why is it so important to you to make sure no one gets close to you?"

He stood up, turning his back on her. He didn't want to see her face, not when just the sound of her voice, gentle and tinged with something he couldn't—or didn't want to—name, was threatening to turn his world upside down. Not when her words were striking very close to the bone.

"It seems so odd," she said, in that same soft voice. "I would think you'd be exactly the opposite. Your family is so close, and you're so close to them . . ."

"Right," he muttered. "The perfect family. Except for one minor little detail."

"One—?" He heard her make a small sound of realization before she whispered, "Your father."

He turned on her then. "What father? I never had one, as I recall. He was too busy fighting a lost cause to bother with anything as trivial as his family."

"Your mother doesn't seem to blame him."

"She wouldn't. She would never hear a word against him. Even though he left her alone to raise us all."

"His trust was obviously well placed. Your family has turned out wonderfully."

"That doesn't make it right!" he snapped, a little stunned by his own vehemence. He started to pace, wishing her office was bigger. He couldn't believe he was talking about this to her; he never talked about it to anyone. But now that he'd begun, he couldn't seem to stop. "She shouldn't have had to do it alone. She had eight children, from Hernan down to me, and I was just born, and she had to do it all."

"Do you think she feels . . . wronged?"

"She never had time to think about it." He reached the couch, then turned back, feeling the anger still building. "But I have. I've thought about it all my life. And I swore I would never, ever do that to anyone. No woman would ever be left alone to raise my kids by herself."

Caitlin's eyes widened. She stared at him for a long, silent moment. "So that's it," she whispered. "That's why all those women, why you never let anyone get close . . ."

"I keep it that way because I like it that way."

"Then I'm sorry for you." Her voice was a mournful thing that made his stomach knot. "I'm sorry for all those women, because I'm sure some of them would have genuinely cared for you, if you had let them. But most of all, I'm sorry for you, because you've cut yourself off from the best thing in life, Quisto."

"We're all better off. A cop doesn't have the greatest life expectancy in the world. Dead or in prison—it doesn't make much difference to a kid without a father."

"So you make the decision for everyone, is that it? How arrogant can you get?"

"That's easy to say—" he ground out, stalking back to stand before her "—when you're not alone with a handful of kids and a truckload of bills to pay."

She stood up, her steady gaze never faltering. "You may think you're being selfless, but I don't think you've learned the most important lesson of all from your mother's strength. A woman is more than capable of doing what she has to. And more than capable of making her own decisions."

She was meeting him toe-to-toe, unflinching. As she always had. Living proof of her own words. She was, behind that soft, seemingly vulnerable exterior, as tough as she had to be. Not hard, not cold, just tough. And in that moment he wanted nothing more than to pull her into his arms and hang on, because right now he needed some of that toughness, needed some of her strength, because he was, as Chance had said, floundering in unfamiliar territory.

He'd always thought he was protecting any woman who might come to care about him; he'd never thought about needing any protection himself. But Caitlin made him feel that way—not that he needed it, but that if he ever did, she was strong enough to do it. And that was such a revelation to him that when she picked up her things, indicating she was ready to leave, he had to stop and remember why he'd been in such a hurry to get her out of there.

And later, as he sat in his car, watching, waiting to make sure Caitlin didn't come back for some reason and wind up in the line of fire, he had far too much time to think. Too much time to spend in unaccustomed self-examination, which yielded results he didn't much care for.

When shouts, squealing tires and echoing thuds, followed closely—but not too closely, he noted with silent thanks to Gage—by the sound of sirens, announced the Pack's raid, he stayed where he was. It was usually difficult, this ignoring of a smaller crime in the hope of solving or preventing a larger one, but tonight, Quisto Romero found it much easier. Because tonight, he wasn't thinking like a cop.

He was thinking like a man probing the boundaries of unfamiliar territory.

"Did you see those flames? Man, the whole front of that place went up!"

"Yeah, thirty seconds, and you couldn't even see inside."

"Gotta hand it to Ryan, he sure knows how to start a fire."

Quisto heard, but didn't react to the Pack's boasting. He'd talked to Gage late last night—or early this morning, he amended with a yawn—when he at last went home after the area was clear and he was reasonably sure Caitlin wouldn't be wandering back to get into trouble. The Trinity West detective had told him everything was under control, that they'd set up the store with some highly flammable material in front—and been waiting with Halon extinguishers behind it, holding it down until the fire department arrived to quickly control what had initially appeared to be an inferno.

"It made for a great show," Gage had said. "For about two minutes. And by then your pals were gone."

"The old man's all right?"

Gage had chuckled. "Yeah. Didn't like the idea of leaving his store to us, though. Ornery old guy."

"As long as he's all right."

"He's fine. The whole thing went down perfectly. Almost too perfectly. The fire was controllable, and the Pack didn't stick around, no civilians got in the way... I kept waiting for the other shoe to drop."

"I know the feeling," Quisto had said, quite truthfully; in cynicism, it seemed, there was little difference between Marina del Mar and Trinity West. Then he had thanked Gage again before hanging up and heading for the warehouse.

And now he had to stifle another yawn as Alarico avidly studied the papers he'd given him. The hit hadn't come until nearly three, and it had been nearly five when Quisto finally got to sleep, and even though he'd slept until afternoon, he was still feeling a bit groggy. But he'd decided to wave some more bait under the man's nose now, when he was flush with the success of last night's attack, small though it might have been. And the slightly blurry copy of James Worthington's insurance papers, listing the appraised value of his wife's considerable jewelry collection, appeared to be serving its purpose quite well; Alarico was all but drooling. It had been worth another stop at Worthington's office, even though he'd ended up cooling his heels for an hour while the busy man finished up a late-afternoon meeting.

A chorus of voices from outside the leader's office drew Quisto's attention; more reveling in last night's success, he supposed. He glanced toward the source of the noise. And froze.

It took him a moment to recognize the new arrival. Several, in fact, as his mind raced through images, faces. Then he had it. Four years ago. Crawford—he couldn't remember the first name. Small-time thief, who'd been considering branching out into narcotics. It had been the first arrest he made with Chance, the week they'd been paired up as partners. That was probably why he remembered it so clearly. Watching Chance convince the not-too-bright Crawford that he didn't have the tools to become a dealer had been an education in itself.

Quisto watched as Carlos clapped the newcomer on the back and began to lead him toward the office. He glanced at Alarico; he was still intent on the shopping list before him. Quisto tugged up the collar of his coat and, grateful that his hair was still damp from his shower, quickly ran a hand over it to flatten it down, a small thing that he knew changed his looks slightly. He didn't know how sharp Crawford's memory was, and knew that he'd been arrested enough times to perhaps not remember each incident clearly, but Quisto wasn't about to take any chances.

He stood up, not wanting to wait until the man got there and risk drawing his attention more than necessary.

"Good work, Rafael," Alarico said. "You can perhaps get more of these before this society ball?"

"I'm working on it."

Alarico nodded, then looked up as the newcomer and Carlos reached the doorway. As Quisto had hoped, Carlos, who had never warmed up to him after that first day, ignored him as they came in. With a nod to Alarico, Quisto walked past them, out of the office, without a word. Crawford glanced at him, looked away, then looked again, but there was no recognition in his eyes, only puzzlement. Quisto kept going.

Damn, he thought as he drove away, this was going to make things very tricky. Obviously something had registered in Crawford's mind, even if it was only a vague sense that he'd seen Quisto before. Somewhere. Out of context, and looking slightly different—his hair had also been much shorter back then, in the very early days of his assignment to narcotics—he thought there was a chance he wouldn't put it together for a while. But sooner or later, the man would probably figure it out, unless he was even dumber than Chance had told him he was. He could only hope his visits to the warehouse didn't coincide with the man's presence very often.

He checked in with Chance then, finding out that Lieutenant Morgan was getting antsier by the hour, called his mother and dodged her question about when he was going to bring that nice girl back again, and called Worthington once more to thank him for supplying the slightly doctored insurance papers that had made Alarico light up like a Christmas luminaria.

And then he just drove for a while, thinking. And wishing he could stop. But there were far too many things roiling around in his mind, and he felt as if he'd lost every amount of certainty he'd ever had. Finally he pulled over at a turnout on the Coast Highway that was a prime spot for watching the sunset. He stared at the ocean without really seeing it, wishing the rhythmic motion of the waves could soothe the chaos in his brain.

* * *

"Sandra, you should at least go to the clinic—"

"No! He'd kill me."

Caitlin sighed and continued to gently cleanse the girl's battered face, wishing she could shelter all the women who put up with this kind of thing, wishing they all had a safe place to stay until they learned it was wrong to stay with a man who treated them like this. Seeing it starting like this, so young, was even more heartbreaking. And no matter what she said, no matter how she tried to calm the girl, Sandra seemed on the verge of falling apart. She wasn't really badly hurt, but she was obviously traumatized, and Caitlin didn't know what to say to her.

Sandra gave a sudden start, and a tiny whimper. Caitlin had already begun to apologize for hurting her when she realized the girl's eyes were fastened on a point over her shoulder. That odd sensation of awareness and knowledge rippled through her, and she knew before turning around that it was Quisto.

"What happened?" he asked from the office doorway.

"A boyfriend who thinks beating up a girl half his size makes him a man."

"Lenny's not so bad," Sandra said through puffy lips, defending the one who'd done it to her, even as she cringed from Quisto's male presence.

Quisto seemed to sense the girl's panic, but instead of leaving, he came forward. Sandra pulled back farther, but her expression became one of puzzlement as he crouched before her so that she was looking down at him. The girl winced when he put his hands over hers, which were clenched into fists in her lap, and held them almost tenderly.

"Anybody," he said to her, in a voice so soft and gentle it made Caitlin stare at him, "who takes his temper, his bad news, his bad mood or anything else out on someone smaller, younger or weaker than he is, is contemptible. There is no excuse for it. Ever."

Sandra blinked, staring at him as if he were some species she'd never seen before. "Lenny's not mean, not really," she said.

"No one has the right to do this to you. No one." Then, even more gently, he added, "But you don't have to deal with that now. You don't have to deal with anything right now. You have time to sort it out in your mind. You don't have to decide anything, you don't have to go anywhere, do anything. Not right now."

As if it were a tangible thing, Caitlin saw the tension drain out of the girl. Somehow, perhaps because of his years of experience with victims such as Sandra, he had found the right words, had known the one thing she needed. Time. Time to sort through what had happened. She stared at him as he continued to talk to Sandra, quietly, reassuringly, and the girl began to nod.

He was being exquisitely gentle with the frightened girl. He was handling her so kindly, she couldn't be frightened of him. And that, Caitlin thought suddenly, was as important as anything else, subtly making the girl realize that not all men were like Lenny, not all men felt the need to control and used violence against the most vulnerable to do it.

This was the other Quisto, she thought. The Quisto she'd learned about at his mother's home, the Quisto who was the favorite uncle to a crowd of nieces and nephews, who was the loving son of an incredible woman, who was the proud godfather to his partner's son. And he was as much that man as he was the tough, cynical cop. A man who held himself apart, a man who denied himself the kind of loving family he'd grown up in, simply because there was the chance that family would wind up having to go on without him. As his own family had had to go on without his father.

"He'll do it again, you know," he said later, as the girl left. The club had closed, Sandra had finally consented to let Caitlin call her mother to come and get her, and the distraught woman had arrived to take her home.

"Probably," Caitlin said with a sigh. She rubbed at the back of her neck, then at her temples, where a dull ache was beginning. "At least her older sister is a nurse. She'll be able to take care of her."

"You've been doing a lot of patching people up lately. You look tired," Quisto said, moving to stand close behind her.

"I am," she admitted. "It's been a terrible day. First poor Mr. Cordero, then this. Did you see his store? It's awful, what they did."

"I saw. But it could have been worse." His hands went to her shoulders. "He wasn't hurt."

"Thank God for that," she agreed fervently. She could feel his heat, and it felt so good that she didn't even try to move away, even though the gentle massaging he'd begun was making her a bit nervous.

"I wish you'd known," she said. "Maybe you could have told someone, and they could have stopped it."

His hands stopped. "I . . . did know."

She turned to stare at him. "You knew? And you let them do it?"

"I couldn't stop them without giving myself away."

"But they set his place on fire!"

"Caitlin, they wanted to kill him."

She paled. "Oh, God."

"I did what I could. I let some people know. He's okay. The damage isn't as bad as it looks, because . . . they were ready. And I've got a little more time."

She lowered her head. "I . . . don't know how you do it. How do you deal with people like that, day after day, year after year, and not think the whole world is like them?"

He resumed the gentle massage. It felt wonderful, and she leaned back against him, surrendering to the warmth he was generating. "Sometimes I do," he said at last. "So I have to keep reminding myself that there are people like you out there, too."

Her mouth quirked. "Naive little fools, you mean?"

She heard him chuckle; it was a deep sound that rumbled up from his chest. "You are many things, Caitlin Murphy, maybe even naive, but you are not now and I doubt you've ever been a fool."

She turned around then, looking up at him. "Thank you."

He stared at her for a long moment. When his gaze shifted to her mouth, she knew what was coming. Knew it and welcomed it. He started to lower his head.

"You're welcome," he said, and before the last syllable died away, his mouth was on hers, and the fire that leaped to life so suddenly between them was set loose once more.

He kissed her with skill, she knew that, knew he'd had much more practice at this than she, knew that should bother her, but how could it, when the low sound he made when she flicked her tongue against his was accompanied by a tremor she could feel beneath her fingers as she touched him? How could it, when in the instant her body sagged against his, he groaned hoarsely, from deep in his chest, as if the sound had been ripped from him against his will?

His hands slid down her back to her hips, to hold her more tightly against him. She flattened her palms against his chest, feeling the beat of his heart accelerate as she felt the insistent nudge of aroused male flesh against her. Driven by an urge she'd never felt before, she moved her hips, as if reaching for him, caressing his body with her own, until he wrenched his mouth from hers with a gasp.

"*Dios mío,*" he panted. His eyes closed, and she saw him take three long, deep breaths.

"Quisto?" she said, her voice sounding much like his as she asked... She wasn't sure what she was asking.

His eyes opened. He stared at her for a moment, and she couldn't deny what she saw in his face. Yes, there was heat and raw sexual need there, but there was more. There was wonder, almost shock, there, as well. And more than a touch of wariness.

"I should have known," he muttered.

"Known... what?"

His mouth twisted ruefully. "That I was in trouble."

Uncertainty flooded her. "Trouble?"

"Honey, I have *never* spent so much time trying to figure out a woman. So much time trying to keep one out of my head. The first time I saw you, I knew you were dangerous, and it had nothing to do with you slapping me. And every day since, I've sworn I wasn't ever going to get to this point."

She wondered again why that *honey* sent such a thrill through her. Perhaps because she had the feeling he had to really think about it, to choose to use it, as opposed to the *querida* that seemed to roll so easily off his tongue. And she knew she was fixating on that because she was afraid to hear what he was going to say next.

A little breathlessly, she asked, "What point?"

He let out a long breath. "The point where I want you so much I can't think of anything else. The point where nothing else matters, even my job. The point where, if you tell me no now, I'm going to curl up and die right here."

Color flooded her face. Never in her life had a man said anything like that to her. She'd long ago decided she was far too much the girl-next-door type to inspire such passion in a man. Especially a man like this. And until Quisto, she'd doubted she could feel such passion in turn. And yet here she was, her heart racing, her body tingling, a consuming heat building low and deep inside her for this man.

"I don't want to say no," she whispered, a catch in her voice.

Quisto took another deep breath. "But?" he asked, his voice as gentle as it had been with Sandra, as if he'd sensed her fears.

"I'm...not much on female competition."

He closed his eyes again, wincing. "Caitlin, don't. This isn't...like that."

"It isn't?"

She heard a long exhalation from him. He opened his eyes again and looked at her intently. "I can't change my past,

Caitlin. I've done what I've done, and that I'm not very proud of it anymore doesn't make it go away.''

"You...had your reasons.''

"Maybe.'' She saw in his eyes the concession that her guess about his motives, and about his absent father's influence on them, had been accurate. "Maybe they were even good ones. And I could tell you I've changed in the past couple of years, and it wouldn't be a lie. But I have no way of proving that to you. Except to say that...this is different.''

She wanted to believe him, wanted it more than anything. Wanted to delude herself, a warning voice in her head echoed.

"I think,'' Quisto added, in a voice so low and rough it sent a shiver through her, "that's why I've been fighting it so hard. Because, deep down, I *knew* it was different. I'm scared, too, Caitlin. You scare me. You, and the way you make me feel. And I've never admitted that to a woman before in my life.''

She believed him. And in this moment, it didn't matter to her what his past had been. It wasn't that Quisto she wanted, anyway. It was the man she'd seen tonight, who had so gently dealt with a frightened girl. The man she'd discovered in his mother's home, the loving son and uncle. The man who had denied himself that kind of loving family, for reasons that made her heart ache for him.

Perhaps she was a naive fool after all, but it was that Quisto she wanted. And if the price was having her heart broken by the charming ladies' man, she would deal with that later, when she had to.

Chapter 15

She had never, Caitlin realized with a little shock, been so naked with a man before. In her few other experiences, it had been a hurried affair, conducted in the dark and leaving her feeling afterward that she had somehow missed the entire point of it all. But her other experiences had been nothing like this. It should have felt odd, standing here beside the now open sofa bed in her office, but it didn't. It felt incredibly right.

Never had a man undressed her with such slow, exquisite care, kissing each inch of skin as he revealed it, as if she were a work of art beyond price. He lingered at her throat, her breasts, her belly, her legs, caressing her with long, lingering strokes punctuated with quick, hot little kisses that set her on fire. Never had her body reacted like this, seeming to respond to him of its own volition, reaching for his touch, rippling under his caresses. Never had she wanted to give herself like this, never had she thrilled to the almost physical feel of a man's gaze on her, never had she been proud, as well as shy, about herself.

But when Quisto looked at her, when his eyes grew hot at the sight of her nudity, when his gaze lingered on her breasts and narrowed fiercely as her nipples tightened as if he'd touched them again, when he let out a soft, low groan of wonder and need as that hot gaze swept over her body, taking in the curve of hip and thigh, and the triangle of red curls she unexpectedly felt no need to hide, she was proud. Still shy, but proud. Proud that she could make him look like that, that she was the one who had drawn his face taut with desire. The one who had brought him to a point of arousal that almost frightened her.

She'd glimpsed him when he took a brief moment, as if he needed to slow down in his touching of her, to discard his own clothes. She'd seen him extract a small foil packet from somewhere and toss it on the bed, thought about a man like him being always prepared, but discarded her qualms; she'd put that dilemma behind her. Now her only fear was of the moments to come; would this really work? For an instant, she wished she had had more experience herself. He had been . . . very aroused. So much so that she'd been afraid to look again.

But she wanted to. She wanted to look at him, as he was looking at her. She wanted to explore every inch of him with her eyes and her hands and her mouth. Even the thought made her pulse race, and heat flashed through her like wildfire.

"Whatever you just thought," Quisto said harshly, his gaze now fastened on her face, "do it."

Her color deepened.

"Please," he said, his voice barely a whisper.

She couldn't deny him. Or herself. Not any longer. For a long moment, she simply looked at him, her eyes taking in the lean, wiry strength of him, seeing vividly now how wonderfully this tightly knit body suited him. Every line, every curve of muscle, was in proportion, flowing from one into the other, speaking of a quiet power that was more of speed and quickness than of bulk. And naked, he was even more beautiful than she could have imagined, reminding her yet again of some statue of an ancient god.

She lifted one hand and placed it, fingers spread, on his chest. The heat of him seared her, making her fingers flex instinctively. Her other hand followed, and she felt his heart accelerate again beneath her touch. She moved her hands slowly, tracing the planes of his chest, savoring the feel of taut muscle beneath sleek, smooth skin.

Her fingertips brushed over his nipples. She saw his stomach muscles contract in the same moment she heard his sharp intake of breath.

"You . . . like that?"

"I like it," he said, sounding a little grim.

She did it again, this time adding the tiniest bit of an edge from her nails to the caress. He groaned.

"Caitlin, honey . . . I know our first time should be slow, and easy, but I . . . You touch me and I—"

His words broke off abruptly as she repeated the movement, liking the way the flat disks of flesh had puckered under her touch. Then she leaned forward, pressing her lips to his chest, midway between her hands. She felt the tension in him, as if it were radiating from his golden-brown skin.

"Damn," he said softly, reverently, wonderingly. "What are you . . . I can't . . ."

She reveled in the stunned, broken sound of his voice, in this proof that he'd meant what he said; this was different. She trailed her hand downward over his belly, until her fingers tangled in the thicket of dark curls. She hesitated then, shyness overcoming her newfound boldness for a moment.

"Yes," he hissed out, as if he'd tried to hold back the plea.

She moved again then, her fingers curling instinctively around him.

"Oh . . ." It was a tiny, awed gasp of wonder as the hot, heavy weight of him filled her hand. She felt his fingers dig into her upper arms, as if he were hanging on to her for support. Tentatively she stroked his length, marveling at the satin-smoothness and searing heat of him. She traced the fascinating masculine contours, lingering at the tip, where she found a tiny bead of moisture. She rubbed at it, and heard him gasp even as she felt that rigid flesh surge and his fingers tighten on her shoulders even more.

He released her suddenly, and his hands came down to grasp hers.

"Sometime," he said hoarsely, "I want to take hours to do this. I want to touch and kiss and taste every bit of you, and have you do the same to me. I want to take us to the edge and then stop, over and over, until we're both crazy for it. But not now. Please, Caitlin, not now."

She shivered at the impact of those hot, impassioned words and the images they invoked. And shivered again when he moved with an eagerness that thrilled her, picking her up and lowering them both to the sofa bed with a restraint he had to visibly fight for. But when he came down beside her, she opened her arms, reaching for him, and he slipped into them with a low sound, something that could have been need or hunger or desperation, or just as easily all of them.

She sensed him trying to bolster that restraint, to make himself go slow. And suddenly that was the last thing on earth she wanted. She'd never felt the hollow ache inside her as fiercely as she did now, knowing that the cure for that ache was within her grasp.

"Please," she whispered as he trailed those hot, biting little kisses down the side of her throat, "don't wait. Not anymore."

He lifted his head. "You're sure? About this?"

"I'm sure that I'll go crazy in another minute."

"I think I already have."

He reached to one side and found the foil packet he'd tossed there earlier, and quickly dealt with it. This time the thought of his expertise was so fleeting that Caitlin barely had time to recognize it, because in seconds he was back in her arms, settling himself atop her gently, starting again to caress her with his hands and his mouth until she thought she would scream if he didn't take that final step and fill the aching emptiness inside her.

And then he did, beginning a slow probing of her body that drove her to the brink of madness. She lifted her hips, trying to take more of him, wanting this more than she'd wanted anything in her life. And then he stopped.

Her hands went to his shoulders, her fingers curving as she gripped him. She moaned, not caring that it was a pleading, needy sound. As if he'd been waiting for that sound, as if it had been a signal, she felt his muscles tighten.

"More?" he whispered, his voice harsh.

"All," she gasped, opening her legs wider in invitation.

He accepted that invitation, driving forward, impaling her with a swiftness that made her cry out at the sudden burst of pleasure, and her body clenched in a fierce welcome of his body sliding home.

A guttural sound broke from him as he froze, buried to the hilt within her. Her hands slipped down his back to grasp at his lean hips, wanting to hold him there, still and full inside her. He seemed to sense her need, or feel a similar need himself; he arched himself against her, as if he couldn't get deep enough.

For a silent moment that seemed to spin out into a million years, he looked down into her eyes. She met his gaze, read there the pure wonder and amazement she could no longer doubt. Whatever he'd known before, this was as new to him as it was to her, this growing, clawing need.

He started to move, slowly at first, in the age-old rhythm. But the heat built too swiftly, turned to flames too fast, and in moments he was thrusting hard and fast, and Caitlin was loving it, lifting herself to meet him, her hands moving over every part of him she could reach, first stroking, but then, as the flames turned into a firestorm, clawing at him in desperation as he drove her closer and closer to an explosion she feared almost as much as she wanted it.

He muttered something, a wild, indistinct phrase out of which she heard only "... can't wait."

Then his hand slipped between their bodies, probing, sliding over sweat-slicked skin, until his searching fingers found the tiny knot of nerve endings that his body had already roused to a raging sensitivity. He touched her there, gently, then insistently, and Caitlin couldn't stop herself from crying out at the sudden rush of fiery sensation. He thrust himself hard into her again, then stroked her again, then repeated it, until the alternation of that circling caress and the powerful invasion had her gasping his name on her every breath.

And then she heard him moan, felt a violent shudder go through him, making every muscle in his body go rigid. He said her name, and then said it again, in a voice that drove her to the very edge of a pinnacle she'd never been to before. And then she felt him grow impossibly larger inside her, heard her name erupt from him once more, felt the convulsive jerk of his hips as he emptied himself into her. That final, helpless movement of his body was the impetus that sent her flying, and with a joyous cry she followed him over the edge.

"Who is he, Caitlin?"

"Hmm?"

"The photo. On your desk. Who is he?"

She lifted her head to look at him. Her hair trailed over the skin of his chest, and as he thought of the various possibilities of having that soft mass trailing all over his body, Quisto felt a flicker of renewed need that amazed him, considering the night they'd just spent exploring each other. For all his so-called experience, he'd never had a night like this. In fact, he'd rarely awoken like this, still in the arms of a woman. But he could no more have left Caitlin last night than he could have walked away from Eddie's murder.

"That's my brother."

"Oh." He didn't think his voice had betrayed anything, but Caitlin, as he'd learned, was more perceptive than most.

"You sound relieved."

He was embarrassed, but he owed her an honest answer, he supposed. "Let's just say that, if he was your type of man, I wasn't quite sure what you were doing here with me."

She looked at him for a long, silent moment. "Is this...a big thing with you? That you're literally not, as you put it, a fair-haired boy?"

"I came to terms with that long ago. But I wasn't sure..." He ended with a shrug.

"If it mattered to me?" she asked.

"Does it?"

"As a matter of fact, yes."

He blinked, startled. During the course of the long, erotic night they'd just shared, his every perception of himself and his world and the way he'd chosen to live his life had been shaken, and his certainty about what he wanted out of that life had been shattered. And Caitlin seemed to be determined to carry that process on, rattling his cage yet again.

"What—" He swallowed and tried again. "What do you mean?"

"It matters to me that you've had to fight harder to get to where you are. It matters to me that your family made their way up from nothing, after leaving everything behind, and risking their lives to do it. It matters to me that you have a sense of your own history that so many others lack."

Stunned by the unexpected fervor of her words, he wasn't prepared when she suddenly moved, levering herself over him, draping her slender, naked body over his as she lowered her head to speak huskily into his ear.

"It matters to me that you're golden-brown and beautiful, that you look like the personification of some ancient, royal race, and that you can turn my muscles to water and my heart into a frantic hummingbird with just a look."

He swore, low and raspy and heartfelt, as his body fairly rippled at her words, the tone of her voice, and the tiny flickers of incredibly erotic sensation that the brush of her breath against his ear sent darting through him. Need, demanding and undeniable, slammed into him, and his body responded with a speed that made him groan even as he reached for her.

And minutes later, as he looked up at her as she rode him so sweetly, her body claiming his with an intimate clasp that made him nearly cry out at her every movement, he knew that his world had been shattered, and no matter how carefully he put it back together, it would never be the same.

He didn't like the way Crawford was looking at him. Or the way he kept glancing away and looking back, in the manner of a man who knew he'd seen someone before, but couldn't place when or where. And he was more sure than ever that it would only be a matter of time before the man remembered.

"Who's Carlos's buddy?" Quisto asked Alarico.

The man shrugged. "A small-time operator he did some time with. He wishes to join us, but, unlike you, he has little to offer."

The words were innocuous enough, but something in Alarico's voice made Quisto nervous. The man seemed a little hyper today. Or tense, Quisto thought. Or maybe it was him; maybe he was just extrasensitive today. Everything seemed changed, different. He nearly smiled in chagrin at himself; one night spent with Caitlin, and he felt like a man released from a hospital after a long illness. But what a night—and morning—it had been. . . .

". . . paid for it."

Belatedly, he tuned back in to Alarico's words. "What?"

"You understand, of course. You are a man who sees the necessity of maintaining a certain image. The boy couldn't be allowed to get away with such a betrayal."

"Er, no. Of course not."

"Such a shame, though. Eddie was a bright boy. It is too bad he had such foolish ideas."

Eddie. For more than two weeks he'd devoted his time to this and this alone, and now here it was, tossed out so easily he couldn't quite believe it. He kept his tone casual, even bored.

"Eddie? Was that his name, the boy you were talking about before?"

Alarico nodded. "I had to have him killed, of course. I could hardly let such treachery go unpunished. No one betrays the Pack to the police and lives."

Alarico knew. He'd known all along that Eddie had ratted on them.

"Is that what he did?" Quisto asked, trying to sound only vaguely interested, knowing he was walking a thin and deadly line.

"He set us up for that raid in Marina del Mar."

Quisto lifted his brows. "Really? A little boy did that?"

Anger contorted Alarico's features, and Quisto regretted being unable to resist that little jab.

"He was a *pachuco,* a punk who wanted to be a big shot, and then couldn't hold his tongue afterward. He should have known we would find out. You cannot hide anything from the Pack for long."

Was that a warning? Quisto wondered. Could he risk going any further?

How could he not? he thought. This was the entire point of his being here. He'd always guessed Alarico had ordered it, but he wanted to know who had actually carried those orders out, who had had the stomach to pump a skinny kid full of a lethal dose of procaine.

Quisto leaned back in his chair, glancing toward the open office door, where he could see Carlos, Carny and a few of the others. Crawford was there, as well, still casting curious glances his way. Lenny, whom he intended to have a private word with later, was conspicuously absent. Nursing sore hands from battering Sandra, no doubt, he thought acidly. Yes, he'd have a little heart-to-heart with Lenny. Soon. But now he had to take the chance Alarico had handed him.

"So," he said easily, "who was the lucky one? Who got to do the little bigmouth?"

"Does it matter?"

Quisto shrugged. "Only to the kid, I suppose."

"He should have thought of that before he betrayed us."

"Um-hmm..."

Quisto smothered a yawn that wasn't feigned; he hadn't slept much last night. Not that he minded. Not when he'd spent those waking hours with Caitlin naked in his arms. And naked in hers.

"Sounds like something Lenny'd enjoy," he said around another yawn that he hoped was giving the impression he wanted, that this was a matter of only mild interest to him. It was only a guess, brought on by the brutal man's treatment of his girlfriend, but the more he thought about it, the more sense it made; who better than Lenny, with a pipeline right to the Neutral Zone in Sandra, to overhear Eddie bragging about helping the cops? And, he thought suddenly, Caitlin had mentioned that Sandra's sister was a nurse. At a hospital, perhaps? Where procaine would no doubt be readily available?

"Who did it is of no importance. What matters is that it was done," Alarico said, but the hastiness of his words and the slight edge that had come into his voice spoke volumes about what he wasn't saying.

Lenny. It was Lenny. It all fit.

Quisto yawned again, purposely this time. Alarico was watching him, closely. He seemed to be waiting for something, watching for some—or perhaps any—reaction. Quisto gave an apathetic half shrug.

"A man must keep his house clean," he said. "And a fool must pay the price for his foolishness. Even a young fool." Then, as if it meant less than nothing, he said with an air of indifference, "Can we get on to something useful? Have you been able to locate a...shall we say, a dealer who can handle our merchandise?"

Alarico said nothing for a moment, a moment Quisto guessed was calculated to make him squirm. He wondered for a moment if the man knew, but his instincts told him no. Besides, he didn't think the man had the control to keep such knowledge secret. He might be suspicious, or perhaps this was simply more of the usual mistrust the Pack felt for everyone.

"Yes, I have," Alarico said at last, and the sense of suspicion vanished.

Maybe, Quisto thought as he half listened, he was just paranoid, because he didn't want to be here at all, because for the first time in his career as a cop, something had become more important to him than the job. A stubborn, contrary, headstrong woman who drove him crazy. In more ways than one.

It was late, well after midnight, when Quisto had reason to remember that thought. Because Caitlin was driving him crazy once again, on the sofa bed in her office. He'd wanted to take her somewhere else, someplace nicer, although his place was out of reach for the moment; if he didn't go home, he could honestly claim he hadn't heard the string of messages he was sure were on his machine, ordering him to call Lieutenant Morgan. He would, soon, now that he had his answers, but not yet. And he would tell Caitlin that he'd learned who had killed Eddie. But not yet.

She'd suggested her place, but despite his curiosity to see where she lived, the moment she looked at him as he walked in the back door of the Neutral Zone shortly after she closed up, the moment he saw the way her eyes lit up when she saw him, he'd known there wasn't a chance he'd last long enough to go anywhere.

As it was, he'd barely made it to the office before he was clawing at her clothes. And the only thing that kept him from feeling like a completely out-of-control animal was the feel of her eager hands dragging his own shirt over his head, then fumbling with his zipper in a way that made him want both to help her with it and make it more difficult, just so that she'd keep touching him.

He hadn't needed to worry about that, he discovered quickly. She had shyly admitted she'd been thinking about this all day, and blushed when she told him how much she liked touching him. He'd responded with a grand gesture of mock submission, lying back to allow her to have her way with his naked body. But he realized now that there was something to this submission business, and the mockery vanished as she proceeded to show him exactly what the appeal was in letting someone do as she wished to you.

No, not just someone. Caitlin. Never before her had he ever thought to find pleasure in this kind of meek surrender, but she was driving him wild. Every tentative touch and caress, every stroke of her hands over his body, soon followed by a searing trail of kisses that followed the same path, tightened him another notch, until he thought he would fly apart if she touched him one more time.

He was shaking, he could feel it, but he couldn't find it in him to be embarrassed, not when she was doing as he'd fantasized, and that mass of soft, curling red-gold hair was brushing over him as she ministered to him in a way he'd never dreamed of.

He was groaning her name like a litany, again and again, as his body both arched toward her touch and retreated when he could bear no more. She kept on, teaching him more than any woman ever had about just how much he could take. And she did it with a kind of shy wonder that seemed to tighten his heart as much as the rest of his body.

He stood it as long as he could, and longer than he ever would have thought. But at last, when he came within a split second of embarrassing himself by losing control when she'd merely been planting a fiery little kiss just above his hipbone, he had to move. In a swift, urgent movement, he rolled her beneath him.

"No one," he said, his voice a raspy sound, "has ever made me feel like this in my life."

Caitlin looked up at him, a little wide-eyed. "No one?"

"No one," he repeated firmly.

The shy pleasure he saw in her expression made him want to return the favor tenfold. And so he began, tracing every line, every curve, of her slender body, finding a spot behind her knee that made her giggle, and a spot low on her belly that made her suck in her breath. He plucked her nipples to exquisite hardness with his fingers, then caught the tight crests with his lips to flick them with his tongue, loving the way she cried out and arched her back for more. Then he suckled her deeply, first one breast, then the other, savoring the way she moaned his name as he'd savored nothing before in his life.

He went back to that spot on her belly and pressed his mouth to it, while his fingers went back to her nipples, rubbing them gently, then harder, until she was twisting beneath the onslaught. In the moment when he heard her moan his name again, he shifted to part the soft red curls between her thighs with his tongue. She cried out as he found and stroked that little knot of nerves. Her hands went to the sides of his head, her fingers threading through his hair as he teased that spot again and again, until she was begging him both to stop and go on.

He kept on until he sensed she was on the edge and he himself could no longer ignore the hot, slick readiness of her flesh, could no longer deny its eagerness for his. When he moved up her body, her arms came around him, as if urging him to hurry. He slid into her so easily it seemed impossible that she was so tight around him; yet another of the paradoxes that was Caitlin Murphy.

He'd barely begun to move when he knew he was about to blow his much-vaunted reputation to bits; if he lasted another thirty seconds, he'd be amazed. And then she made it a moot point; at the depth of his thrust, when it was taking everything he had to hold back, she cried out his name and her body clenched around him with an exquisite pressure that was the most beautiful thing he'd ever felt.

He held on, wanting to luxuriate in the incredible experience of feeling her pleasure so clearly, but that sweet, rhythmic squeezing was too much, and with a throaty growl of her name, he let himself go. It was explosive, a burst of swirling heat and sensation that made his vision fade and his ears ring, and made it seem that any part of him that wasn't touching her had gone numb.

He collapsed atop her, gasping, unable to move. He vaguely felt her arms tighten around him, and tried to return the embrace, but he couldn't seem to move. His head was nestled in the curve of her shoulder, and he couldn't, didn't want to, lift it. He felt as if he'd poured himself into her, body and soul. And she was holding him, so safe and sound, he felt sheltered in a way that he couldn't remember ever experiencing. In a way, he realized somewhat dazedly, that he never would have allowed himself to feel before.

"Caitlin," he said. Or tried to; he wasn't sure it came out right.

He tried to move again, managed this time to tense a couple of muscles, then gave up again. He felt her hand slide down his back. Her palm flattened against the small of his back, pressing him harder against her, into the cradle of her hips. At the movement, a little tremor, an echo of the explosion that had been so shattering, rippled through him. It took what little strength he'd regained.

"Sorry," he murmured. "Can't...move."

"Shh..." she said soothingly, stroking a hand over his hair. "Rest, Rafael."

Rafael. She'd called him Rafael. He hated that name. So why did it sound so good when she said it? He was still wondering why as he drifted into sleep.

He didn't know how long it had been when something brought him groggily awake. He felt a soft, warm weight pressed against him. It felt very, very right, and he wanted nothing more than to cuddle it close and go back to sleep. The warm shape against him shifted, murmuring.

Caitlin.

The realization that he hadn't dreamed last night brought him fully awake in time for the second ring of the phone that had awakened him in the first place. He sat up sharply, wondering who would be calling the Neutral Zone at this hour.

Caitlin sat up in turn, pushing her hair back. She flipped on the small lamp beside the sofa bed, then moved as if to go for the phone. Quisto held her back as the third ring came and the answering machine came on, playing her breezy greeting.

"Let the machine get it. Nobody needs to know you're here."

"But it's the middle of the night. Nobody calls unless it's an emergency—"

"If it is, then you can pick it up."

She started to continue her protest, but stopped when the beep came from the machine. A low, gruff, unrecognizable male voice spoke, clearly audible, though it was barely above a whisper.

"Romero. I know you're there."

There was an instant's pause as Quisto considered picking it up. Then the voice said two more words. Short. Deadly.

"Crawford remembered."

The click as the connection was broken echoed in the silence.

Chapter 16

"Just do as I ask, Caitlin, please."

"Who's Crawford?"

It was the second time she'd asked, and for a second time he put her off. "It doesn't matter. Just hurry. I want you out of here. And you can't go home, either. They may know where you live. Go to your parents' house."

When she backed away from him a step and planted her hands on her hips, Quisto sighed. He should have known she'd react like this. She'd gotten up and dressed willingly enough, but then she'd turned to him expectantly, obviously waiting for an explanation that he didn't want to give her.

"I'm not going to my parents' house."

"Caitlin—"

"I'm not going anywhere without knowing why."

"Oh yes, you—" he began, but he stopped when he saw her chin come up. He should have learned by now that she didn't respond well to unexplained orders. "Honey, please," he said, not even caring about the pleading note that had crept into his voice.

Color stained her cheeks at the endearment. She eyed him for a moment, looking thoughtful now, rather than angry.

"That was a warning, wasn't it? Something about the Pack?"

"I don't have time to explain it now—"

"And you wouldn't even if you did have time, would you? No, you just want me out of the way, so you can do some stupid macho thing like face this alone, right?"

He was teetering on the edge of simply grabbing her, throwing her over his shoulder and marching out, like some primitive cave dweller. He was feeling a bit that way. She made him feel that way. And only the knowledge that she'd fight him every step of the way stopped him from doing it.

"You have some funny ideas about women, Rafael Romero," she said, glaring at him. "You think we need protecting from everything. Well, I, for one, don't need or want to be lied to, simply because your misguided machismo, or whatever it is, tells you I can't handle the bad along with the good."

The only thing he could do for a moment was to wonder, inanely, when he'd become *Rafael*. And then he remembered the moments last night when she'd convulsed around him, when her body had claimed his so completely. The name that burst from her lips had been *Rafael*. And he had loved the sound of it. As he'd loved it when she whispered it to him as he drifted off to sleep.

"Who's Crawford?" she asked a third time.

He looked at her for a long, silent moment. The idea of her getting in the middle of this went against every belief he'd ever held, as a man and as a cop. But this wasn't just any woman, this was Caitlin. Caitlin, who had left a plush, cushy life behind to do what she thought was most important, who had opened this unlikely place and kept it going in the face of incredible odds, who faced down the ugliness every single day and refused to let it win.

This was Caitlin, who had turned his world upside down and made him feel as if he were the one being sheltered in the night.

"Crawford's a guy Chance and I arrested, four years ago."

Caitlin, as usual, was quick to realize what it meant. "And he just now remembered who you are?"

"Apparently."

She glanced at the phone. "But who was that?"

"I don't know. And we don't have time to figure it out. Come on. It won't take them long to learn I'm here—"

"How?"

"Honey, they've been watching this place all the time." This time, when he took her elbow, she let him move her along, through the office door. "And they could be here any second. Come *on!*"

"I'm not leaving. Not until you at least call for help. You're a cop, for God's sake! Why won't you call the police?"

"Damn it, this is no time to go all stubborn on me. You could get caught in the cross fire!"

"And you already are! I'm not walking out and letting you do some grand solo act."

"And exactly what good do you think it's going to do if I have to worry about you, along with the rest of this falling apart?"

"Don't worry about me. Just call the cavalry."

"And write off my job," he said grimly.

"What do you mean?"

"We don't have time for this."

He tried to urge her toward the back door, hoping the Beemer was still there; every time he parked it in this neighborhood, he wondered how much of it, if anything, would still be there when he went back. Right now, he'd settle for the weapon he'd foolishly left behind in his haste to get to Caitlin.

She began to move this time, but not nearly as quickly as he wanted.

"What did you mean, write off your job? Why would calling for help do that?"

He let out an exasperated breath. "Because I'm not supposed to be doing this at all."

She blinked. "What?"

"I'm on my own, Caitlin. I told you, I was ordered off."

"But... I thought you just said that because you were going under cover..."

He shook his head, still trying to get her to hurry. "No. My brass, and the brass at Trinity West, both ordered me to back off. I don't know why. As far as they're concerned, I'm a loose cannon. Now, can we please get out of here before the Pack sends a hunting party out?"

"You can't do this alone! Surely Chance will help you."

"Yes, he will. He's never let me down yet. And I'll call him. But not until you're safely out of here."

She stopped in her tracks. They stood face-to-face, her stubborn determination not to abandon him showing clearly in her face, making him even more desperate to get her out of here before the Pack came after him. And he knew they would; being taken for a fool would goad Alarico far beyond any caution about killing a cop. And he'd already gotten away with killing a police chief; a mere detective wouldn't cause him much worry.

"Call now."

She wouldn't back down. In her own quiet, consistent way, she was as strong as he was, perhaps stronger. And probably braver, he thought wryly. She had the kind of strength that let her be gentle and giving, and yet never compromise her beliefs. Like his mother, she had an integrity that went to the core, unshakable and never wavering.

"Call now, and I'll run out of here if you want."

He shook his head in wonder. She was the most incredible woman he'd ever met. And damned if he wasn't going to do what she said.

He walked back to the office and picked up the phone. Chance answered on the second ring, sounding awake and alert, if a little breathless and not particularly happy. Quisto had a good idea of what he'd interrupted, but he couldn't help it.

"They burned me."

"Where are you?"

"The Neutral Zone. I'm going to try and get Caitlin out of here, but they may already be on the way."

"So am I."

Chance hung up even before Quisto did. That was it. No questions, no hesitation. The man was one in a million, Quisto thought, as he turned and strode back into the main room.

"He's coming. Now will you go peacefully?"

"I—"

A noise behind him told him they'd delayed too long. He whirled, pushing Caitlin behind him. Being Caitlin, she refused to stay, and stepped to one side as Alarico strolled in through that damned open back door. He carried an automatic pistol with a menacingly large magazine protruding from it in his right hand, and his face was an ominous mask of barely suppressed rage and evil anticipation. Ryan was close behind him, his expression, as it almost always was, unreadable. His knife was at his belt, as usual, but apart from that, he appeared unarmed.

Not, Quisto thought, that the man wasn't weapon enough himself.

Alarico gestured with his pistol, and Ryan moved toward them. Quisto tensed, but stayed still when Alarico shifted his aim, pointing the deadly weapon at Caitlin.

"Don't talk," Quisto whispered to her harshly, praying that for once she'd listen and not draw any attention to herself.

Then Ryan was there, seeming even bigger than usual. He quickly searched Quisto, who was cursing himself silently, thinking of his own small weapon, still in the compartment behind the speaker in the Beemer. His haste could get them both killed. Ryan's searching fingers paused for a split second over the small knife hidden by his belt buckle. Quisto held his breath, waiting. Not that the little weapon would do him any good, even if he could get it out, but it was all he had.

But then Ryan moved back.

"Clean," he said, with his usual succinctness.

"Really?" Alarico lifted a brow. "A cop with no gun?"

Ryan didn't move away, but stayed close behind Quisto, as if to guard against any foolish moves. It wasn't necessary, Quisto thought; he wasn't about to try anything on Ryan. Especially with Caitlin in the middle of things.

"Or," Alarico said, with a leer that made Quisto's skin crawl, "perhaps a cop with other things on his mind?"

Quisto didn't answer, didn't respond to the words or the lurid expression. His mind was racing, turning over possible ways out of this. It didn't take long; there weren't many options. He kept quiet, kept his expression even and unworried, even let the tiniest of amused smiles curve his lips. If he could convince Alarico he wasn't worried, the man might begin to wonder why. And he just might get nervous enough to make a mistake.

Which didn't, he thought sourly, do a damn thing to get Ryan off his back. He had the distinct feeling that that man didn't make mistakes. Ever.

"I suspected you all along, you know."

Quisto shrugged; the negligent gesture seemed to infuriate the man, to prod him into giving free rein to his triumphant gloating.

"I knew you would show up. Sooner or later. My plan worked perfectly. I knew killing that little *pachuco* would smoke you out."

"What?" Caitlin's voice echoed with shock.

Alarico laughed, a chortling, jovial sound that gave the lie to his look of evil glee. "Such an innocent still," he said. "Do you think I cared about that ridiculous child?" He shifted his gaze to Quisto. "It was you I wanted. The cop who interfered with my plans for Marina del Mar."

"So you murdered a fourteen-year-old boy?" Caitlin asked incredulously. Quisto put a hand on her arm, and shook his head sharply when she looked at him. She subsided into silence.

"The boy meant nothing," Alarico said. "He was merely the means to deliver my message. I know how cops think, with all their stupid ideas of honor and duty. I knew once they discovered it was murder, the cop he'd talked to would come sniffing around." He looked Quisto up and down with the first evidence of genuine curiosity. "Although, I admit, I had not expected someone like you. What are you doing, *vato,* working for those rich bastards, when they look down on you as if you were nothing?"

Quisto ignored this jab, as well. "I got your message. Hang around here a little longer, and you'll get my answer."

"I'm afraid I can't do that," Alarico said, with an air of genuine regret. "I liked you, Romero. I'm sorry it turned out to be you." He glanced at Caitlin. "And I'm sorry your woman must die with you."

Quisto felt Ryan go very still behind him. He waited a split second, but the big man didn't speak.

"She has nothing to do with this," Quisto said.

"Ah, but she does. If little Eddie hadn't been so eager to impress her, he might never have gone to you."

Caitlin made a tiny, distressed sound that stabbed through Quisto like an ice pick driven deep.

"Let her go," he said. "She can't hurt you."

"But she does," the man repeated, still with that air of regret that seemed almost real. "She hurts me by her very existence here, under our noses. She is giving the young people dangerous ideas."

"You mean that they don't have to grow up into scum like you?"

"Enough," Alarico snapped, stung out of his mocking air of regret. "I have left her alone, because she is only a woman, but she has become too annoying to ignore any longer. She dies with you, *scum.*"

"No." Ryan's voice was low and harsh, and, Quisto thought, oddly strained. Alarico stared at the big man. In a voice much more like his normal, offhand tone, Ryan continued. "Kill Romero if you have to. People think risking their neck is part of a cop's job. They'll be mad for a while, but it won't last. The cops will still be after us, but we can handle that if we have to. But they won't forget her. She's young, innocent, a do-gooder. The same reasons as before are still true. The press will eat it up. She'll become a martyr, give the citizens of this town a rallying point. From the east side to Trinity West, they'll be after us. People who never would before will call the cops. They'll make it impossible to do business."

It was a veritable speech from the taciturn man. All of it dispassionate and coldly logical. But it wasn't going to work this time, Quisto thought.

"I must disagree this time, *amigo*," Alarico said. "She is going to be a witness to a cop-killing. It is much too dangerous to let her live."

Alarico *wanted* to kill them both; Quisto could practically smell it. The man had been fooled, and now he was out not just to send another message, but for revenge.

As if he'd sensed it, as well, Ryan shrugged. "You're the boss." He looked at Caitlin, letting his mouth curve into a smile that made Quisto want to jump him, no matter that it would get him killed instantly. "It's just a waste of a beautiful woman."

Alarico laughed. "And one you had your eye on yourself, eh, *amigo?*"

"I wouldn't have minded a taste."

The leader laughed again. "So take her. She can die now or later, it makes no difference."

Ryan's face took on a considering expression as he looked Caitlin up and down.

"Take her now," Alarico suggested. "So our friend can enjoy knowing his woman is being—"

"Stop it!" Caitlin looked up at Ryan in disbelief as he started to move toward her. "You can't do this!"

"What's wrong, Irish? Too good to be screwed by an Indian?"

Caitlin's eyes widened at his harsh words, her shocked betrayal obvious enough to make Alarico laugh once more.

"Bastard," Quisto swore as Ryan brushed past him.

But then a whisper as faint as a summer breeze stopped his rage dead.

"I'll get her out. You're on your own."

Quisto knew he had no time to wonder whether the man meant it. He either had to trust him or not, right now. But when it came to Caitlin's life, he found he didn't want to trust anyone. But he would.

Then Caitlin took things out of his hands, reacting the moment Ryan reached her. She began to fight, clawing at the big man wildly, heedless of the fact that she couldn't possibly win. Yet Ryan didn't do as he so easily could have done, overpower her with sheer strength and weight or knock her senseless. It was as if he didn't want to hurt her, despite the fact that she was landing several blows Quisto knew must have hurt; Caitlin wasn't a weak woman.

That made the decision for him. He might not know what Ryan's game was, but he knew Alarico had one intent only. He shifted his focus to the leader, but at that moment it all came apart.

Somehow, Caitlin broke loose. Alrico's weapon came up. His target was unmistakably Caitlin as she scrambled away from Ryan. In that split second, Quisto's nightmare image of her, lying on the floor of this very room in a pool of her own blood, flashed through his mind again. And in that instant of seeing himself lose her forever, he realized what he knew he should have seen long ago. He loved her.

Without a second thought, he launched himself at Alarico. The man sensed the attack and began to turn. From the corner of one eye, Quisto saw Ryan move. The man grabbed Caitlin. But Quisto was committed; he couldn't stop now. He hit Alarico low and hard. He heard the leader grunt in the same instant he heard the gun go off. Heard four, maybe five, shots in rapid succession. Heard the ping of bullets hitting the walls as Alarico went down, before the pistol flew from his grip.

And then he heard Caitlin scream. And heard a thud. The unmistakable sound of a body hitting the floor.

Chapter 17

Alarico fought hard. And dirty. But Quisto had learned to fight on the same kind of mean streets. And he was driven by a fierce rage, born out of the growing terror that his nightmare image of Caitlin's death had been born not of fear but of premonition.

He connected with a vicious jab to Alarico's jaw. Next he tried to get the man in a choke hold, but Alarico dodged out of his grasp. Quisto followed, spinning to cut him off. It cost him a painful blow to the belly, driving the wind out of him. Gasping, he went down to one knee. Alarico was on him in an instant, kicking, pounding. Quisto ducked his head and rolled. He fought back, stabbing out with one leg to sweep the leader's feet out from under him. The man came down hard, but was up again and charging in seconds.

It was all he could do to hold his own against Alarico's brutal attack. He couldn't spare even a split second to look for Caitlin. He was learning how Alarico had risen to his position. He took advantage of every slip. And if they didn't come, he made them happen. Quisto wasn't at all certain he could win this. And all the while, that image of Caitlin burned in his mind.

They went down in a heap, Quisto landing as many blows as he took. There was no room for grace or planning or fancy moves. This was street fighting at its brutal ugliest. And Quisto knew now just how far he was from those streets. Alarico landed three successive punches to his head, making Quisto's vision dim and his ears ring. He drove an elbow upward blindly and caught a vulnerable spot. Alarico grunted. Quisto rolled again, this time coming up on top. Alarico wasted no time. His knee came up in a driving motion. Quisto twisted sideways, barely avoiding a blow to the groin that would have incapacitated him. The motion overbalanced him, and he went down hard on his right shoulder.

When he regained his balance, Alarico was going for the gun on the floor. In the instant before his outstretched fingers reached it, there was a quick kicking movement just at the edge of Quisto's range of vision. A foot, sending the pistol skidding across the floor. And in the instant when Alarico scrambled after it, Quisto saw his chance. He dived sideways, hard and fast, slamming Alarico up against the block wall. A hollow thud echoed eerily as the leader's head hit the cement. Quisto jammed his forearm against the man's throat, then realized it wasn't necessary. Alarico was slumping dazedly.

Quisto sagged to his knees, feeling as if he'd gone through the Pack's initiation all over again, only worse. His head was reeling, his vision blurry.

Caitlin. Oh, God.

Adrenaline shot through him, and his head came up. He heard noises from the direction of the door, but he ignored them. He looked to where she'd been and saw nothing but the pool of blood that had been so vividly present in that nightmare vision.

"Caitlin," he whispered, staggering to his feet.

"Hey, partner. You look like hell."

Chance. Chance was here. He would help. Quisto turned to look at his old friend. But before he could formulate any words, there was a rush of movement to the other side of him. He tensed, half expecting another attack, even as he wondered why Chance wasn't moving. He spun around, staggered again, then stopped, staring as Caitlin flung herself at him.

"Oh, God, I thought he was going to kill you."

Her hands were moving over him, probing, as if searching for any irreparable damage.

"Cait—Caitlin?" he whispered.

"Are you all right? You look awful, but—"

He grabbed her then. His hands gripped her shoulders and held her away from him as he searched her in turn for signs of damage. "You . . . I thought . . . I heard shots."

He felt her shiver. "God, it was awful. All that blood."

"Caitlin," he said, giving her a little shake. "I thought it was *you* who was shot."

Her eyes widened. "No. No, it was Ryan. I swear, Rafael, he stepped in front of me, as if he meant to . . . to . . ."

She broke off, shaking her head. Quisto heard the familiar ratcheting sound of handcuffs, heard Alarico's whine of protest, and knew Chance was taking care of business.

"You're really all right?" he asked her, unable to quite believe it.

"I'm fine."

"Thank God," he breathed, his head sagging in relief.

Then something registered; she was wearing those paint-spattered jeans, and white high-tops. A memory played back in his mind, and his head came up.

"It was you," he said, staring at her. "You kicked the gun away from him."

"I had to do something."

"So naturally you waded into the middle of everything."

"He was going to kill you!"

He had no answer for that. So, despite the various pains that were making themselves known, he pulled her into his arms. She clung to him, and he felt tiny shivers of reaction going through her. He felt more than a little that way himself, and wondered that his knees hadn't give out on him already. They stood there for what seemed like an age, saying nothing, just holding on.

"Ahem." Chance coughed delicately. "Sorry to interrupt, but could somebody explain something to me here?"

Quisto raised his head, knowing he was grinning like an idiot, but not caring. Caitlin was all right. He'd thought she was dead, but she was here, alive and well, and so warm in his arms that he knew he'd never be cold again as long as she was with him.

"What part don't you understand, partner?" he asked.

"That," Chance said, pointing.

Quisto followed the direction of the gesture, as did Caitlin. The blood. The blood he'd thought was Caitlin's. He drew back slightly and looked at her. She shook her head.

"I told you. He got between us. That man—" she gestured with distaste at the handcuffed Alarico "—and me. As if he'd meant to. And then the gun went off... and he went down. Hard. But when I looked again, when it was over... he was gone."

"Who was gone?" Chance asked.

"It's a long story, partner. And I have a feeling I only know the half of it."

"I never even heard him move," Caitlin said.

"That," Quisto said wryly, "doesn't surprise me. Even shot."

"I found this near the blood," Chance said. "Look familiar?"

He held out a small object. Quisto took it, inspecting it with interest. It was a tiny wood carving of an owl, barely two inches tall, with a wide-eyed expression that could only have been called whimsical.

All the images of Ryan and his knife, that dangerous-looking blade, always moving, carving away at pieces of wood small enough to be easily hidden by his big hands, flashed through Quisto's mind. He stared at the little figure in amazement.

"It's adorable," Caitlin said softly. "Look at that face."

"So that's what he was doing with that knife all the time."

Caitlin took the tiny bird from him. "Ryan? Really?"

Her voice had risen in surprise, and in apparent response to her utterance of Ryan's name, Alarico was stirred to shrill defiance.

"He'll make you pay! Ryan will be back, and he'll make you both pay!"

"You want me to take him somewhere?" Chance asked, gesturing with a thumb at Alarico without looking at him.

"The pier," Quisto said. "And drop him off."

"Okay."

Alarico yelped. "You can't do that! You're cops!"

"Damn, he's right," Chance said glumly.

"Yeah. I forgot for a minute we have to be the good guys, no matter how bad the bad guys are." Quisto sighed. "I'd better call Trinity West."

"I'll do it. You're going to be in enough trouble."

"*I'll* do it. I'm already in trouble—no sense you joining me. Not with a promotion in your near future. But thanks for the rescue work."

"Sorry I couldn't get here sooner." He smiled at Caitlin. "But you didn't need me, anyway."

Caitlin blushed. Quisto hugged her. "No, I had all the help I needed."

"We seem to be making a habit of getting our butts saved by our women, don't we, partner?" Chance said, grinning.

"Yeah," Quisto said. "Now get out of here while yours is still savable."

"Sure thing," Chance said. Then, with a sideways grin, he added, "Rafael." He strolled out, whistling cheerfully.

Quisto's mouth twisted ruefully; he was going to be hearing about this. A lot. He could just feel it. Along with everything else he was going to be feeling, he thought, flexing muscles he just knew were going to knot up on him later.

"'Our women'?" Caitlin asked softly.

He knew what she meant, but he wasn't about to discuss it in front of Alarico. So he answered the question she hadn't asked, instead. "Yes. Shea saved his life on the case where they met. Like you saved mine tonight."

"I didn't—"

"You did. If he'd gotten hold of that pistol..."

He hugged her again, tightly. And then he went to call Trinity West.

"They picked up Lenny this afternoon."

"Good," she said. "Not only for Eddie, but for Sandra, too."

As she sat on the comfortable sofa and watched him pace the room, Caitlin sipped at the wine he'd poured for her from a bottle he'd brought home. His apartment was nice, she thought, and there was definitely something soothing about looking out and seeing the lights reflecting on the water. The place was marked with little touches she would never have expected; drawings from his nieces and nephews on the refrigerator, and a collection of family photos on one wall, smaller than his mother's, but still as warm and touching.

"I talked to Mrs. Salazar today, while you were at Trinity West," she said.

He turned to look at her. "Good. I didn't have time to do that."

She smiled at him. "She told me what you did. That you paid for Eddie's funeral."

He looked startled, then glanced away, as if embarrassed. "It seemed like the least I could do."

"Besides risking your life to find out who killed him?"

"That's different."

"Perhaps," she said. But it all stemmed from the same source, that part of him that he kept so hidden except from his family. And maybe Chance and *his* family. She smothered a sigh, wondering just how big a fool she was to hope that he might share that part of himself with her.

But she was glad he'd brought her here, to his home, to rest while he tackled cleaning up the multitude of details. She'd had to give a statement, but it had been nothing compared to the grilling she guessed he'd been through all day long. He hadn't returned until well after dark, and despite looking exhausted, and turning down her offer to fix him something to eat, he hadn't stopped moving.

"You're not sitting down," she said after a few more minutes of watching him crisscross the floor. "Did they take that big a bite out of your backside?"

He stopped pacing and gave her a sheepish grin. "Big enough. And everybody wanted their turn. I got chewed out by everybody with stripes or better at Marina del Mar, then got it all over again at Trinity West, from everybody except the chief himself."

"You're not really going to get...fired, are you?" She was still feeling a bit guilty; she'd thought the worst of him, when all along he was risking his job, working alone and on his own time.

"I don't think so. Trinity West was happy enough to have Alarico in custody on felony charges that will stick. The trial could get a little dicey, but I think the Trinity West brass may decide to overlook the little detail of them ordering me to keep my nose out of it." He paused, giving her a solemn look. "I didn't tell them about Ryan."

She let out a breath of relief. They'd talked about that, but she wasn't sure he believed her, about Ryan intentionally getting between her and Alarico, taking the bullet that would have struck her. But he hadn't denied the possibility.

"I'm glad," she told him. "I hope...wherever he is, that he's all right."

"I talked to Gage. He told me something strange, about the firebombing at the Corderos' store."

"What?"

"He said the bombs were fairly sophisticated, not your typical Molotov cocktail. Some sort of gunpowder-and-gasoline combination that reacts almost like napalm. But they were underloaded."

Caitlin's forehead creased. "I don't understand."

"They were duds, in a manner of speaking. Made a big flameup, but then died out. Even if the Trinity West guys hadn't already been inside with Halon extinguishers and the fire department hadn't been waiting a couple of blocks away, Mr. Cordero wouldn't have lost much."

"But why would the Pack make duds?"

"The Pack didn't. Ryan did."

Her eyes widened. Quisto nodded. "I still don't know what his game is, but he's more than what he seems. And if you're right, we owe him. A lot."

"Do you think that call . . . was him?"

"I don't know. But it seems . . . possible. Maybe even probable. What I don't know is why."

"I wonder if we'll ever have the answer?"

"I don't know," he said again as he resumed his pacing. "And I don't want to go poking around without knowing what I might stir up."

"What about your lieutenant?" she asked after a few moments. "Was he angry?"

"Morgan? Oh, he did his share of chewing. Told me if I ever pulled anything like this again, I'd be sorry. Then told me to take a couple of days off and reflect on my own foolhardiness."

"Lieutenant Morgan sounds like someone I'd like."

He grinned at her pointed tone. "He's a good man."

And then he started pacing again. She watched him for a while, wondering what was eating at him. It seemed everything was turning out as well as it could, under the circumstances.

Suddenly, right in front of her, he stopped his restless crisscrossing and turned to look at her. Her breath caught; decisiveness was written all over his face. He sat down beside her.

"Why wouldn't you go last night?"

She blinked. "What?"

"You had to know you were in danger. Why wouldn't you just leave?"

"I . . ."

She lowered her eyes, unable to meet his gaze when she didn't know what to say. She knew why she hadn't left, even though she'd been very afraid. But she couldn't tell him, couldn't even admit it to herself. Because she was very much afraid she'd done the most foolish thing she'd ever done in her life.

"You—you were in danger, too," she stammered at last.

"That's not an answer, Caitlin. Why didn't you just leave and let me handle it?"

She tried to pull herself together. She made herself look at him, even though it took every bit of her nerve. "It's a good thing I didn't," she pointed out.

His gaze narrowed, becoming so intense that for the first time she couldn't meet his eyes. She looked away. And heard his breath catch.

"Caitlin..."

"What?" she said, her eyes still lowered.

"Look at me."

She shook her head, feeling decidedly childish, but unable to do as he asked. She just couldn't deal with this, couldn't deal with knowing that she'd made such a fool of herself, falling for a man who had more women on a string than she had dings in her poor old car.

Then she felt the gentlest of touches as he crooked a finger under her chin and tilted her head back. Still, she tried to avoid looking at him.

"Caitlin, please. I need you to...look at me."

Steeling her nerve, she at last did as he asked. "Why?"

"Because I want you to see I mean this."

"Mean...what?"

He took in a quick, deep breath. "I love you."

Her heart seemed to quiver for a moment, forgetting how to beat. Then it began anew, racing as if to make up for that frozen instant.

"I love you," he said again, as if in reaction to what she was certain was her look of shock. "And I've never said that to a woman in my life."

I've dated a lot of women, but...I never told anyone I loved her.

His voice echoed in her mind. Was it true? Could she believe him? Did she dare?

"I don't blame you for doubting me," he said. It was he who lowered his eyes then. "I don't exactly come with good references—not about this, anyway. All I can do is tell you how I feel. And that I mean it." His eyes met hers again. "You're the most incredible woman I've ever met, Caitlin. You made me really look at myself. And why I was...the way I was. And I didn't much like what I saw."

"I...But you think I'm—"

"Wonderful. Brave. Stubborn. Smart. Gutsy. Beautiful. Gracious. Gentle. Ornery. Charming. Want more? I can go on for a long time. Oh, and sexy. God, don't let me forget that. As if I could."

She knew her cheeks were flaming, but now she couldn't look away. "Rafael," she breathed.

His mouth quirked. "I'm so far gone, I even like that." His eyes took on a sudden heat. "I especially like it when you say it with that little catch in your voice, like you did the first time, in bed, when you were just about to—"

He stopped suddenly. She was grateful, she would no doubt have been embarrassed if he went on, but she wasn't sure why he'd done it. She didn't think her thoughts had shown in her face, but he seemed to read her rather easily. He grabbed her hands and held them tightly.

"Caitlin, listen to me. I can't prove this to you—only time can do that. I can only tell you. What I feel for you is nothing—*nothing*—like anything I've felt before. Because you are nothing like any woman who's been in my life before. And I swear to you, if you can...believe that, you will be the *last* woman in my life. Forever."

"Oh, God," she said, trying to stop herself from shaking.

"I love you," he repeated for a third time. "And whether you love me back—" His voice broke, and she saw him swallow before trying again. "Whether you love me back or not, I'll never be the same. I'll never go back to what I was. You were right, I was holding myself apart, afraid I would cause some woman as much pain as my father caused my mother. But I'm not my father. And I can't change what he did, either. Or make up for it. He made his choice. And I've made mine.''

"Oh, Rafael . . .''

She couldn't get any more words out past the tightness in her throat. He looked away, then back, then away again. And, in a voice that was a little shaky, he said, "Caitlin, I understand if you don't—''

She finally got it out. "But I do!''

He gaped at her as if stunned. "What?''

"I do love you!''

"You . . . do?''

"That's why I couldn't leave you there to face the Pack alone.''

"God, Caitlin,'' he said, the words coming on a breath of relief so powerful it made her smile. "I hoped that was why, but I didn't dare . . . You mean it?''

She nearly smiled. He was doubting her? "I mean it,'' she said.

He pulled her into his arms and kissed her urgently, fiercely. And then tenderly, so tenderly it brought tears to her eyes. And much, much later, when she lay snuggled beside him in the darkness, after he'd promised her that he was going to hear her cry out, "Rafael!'' again and again and again, and had proceeded to keep that promise, he brought tears to her eyes once more.

"Right over the root beer,'' he said out of the blue.

"What?'' she asked, wondering what on earth he was talking about.

"On the yellow wall,'' he explained sleepily. "Right over the root beer. That's the spot.''

She laughed. "The spot for what?''

"Our wedding picture.''

She'd never known it was possible to laugh and cry at the same time.

Epilogue

He was going to miss Chance. But it hadn't really been a surprise; he'd known his partner would ace the sergeant's test and it would be the end of the four-year partnership anyway. They would always be close, but that day-to-day intensity would be gone. It didn't really matter. They had other ties now. The close-as-family kind of ties. Ties like being each other's best man, like Quisto's little godson, and maybe, someday, a baby for Chance to be godfather to. And for Quisto's mother to spoil. And Caitlin's parents, as well, who, while they hadn't been happy at her continued refusal to move back to Marina del Mar, had been somewhat relieved that she'd chosen to marry a cop, making Quisto wonder with some amusement what they'd been afraid she might do.

And Chance's promotion had made this decision easier. Even the thought of going back on the street in uniform didn't bother him. He would have wound up there eventually, anyway, when his rotation in detectives was over. Besides, not only would he be closer to the Neutral Zone—which he knew perfectly well his wife was going to insist on keeping open—but it would help him learn this place, become part of Trinity West, something he'd have to do if he hoped to win a detective slot later on.

He'd been toying with the idea of applying for a transfer ever since he'd realized how much satisfaction he'd gotten out of this operation—despite the no-doubt-deserved dressing-down he'd also gotten. He'd always felt gratification at putting the bad guys away, but he hadn't really thought about being able to actually help, maybe to change things at the source. Perhaps because, for the most part, the people in Marina del Mar didn't really need that kind of help; they only needed protection. But Trinity West did need it. Trinity West was different. Just as Trinity West cops were different.

The chief of Trinity West certainly was, anyway, Quisto thought as he sat across the desk from the man. Miguel de los Reyes was indeed a different man. There was little outward sign of the injuries that had nearly killed him when he went down in the hail of bullets that took the life of his predecessor. Tall, lean, with patrician features and dark hair silvered at the temples, he was an impressive man, with oddly colored light gray eyes that seemed to peer into you, probing far past the surface.

Maybe you're just feeling a little exposed because he has the final say on your transfer here, Quisto told himself wryly. And you haven't done much to endear yourself to the brass around here. This man hadn't been the dispenser of a lecture yet, but Quisto knew it had to be coming.

Even as he thought it, de los Reyes addressed the situation with blunt honesty.

"I don't like cowboys, Romero."

"No, sir," he said.

"That the final results were good, and you did some fine police work, doesn't excuse your recklessness."

"No, sir."

"Your record at Marina del Mar is excellent."

"Thank you."

"I appreciate your reasons for asking for this transfer. And may I say, your wife is a woman I greatly respect."

Quisto smiled at that. "She deserves that respect."

"She does," de los Reyes agreed. "I've also had some good words put in for you by some people I trust a great deal."

Quisto blinked. He hadn't expected that.

"And," the chief added, "a warning from somebody else."

Quisto didn't miss the implication that the warning had come from somebody de los Reyes didn't trust quite so much. Robards, he wondered? No doubt.

"Your record speaks for itself. What I have to decide," the man said, leaning back in his chair and fastening that penetrating gaze on Quisto, "is if I can trust you. Trust you not to pull a stunt like this again. There were reasons we told you not to pursue this. Reasons we weren't at liberty to divulge to you."

Robards hadn't told him anything, Quisto thought, but said nothing.

As if he'd read his thoughts, de los Reyes nodded. "I realize the manner in which you were told left something to be desired in the way of professional courtesy. I'm dealing with that. But for you, I have two questions."

"Yes, sir."

"First, I wish to know if, were a similar situation to arise again, you would follow the same course as in the Salazar matter."

"Given the same circumstances, the murder of a boy who trusted me?" Quisto asked.

"Yes."

Quisto considered the question carefully, sensing that Miguel de los Reyes was a man who valued honesty. With a sigh, realizing he could well be destroying his chances with this man, he gave him the truth.

"I'm afraid so. Sir."

He didn't look surprised, Quisto thought. And he began to wonder who his new partner at Marina del Mar would be, since he apparently wouldn't be making this transfer.

"And if it were I who personally ordered you not to, with my promise that I had good, valid reasons?"

This time it was Quisto who gave the other man a penetrating look. He stared into the light gray eyes. They returned his gaze steadily, unwaveringly. He wasn't sure what he was looking for, or even if it had a name. He only knew that in some men he found it, and in others he didn't.

He found it in Miguel de los Reyes.

"In that case," he said softly, "until and unless you gave me reason not to, I would trust you."

Something flickered in those gray eyes. After a moment, de los Reyes nodded. He stood up. Quisto did the same, wondering what had just happened.

The chief of Trinity West held his hand out across his desk.

"Welcome to Trinity West," he said.

Quisto blinked. Then grinned. And shook the hand of his new boss. "Thank you, sir."

"Don't make me regret it."

"No, sir!"

"And give your wife my best regards."

"I will."

Moments later, he was in the large anteroom, feeling a little dazed. He'd been heading for this for over a month now, going through the whole complicated process of changing departments, and now that it was done, he felt a little disoriented.

The woman who had been waiting to see Chief de los Reyes went into the office Quisto had just exited, leaving him alone for the moment. He looked around, wondering what it was going to be like to work here, in this place that was so different, both physically and in attitude.

He'd been too nervous beforehand to pay much attention to this room, other than to notice the row of photographs and plaques on the walls, but now he couldn't help seeing that it was sort of a shrine, or a hall of fame, commemorating Trinity West officers who had been honored for valor. He wandered along, looking and reading, wondering how many of these men were still here.

Cruz Gregerson, for one, he thought as he recognized the man's picture beside the newest plaque. Last year, it was dated. Honored for defusing a bomb when there'd been no time to call out the bomb squad. Quisto grinned. His feeling that Gregerson had a cool head was obviously an accurate one.

He turned the corner of the room, toward some much older photos and plaques. He walked along, thinking it was like watching a parade of history, seeing the changes of time as he slowly circled the room and came back to more current images.

He let out a low whistle when he realized the last three photographs he'd looked at were of the same man, the legendary Trinity West cop he and Gage had talked about. Clay Yeager. Honored three times for risking his life to save someone else's. And then, Quisto thought, unable to stop the tragedy that had destroyed his own life, and left him forever changed.

Suppressing a shudder, Quisto walked on, heading back toward the most recent photos. More than ever now, with Caitlin in his life, he could imagine the pain of that kind of loss. He didn't know if he would have had the strength to survive what Yeager had gone through. He didn't even want to think about it, about how the man must have felt—

Quisto stopped dead, staring at the last photo before the one he'd already seen of Cruz Gregerson.

It was, like the others, a tribute for extreme valor. In this case, a cop who had risked his life, and had indeed nearly died of smoke inhalation after pulling three small children from a blazing house two years ago. And, like Gregerson's, this was a face he knew. It would take more than the short hair that seemed so startling in the photograph to disguise that unmistakable visage. He knew that brooding intensity, those dark, commanding eyes. Eyes in which, he only now realized, he'd found that same nameless something he'd found in the eyes of Miguel de los Reyes, that same something that had made him trust in a moment of great danger, despite all the evidence to the contrary.

And he had his answers now, including exactly why the Trinity West brass hadn't wanted him poking around the Pack.

He didn't need to read the name beneath the photo to be certain. But he read it anyway.

Ryan Buckhart.

*   *   *   *   *

Watch for the next book in the
TRINITY STREET WEST *series from Justine Davis*
and Intimate Moments—
coming your way in summer 1996!

COMING NEXT MONTH

#703 SURVIVE THE NIGHT—Marilyn Pappano
Heartbreakers

Framed! Escaped convict Dillon Boone had no choice but to do the unthinkable: take Ashley Benedict hostage. Her home provided a place to heal his wounds, while her arms promised love and acceptance...if only they could survive the night.

#704 DRIVEN TO DISTRACTION—Judith Duncan
Romantic Traditions

If anything, Maggie Burrows's life was pretty darn sedate. Then Toni Parnelli moved in next door—and immediately put the moves on Maggie. He was a younger man, determined to break all the rules—and more than determined to break down Maggie's reserve.

#705 A COWBOY'S HEART—Doreen Roberts

Sharon Douglass had loved and been left by her cowboy, and now their son wanted to follow in the footsteps of his rodeo-riding father...a father he didn't even know. Then Mac McAllister returned to Sharon's ranch expecting to save the day—but instead he got the shock of his life....

#706 BABY OF THE BRIDE—Kay David

Rachel St. James found herself the proud *almost*-mom of a beautiful baby girl—but with no husband in sight! Desperate for the adoption to go through, she proposed nick-of-time nuptials to friend Paul Delaney. Now the last thing the convenient groom wanted was for their marriage to end....

#707 BLACKWOOD'S WOMAN—Beverly Barton
The Protectors

Though Joanna Beaumont had learned the hard way about life's darker side, she still was every bit the romantic. Especially when it came to cynical J. T. Blackwood. His harsh demeanor beckoned her to heal his wounds—even as she welcomed his tender protection from the terror of her past.

#708 AN HONORABLE MAN—Margaret Watson

She'd ruined his life two years ago, and now Julia Carleton had the audacity to ask for his help. Well, ex-cop Luke McKinley would just have to say *no*. Only he couldn't. Not when his silence could mean harming innocent people...or the woman he'd fallen for, despite the odds.

MILLION DOLLAR SWEEPSTAKES

Alicia Scott's

THE GUINESS GANG

Elizabeth, Mitch, Cagney, Garret and Jake:

Four brothers and a sister—though miles separated them, they would always be a family.

Don't miss a single, suspenseful—sexy—tale in Alicia Scott's family-based series, which features four rugged, untamable brothers and their spitfire sister:

THE QUIET ONE...IM #701, March 1996

THE ONE WORTH WAITING FOR...IM #713, May 1996

THE ONE WHO ALMOST GOT AWAY...IM #723, July 1996

"The Guiness Gang," found only in—

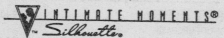

INTIMATE MOMENTS®
Silhouette

As seen on TV!
Free Gift Offer

With a Free Gift proof-of-purchase from any Silhouette® book,
you can receive a beautiful cubic zirconia pendant.

This gorgeous marquise-shaped stone is a genuine cubic
zirconia—accented by an 18" gold tone necklace.
(Approximate retail value $19.95)

Send for yours today...
compliments of ▼ *Silhouette*®

To receive your free gift, a cubic zirconia pendant, send us one original proof-of-purchase, photocopies not accepted, from the back of any Silhouette Romance™, Silhouette Desire®, Silhouette Special Edition®, Silhouette Intimate Moments® or Silhouette Shadows™ title available in February, March or April at your favorite retail outlet, together with the Free Gift Certificate, plus a check or money order for $1.75 U.S./$2.25 CAN. (do not send cash) to cover postage and handling, payable to Silhouette Free Gift Offer. We will send you the specified gift. Allow 6 to 8 weeks for delivery. Offer good until April 30, 1996 or while quantities last. Offer valid in the U.S. and Canada only.

Free Gift Certificate

Name: _____

Address: _____

City: _____ State/Province: _____ Zip/Postal Code: _____

Mail this certificate, one proof-of-purchase and a check or money order for postage and handling to: SILHOUETTE FREE GIFT OFFER 1996. In the U.S.: 3010 Walden Avenue, P.O. Box 9057, Buffalo NY 14269-9057. In Canada: P.O. Box 622, Fort Erie,

---

FREE GIFT OFFER   079-KBZ-R
ONE PROOF-OF-PURCHASE
To collect your fabulous FREE GIFT, a cubic zirconia pendant, you must include this original proof-of-purchase for each gift with the properly completed Free Gift Certificate.

079-KBZ-R

It's time you joined...

THE BABY OF THE MONTH CLUB

Silhouette Desire proudly presents *Husband: Optional*, book four of RITA Award-winning author Marie Ferrarella's miniseries, THE BABY OF THE MONTH CLUB, coming your way in March 1996.

She wasn't fooling him. Jackson Cain knew the baby Mallory Flannigan had borne was his...no matter that she *claimed* a conveniently absentee lover was Joshua's true dad. And though Jackson had left her once to "find" his true feelings, nothing was going to keep him away from this ready-made family now....

Do You Take This Child? We certainly hope you do, because in April 1996 Silhouette Romance will feature this final book in Marie Ferrarella's wonderful miniseries, THE BABY OF THE MONTH CLUB, found only in— ▼ *Silhouette*®
™

You're About to Become a *Privileged Woman*

Reap the rewards of fabulous free gifts and benefits with proofs-of-purchase from Silhouette and Harlequin books

Pages & Privileges™

It's our way of thanking you for buying our books at your favorite retail stores.

**Harlequin and Silhouette—
the most privileged readers in the world!**

For more information about Harlequin and Silhouette's PAGES & PRIVILEGES program call the Pages & Privileges Benefits Desk: 1-503-794-2499

Silhouette®

SIM-PP114